The Silkie's Call

by

Laura Browning

The Silkie's Call

Cover Art by *Angela Anderson*

The Wild Rose Press
PO Box 708
Adams Basin, NY 14410-0706
Visit us at www.thewildrosepress.com

Publishing History
First Black Rose Edition, 2010
Print ISBN 1-60154-840-0

Published in the United States of America

She fumbled in the dark to find her crutches.
Slowly, carefully, she negotiated the slope down to the dock. It had always been the place she came to whenever her heart was heaviest. She had come here when she was seven and her mother had just died. She had come here again when she was fourteen. Now she was back, seven years later. As she stared down into the water lapping at her toes, her gaze went to her legs. Taylor was right. You couldn't tell, just looking at her, that her legs were next to useless.

Annabel dragged her hand across her eyes with sudden decision. Without bothering to remove the t-shirt she slept in, she dove off the end of the dock and swam out and away. At least here she felt at home, felt normal.

"A little late for a swim, isn't it, Annabel?"

The deep voice startled her. Cay! She floundered. Unable to effectively use her legs to tread water, she frantically scissored her arms to regain her equilibrium. Hard fingers closed around her upper arms. He grabbed her, holding her pressed against him while he stood, his feet firmly planted on the bottom of the bay.

"Leave me alone, Cayden!" she protested, arching away from him and pushing at him with her hands. Even as her mind panicked her body reacted to him. No, not again! At that moment she hated her body even more. Even in the darkness, she saw his nostrils flare as the scent of her arousal rose up to him. She didn't want this; it was too painful. He was in her past and he should stay there, not see her like she was, not see her as a cripple! "Go away!"

Dedication

To Harvey—You were right. Thank you.

Chapter 1

"You don't have to finish this right now, Poppy," Taylor said as he watched her cover her eyes with her hands. "I could take you back over to our place."

Taylor still persisted in calling her by her childhood nickname of Poppy. But now, at the age of twenty-one, she was known to everyone else as Annabel Barton. Placing her hands back down on her father's desk, she stroked the leather surface of the blotter with loving fingertips. Sadness, regret...what was it she truly felt when she thought of her father? Along with those emotions, there were good memories as well.

She smiled as she looked up at her cousin Taylor. With parents like George and Helen, who would have thought he would turn out to be such a good friend? It was too bad they were cousins. Not only was he fun, generous, and her best friend, he was damn fine looking! With his blond-streaked hair and sapphire eyes, they were often mistaken for brother and sister, something that constantly angered Helen Stokes. Annabel sometimes felt that resemblance was part of the reason her aunt disliked her so much.

"I do need to do this, Taylor. At least make a start on it. It's been a month since Daddy's funeral."

"Yes, and you've already gone through the apartment in New York, cleaned it out, and put it on the market. You're driving yourself too damn hard. Why don't you take a break and enjoy a few weeks up here to just relax. It's been years since you've been here."

She looked out the window. Yes, seven to be exact, and she hadn't wanted to come back now. She had few fond memories of the bay and the sound. Seven years ago, she'd come here as a normal, healthy, if somewhat lonely, fourteen-year-old and left as a physical wreck. At least she had never had to worry about anyone trying to push her onto the field hockey team, she thought cynically. Nor had she been obliged to make her debut at the debutante ball. No, she'd never danced with her father nor needed Taylor to serve as her escort.

Instead, she spent seven years learning to move out of a wheelchair to the point where she could manage with crutches for at least part of the day. She was focused and determined. Everyone commented on how mature she was, how well she handled her personal tragedy. And she never let them see her private pain, never told anyone of the dreams that haunted her, of the voice she heard over and over. *No matter what anyone tells you over the next few years, believe me. I love you.*

But she had quit believing. Oh, not for the first year, or even the second or third, but by the time she left for college she quit believing she ever meant any more to Cayden Clifton than a chance to play around with a naïve little virgin. At least until she chickened out. And she began to believe what her father and Aunt Helen told her. That he deliberately turned his back on her when he heard she would never walk again.

Being here in this house was a reminder of that last summer. It made her uneasy. She had moved on. The accident had forced her to. And she didn't want to be here now. But she did need to sort through her father's belongings. Then she would put this house on the market too. She planned to finish her degree in finance this year, and then she would go after a Master's. This was just a temporary and unpleasant interlude. An obligation she must fulfill.

"I had your boat sailed up here for you. It's docking now."

Annabel's head snapped up and she glared at her cousin. "Taylor! You had no right. I don't want to stay here."

"You need a fucking break!" His lean face reflected the stubbornness coursing through her veins.

"But not here!" She clenched her hand into a fist when she saw it tremble. There were too many memories of sneaking out to meet Cayden, of swimming in the dark water, the way the moonlight shone in his dark eyes. And his kisses. Even as young as they were, the longing was there. Longing from which they both shied away, too naïve and hesitant to do anything about it.

Taylor sat in the chair across from her, crossing his legs and staring at her with an intensity that made her shift in her seat. "Don't practice your legal eagle crap on me. I won't stay here." He had just finished law school and would soon join a practice in the city.

"Why is that, Poppy? What the fuck happened that last summer you were here? Was it something with that guy Cayden Clifton?"

"Don't talk about him." she snapped.

Taylor watched her, his eyes never wavering from hers. "He used to ask about you."

"You've seen him?" A shaft of longing hit her right in the heart, and she hated herself for it. Hated herself for caring when Cayden so obviously didn't.

"Not for several years. He had a big fight with his family. I got the feeling he was out on his own. He worked around here for a summer. Hiring out as crew at the yacht club and then he disappeared. His parents have been back, but he wasn't with them. Just the other brother, the younger one."

"I really don't want to talk about this," Annabel said coolly but firmly, shutting the door on any further conversation about Cayden.

Taylor studied her for a moment. "Come out with me. Take the wheel and I'll crew, Captain."

His grin disarmed her. She was never able to resist it.

Her father had installed a ramp all the way from the house to the dock years ago, perhaps hoping she would come back during the summers, but she put her foot down and created such a scene when he suggested it that he finally just gave up. Remorse ate at her now when it was too late. He'd made such an effort, and she'd rejected it. She squeezed her eyes shut. More than rejected, she had positively thrown a tantrum. Sometimes she hated herself as much as she hated her condition.

While she had healed her relationship with her father on many levels, she'd kept some parts shut off from him in the same way that he'd shut her out. She'd never been able to touch or heal some of his deepest grief. And that was what had finally overwhelmed him once she'd left for college. When she'd come home for holidays and breaks, she'd seen that he was deteriorating, but she'd been helpless to do anything about it. She hadn't understood it. The grief had been about more than her mother, but he'd never talked about it.

She didn't understand it. The grief was about more than her mother, but he would never talk about it.

Then came the call right after she finished her finals, the call that he had been found dead inside the New York apartment, an empty bottle of sleeping pills by his side. *You have your wish now, Daddy. You can finally be with Momma.* It was what he always wanted. She had known it ever since she was seven. Somehow, she had never been enough to hold him. Even his career as a writer had never been enough.

From the moment her mother died of cancer, her father had been little more than the walking dead. He would have willingly turned her over to Aunt Helen until Annabel's accident changed that. In fact, he had planned to, but the accident forced him to go on for a few more years. She had no doubt that had she not been paralyzed that summer when she capsized the *Silkie*, he would have ended his life years earlier.

She walked carefully down the ramp now, balancing on the crutches that hooked around her forearms. Taylor strode on ahead, getting the *Revenge* ready to go. He hopped back onto the dock when she reached the side of the boat and lifted her in. While Annabel would have rejected such help from most people, she accepted it from Taylor. He was more family to her than anyone, and she loved him like a brother.

"Ready?" he grinned as he untied the lines fore and aft and jumped in.

She smiled back at him. "Yes, but you're not. Lifejacket, Taylor. You know my rule."

It had saved her seven years ago. It was perhaps the one smart choice she'd made that day when she was fourteen, deciding to put on the lifejacket. If she hadn't, she would have drowned. The boom had cracked her skull before it damaged her spine, leaving her not only semi-conscious in rough seas, but partially paralyzed from the waist down. Without the lifejacket, she would have been helpless to stay afloat.

She remembered very little from that day, only what her father had told her. That Carrick and Cayden Clifton found her and pulled her out. She'd heard the story of how the Coast Guard took her by cruiser to the station and then airlifted her to a trauma center.

Annabel jerked herself back to the present. Taylor dutifully donned a lifejacket and was busy unfurling the sails, so she started the small motor on the boat and came about to head out into the bay.

"Hey, Poppy! Did you wear your suit under your clothes?"

"Yes. Why?"

"Let's go to that cove you used to visit and go for a swim."

She blanched. "Not there, Taylor."

He stared at her. "You can't let him haunt the rest of your life, you know."

"Who?" she asked innocently.

"Clifton. Make some new memories, Poppy."

So in the end, she set off in that direction. It didn't take long to reach the cove. The *Revenge* was faster than the *Silkie* had ever been. They dropped anchor in the middle of the cove and Taylor set the ladder on the stern so that she'd be able to get back in. After stripping down to his trunks, he dove over the side. Annabel took her time, keeping her gaze carefully away from the small beach where she and Cayden first kissed each other.

Using her arms to keep her balance, she sat on the edge of the *Revenge* and swung her legs around. To a casual observer, she looked perfectly normal. She now had enough control that she was able to maintain muscle tone in her legs, and when she was in the water, could even swim using a dolphin style kick that relied heavily on the muscles in her abdomen and back to create momentum. That at least was something that hadn't been taken away from her. She had always loved the water, and even her accident hadn't changed that.

It felt wonderful to swim in salt water again. It had been a while. At school, she regularly exercised in the pool, not only using aqua therapy to work her body, but swimming laps to make her stronger. The salt water was so buoyant she could spend more time swimming and less time trying to stay afloat. She sighed blissfully and floated on her back, staring up at the gulls wheeling and turning overhead.

****

Cayden sensed her as soon as she hit the water. The shock to his system almost made him forget to hold his breath as he shot through the water. Breaking away from the school of fish he pursued, he turned out of the sound to search the bay. He followed her scent and her sound as carefully as any predator in the sea. And as a bull seal at full maturity, that's exactly what he was, a predator. Seven years. Or not quite seven years, so he couldn't go to her, not until the seventh day of the seventh month, but he could look. He would look because he could do nothing else.

If he could just see her again. Did she remember what he'd told her? Was that why she was here? He didn't dare hope for that much.

It had been a long seven years, he thought bitterly, separated not only from her, but from his family as well. He closed his eyes as he remembered what happened after Bell's accident. They had taken her away while he watched, his father holding his arms in a vise-like grip to prevent him from following. He'd tried to see her, but Carrick forbade it. Then when he managed to sneak into the hospital in the city, a place he never wished to see again, Phillip Barton physically barred the door and then had him removed by armed security guards. He'd tried again the next day, and this time he'd been arrested. Carrick and Catriona had come to get him.

But it wasn't just human law he had violated. His father soon broke the news that they must travel to the islands off Scotland, the ancestral home of the Silkie, to appear before the Council of Lords.

"But why, Dad?" Cayden had asked.

Carrick sighed. "You answered the call of a female and didn't fulfill your responsibility to mate with her. The Council doesn't understand human beliefs about age and sex. In their eyes, you've flaunted our traditions, and because you are my son, they will make an example of you."

And they had. What had made it even worse was that Carrick had to sit in judgment on his own son. The outcome was a foregone conclusion. He was banished for seven years to live on his own. His mother cried, his brother, Ciaran looked coldly victorious, and his father slipped a piece of paper into his hand even as he embraced him one last time. Cayden was escorted from the hall and turned out into the night. Shunned by his own kind, he sought shelter with humans while he figured out what to do.

His father had given him a letter with instructions about where he could access a bank account set up for him. "Use this as an opportunity to grow, my son," his note had said. "I have supplied you with enough funds to provide for you, if you are thrifty. Learn all you can. On the seventh day, of the seventh month, in seven years, we will find you again."

So Cayden had returned to the sound and the town on the bay. He'd found a job cleaning and fixing boats during the off months and crewing during the summer. He'd finished high school and then gone to college, completing a degree in Marine Management. It hadn't been easy. His father had left funds for him to survive, not to pay for an education, so Cayden had spent the seven years working hard and fitting in classes around whatever jobs he'd been able to find.

And he'd tried to forget Annabel Lee Barton. Poppy to nearly everyone in her family, but to him she had always been Bell. His beautiful Bell. He hadn't found anyone else, and he'd never forgotten her. For seven years, he'd lived in the hope that he would find her again.

Now she was within reach. If she called to him again, he would go to her. He had to. As a Silkie, it was his nature to please the human who sent for him, and Annabel Barton was the only female who had ever called to him. The only female he had ever wanted.

He hovered at the entrance to the cove, his dark eyes examining the small sloop anchored there. *Revenge.* From there his gaze scanned the cove, coming to rest on two heads bobbing close together in the water. Her laughter traveled across the surface to him, at once arousing yearning, jealousy, and anger. Damn her! How could she sound so carefree when he had spent seven years agonizing over her, longing for her?

He ducked under the water and swam closer, hovering in the depths below them, scenting and listening. He saw the long, slender length of her legs and the way they blended so smoothly into her rounded ass, her flat belly and the slight protuberance of her sex. The cold water had tightened her nipples until they poked, pebble hard, against the thin material of her suit. His Silkie instincts roared to life. Cayden wanted to take her in his mouth, suckle her breasts and bury his erection in the soft folds between her legs.

He started to move on the human male and then realized two things. His seven years had not yet ended, and the man with her was Taylor Stokes. Some of his jealousy evaporated as he realized she was with her cousin.

"I told you, Taylor," she protested. "I don't want to go to the yacht club. It was bad enough before. It would be torture now."

"No one will pay any attention."

Her laughter had a hard edge to it. "Please! Just leave it alone. All I want to do is go through everything at the house and get it sold. After that, I never want to see this hellhole again."

She swam away from her cousin then, her stroke just as strong and graceful as it had always been. Cayden watched her with a longing so great he was afraid to stay any longer. Turning swiftly, he torpedoed his way out of the cove and into the waters of the bay. He had to stay away from her. There were just two weeks remaining, but even then, she had to call him.

And now he feared she wouldn't. She'd said as much. She wanted to get away from here. While he remembered their summer with longing, she apparently had no such similar feelings. Hope disappeared to be replaced by anger and bitterness.

****

Annabel pulled herself back up the ladder. It was a slow process, and not particularly graceful, but it was a damn sight better than it had been. At least now she could rest her weight on her legs even if she still did most of the actual lifting with her upper body. Taylor wasn't far behind her, levering himself back into the *Revenge* without using the ladder.

"Come on, Poppy! Let me take you out to dinner, even if it's just so I don't have to eat your cooking."

She turned her face away unhappily. Taylor was so good to her, and she did always have a good time with him.

"Taylor, it's just... I'll have to use the chair."

He knelt next to her. "Poppy, the only one it bothers is you. Yes, people might look at first, but you make them forget when you let yourself forget. Come on. Put on something pretty and let me take you out."

She brushed the hair off his dear, dear face. "You don't know how often over the years I've wished you were my big brother. You have always been there for me, Taylor. Out of everyone in our family, including my dad, it's always been you."

He tweaked her cheek. "Somebody has to look out for you, Popper."

Chapter 2

Cayden saw them at dinner on the terrace that night. He had finished cleaning up several boats that were out on day trips and now he was headed back to put his supplies in the maintenance shed when he looked up. Taylor's back was to him, and he saw Bell sitting across the candlelit table. She looked incredibly lovely. Her honey colored hair was swept up off her neck in a loose knot, showing the slender column of her throat and her bare shoulders to advantage. He stopped and simply stared. If anything, she had grown more beautiful in the last seven years. She paused in her conversation with Taylor and looked up. A puzzled look crossed her face as she gazed out at the marina, her eyes searching.

Cayden ducked his head and kept going. He had already run afoul of the traditions of his clan, and he wouldn't do it again, not when he was this close. He wouldn't survive seven-year banishment.

****

"What's wrong?" Taylor asked as they finished their meal.

Annabel shook her head. "Nothing. Just a strange feeling for a moment. I guess I'm more tired than I thought."

"Would you like to go home?"

"Yes. I think that would be best. And thanks for helping me fix up the spare room off the kitchen. That will save me trying to negotiate the steps every day."

"Hey, I just appreciate you putting me up until

Mom and Dad get here to open up the house. You're sure you don't mind?"

She smiled. "Positive. You're doing me a favor. I suspect I'll need the help getting things out and moved around."

Taylor grinned. "Happy to be your hired hand, Poppy, you know that."

"Then play the gentleman and wheel me out of here."

Hours later, Taylor was sound asleep in what had been her father's room upstairs, but Annabel lay wide awake in the former storage room off the kitchen. She was restless and unsettled. What sleep she'd managed was disturbed by dreams of her summer with Cayden. She tried so hard to put it behind her, and during the day when she was busy doing other things, she truly didn't think about it or him, but night was a different story.

She would remember how he taught her to hold her breath. She was never as good as he was, but she had reached the point where she could stay under for just over four minutes. Then there was the skiing. His father, Carrick, and Cayden both helped her learn, but she was never as proficient at that as she was at sailing and swimming. Now of course, it wouldn't matter. Skiing was out of the question.

I love you Annabel Lee...I never left you. I was coming back to you.

But it was a lie. He never came back. And if that was a lie, then everything else about that magical summer was too. His kisses, his touch, and the way they had held back, knowing they were too young and thinking they had all the time in the world. All of it was a lie.

Annabel punched her pillow and pushed up into a sitting position, using her hands to move her legs until she sat on the side of the bed. She had done too much today, and now she was paying the price for that. She ached. She knew better. She knew from bitter experience in the past that she had physical limits, and they were a lot more confining than before her accident.

After shifting from the bed to her chair, she wheeled into the kitchen and made herself a cup of tea. Then she rolled down the hallway to her father's office. It seemed almost sacrosanct to enter it on her own, especially when her intention was to go through the items in his desk drawers.

After setting the cup on the blotter, she started with the center drawer. Her father had been a pack rat when it came to his office. She doubted seriously that he had ever thrown anything away. Half-used pencils were shoved in the drawer simply because their erasers were already exhausted. Loose change dotted the bottom of the drawer underneath piles of old receipts, phone messages, and notes he jotted to himself. There wasn't much in this drawer to sort; it was simply a matter of cleaning it out.

That done, she turned to the drawer on the right. The top drawer was filled with unused writing supplies: paper for the printer, pens, pencils, paper clips, and all the usual things. Below that were the drawers large enough to hold files. Now the going was slower. These drawers contained partial manuscripts, records of household bills, and copies of contracts for other books. Part of the danger was getting caught up in reading everything, Annabel thought with a sad smile, but she continued to plug away and soon had the first of the file drawers knocked out, too.

The bottom drawer contained journals. Her eyes widened. She never knew her father kept personal journals. She had always just assumed that all of his writing was for publication. The last entry in the small book on top was dated just a week before her father's suicide. She ran her hand over it. So he had come back here one last time. Annabel's hands shook as she picked it up.

Dear Emily,

Annabel looked up, a frown on her face as she stared off into the distance and then she flicked back several pages. Each and every entry was written as a letter to her mother. Her eyes clouded with tears. Her father's grief and despondency had run far deeper than she ever suspected. She turned again to the final entry.

It will be fourteen years in July since the cancer took you, but you and I both know you were gone before then. You really left me two months earlier when you made the decision to stop fighting. I've made my decision as well. It's time for me to stop fighting. Annabel has just one more year of college remaining, and I've put all our finances in order so that she will want for nothing.

You would be so proud of her, Em, the way she's fought through the obstacles she's faced in the years since that awful summer. She's as strong as you, and far, far stronger than I ever was. I can leave now knowing that she will be all right. Annabel is a fighter. I look forward to seeing you soon, my love.

She slammed the journal shut, put her face in her hands and cried for the shell of a man her father had become. *You're wrong,* Annabel thought. *I'm not as strong as you think, and I don't feel very strong now.* She only vaguely remembered her father from when her mother was healthy, just as over time, her memories of her mother had faded to moments, snapshots taken out of time and context. They could only be viewed like a slide show now. They were incomplete.

After a few minutes, she wiped her eyes and stared down at the drawer. It was filled with similar composition books. How far did they go back? While she couldn't bear to read them now, Annabel pulled them out one by one to check dates and put them in order.

Fourteen years. They went back to the year her mother died. Annabel looked over to the drawers on the other side of the desk and yanked open the bottom drawer on that side. More journals! She slammed the drawer shut. She couldn't face any more than what she looked at right now.

She pulled the one dated that summer she was seven from the top of the stack and it fell open to a date just a month after her mother's death.

Poppy disappears every day right after breakfast and she's gone until dinner. I guess I should worry. I know you would, Em, but I can't right now. I miss you so much and part of me is glad Poppy's not around. Is that so terrible of me? Every time I look into her face, I see you...oh not in the coloring, that's all my side of the family, but in the shape of her face, the lift of her brow and the expressions. She's all you, and right now it's so hard to look at her, knowing that she is the only reason I must go on.

But I won't let you down, Em. I promised I would stay to take care of her, and I will. Until I'm sure she can handle things on her own, I will be here for her just as I told you.

She had always suspected it. Now it was in black and white. Had she not been here, her father would likely have killed himself years earlier...probably right after her mother's death. Annabel shivered, but she couldn't feel contempt for her father. She understood.

It was very nearly what her mindset was following her accident. Cayden disappeared, and the doctors told her she was paralyzed. It was a very, very dark time. They gave her painkillers while the bruising and the fractures healed, and she was grateful for them. Her father and Taylor were there to offer her encouragement. How hard that must have been for her dad!

"Poppy?" Taylor leaned in the doorway, his chest bare and his boxer shorts resting low on his hips. "It's almost dawn. How long have you been down here?"

"I don't know. I couldn't sleep, so I got up. Gosh, I guess it's been hours. I started going through Daddy's desk."

He walked closer, running his long fingers through his hair, so similar to hers in the way it bleached out. "What's all this?" he asked in his morning voice, still roughened from hours of sleep.

"Journals. Daddy kept them." She looked up at Taylor. "These go back fourteen years."

His brows disappeared beneath the hair that hung over his forehead. "These? Does that mean there's more?"

Annabel pulled open the drawer on the opposite side and Taylor peeked inside. "Damn! How far do those go back?"

"I don't know. I haven't sorted through them. I'm feeling a little overwhelmed right now."

Taylor pushed the drawer shut. "Let's get cleaned up and get some breakfast, and then I'll help you with them." He looked at his cousin's pale face. "How you feeling?"

She sighed. "I did too much yesterday, Taylor."

"Legs hurt?"

She nodded.

They knew each other so well. She knew he could see it in her face, what she would never ask. Taylor's mouth thinned. "Let me massage them for you, Poppy, and help you with some exercises. You know you'll start cramping otherwise."

She looked away from him, her chin tilted, but after a moment, she nodded. As he moved her legs for her, she stared up into his face.

"Why are you so good to me?" she asked, truly

17

puzzled by this cousin who didn't seem to fit with the rest of his family.

He smiled, not his normal fun-loving grin, this smile was gentle and sincere. "You're the sister I wish I had."

"You've got Sydney."

Now he did grin. "Like I said—you're the sister I *wish* I had."

"Come on. Sydney's gotten better since she married what's-his-name, the third."

"Thomas Remington Hensley, the third? Better known as Trip?"

Annabel grinned. "And such an original nickname."

"Meow. You must be feeling better. Is the valium kicking in?"

"My life as a drug addict," Annabel murmured happily in a fog.

****

Cayden crewed for a boat making a run up to Boothbay Harbor. He had learned to enjoy sailing over the last several years, though he still preferred to travel in the water rather than over it. Still the trip to Maine would be a break, and it would get him away from the temptation of Bell for at least the next week.

At this point, he felt getting away was the best way to avoid running into Bell by accident. While he waited in Maine, he would fish and swim on his own terms. The guy he was crewing for didn't give a flip what he did once they reached Maine. Then all he had to do was transform and show back up in time for the return trip. By then, there would be only a couple of days left before his seven years of banishment would be over. He could let Bell see him. And he could see his family.

There had been no contact with his parents, his brother, or any Silkies for that matter, for the last seven years. He hoped they would show back up for his birthday. In fact, he sent up prayers every day for that to happen. It was almost as fervent a prayer as his desire to be with Bell once more. Almost.

****

Annabel decided to leave the office for a while and tackle her father's room first. It took them about three days to sort out the items she wanted to keep, but there were very few of those. Most of what she sorted went to charity, and a few things simply needed to be thrown out. When that part of the house was done, Taylor helped her back downstairs and fixed her a cold glass of lemonade.

He popped the top on a beer and took a long pull on it.

"You know we'll have to celebrate your twenty-first birthday next week," he told her, looking at her over the edge of the can.

She laughed. "Hmm. If I don't take my drugs, then I might actually be able to have a drink."

"It's the law," he assured her with a grin. "You have to have at least one drink when you turn twenty-one."

"Maybe a glass of wine."

"It's a date."

He took her out for a drive along the island just so they could get some fresh air. He still had the Miata his father gave him when he was sixteen.

"Now that you're going to be an attorney, are you getting the big car to go with the big job?"

"Not likely, Poppy. I like this old thing. It's fun. Besides, you know what it's like in the city; I never use a car. I can walk or grab a cab."

"You know, I used to really look forward to when I would turn sixteen. I used to dream about you teaching me to drive, or Daddy taking me out in the Volvo."

"You could still learn."

She shook her head. "No. It's enough for me to be at a point where I can sail. And I have to thank you for that too. If you hadn't convinced me...no forced me...to get back on a boat, I probably never would have."

They returned to her dad's office early the following morning to continue cleaning it out. She had boxed the journals to keep and was going through the remains of what was in the second drawer when her hand hit something wedged in the back of the compartment. She pulled, but it wouldn't come out.

"Taylor?" she called to him. He was in the kitchen fixing them breakfast. "Can you give me a hand?"

He showed up in the doorway, wiping his hands on a towel. "What's up?"

"There seems to be another journal, or something, wedged in the back of the drawer. I can't get it out."

"No problem." He flopped down on the floor at her feet and reached into the back. After twisting his hand around and manipulating the angle of the drawer, he finally came out with a simple composition book. "Ta da! All this for one little notebook."

He handed it to Annabel and she flipped idly through it. "Yeah, but this one's a lot older. The rest of them started around the time I was born. The first date in this one goes back almost twenty-five years."

Taylor rolled his eyes. "Ancient history, then. Tell you what. While you read it, I'll finish breakfast."

He hopped up with a grin and headed back to the kitchen. She stared after him. He would leave at the end of next week. That's when Uncle George and Aunt Helen would arrive to open their house. She would be on her own then. While that didn't really

20

bother her, she had gotten used to having Taylor around, and she would miss him. He could always make her smile.

Annabel opened the notebook and paged through it. Like the other journals written while her mother lived, these entries were not addressed to her mother. She began reading about a year into the journal.

I'm going up this weekend to open Grandmother Taylor's house on the sound. I couldn't believe she left me the property in her will. What great good fortune! It will be the perfect place to write and get away from the city—not to mention a great place to raise kids. I'm seeing a wonderful girl—Emily Wainright.

Wow! Annabel thought. The beginnings of her father's relationship with her mother. She flipped a few more pages and read some more.

As it turns out, Emily's older sister, Helen Stokes, has a place not far from grandmother's house. She's going to give me a lift up there this weekend, as she was getting ready to open their house as well. She's a lot different than Emily, but really a fun person to be around. I can't say the same thing for her husband, George Stokes. Kind of a stick in the mud, but Helen seems happy with him and they already have a young daughter, Sydney.

Annabel skipped a few pages, but noticed that her father's handwriting seemed agitated in a series of entries, so she stopped and began reading again. This time her hands began to shake.

No one expected the storm. It blew up out of nowhere. Helen and I were already here working on getting the house open when it struck. We were stranded without electricity. It was all supposed to be harmless fun. I got out a bottle of wine and some cheese and crackers...oh God! I can't believe what I've done. I don't think Helen can believe it either. We didn't mean for it to happen. Things just kind of got out of hand, and the next thing I knew, we were in bed together. I won't lie. It was a long night, and the sex was great, but Em's SISTER? She would kill me if she ever found out.

Aunt Helen? Her father had screwed Aunt Helen?

Annabel felt suddenly almost physically sick. She looked at the date on the entry and paled even more. Cautiously, she turned more pages.

Helen called me in tears. She's pregnant. I didn't want to ask how she was so sure it was mine, but I do know I didn't use anything that night. I just assumed she was on the pill. Obviously not. And an abortion is out of the question. She doesn't want to leave George, and I sure as hell don't want to lose Emily. But I'm also not sure I like what she's suggesting. She believes she can fool George into thinking the baby is his if I'll just keep my mouth shut.

It would make life easier on everyone. I agree with her on that. But it will mean turning my back on my own child.

She stared at the confirmation in front of her unseeingly, her hands absently stroking the paper. Taylor Stokes wasn't her cousin. He was her brother! She bit her lip to still the bubble of hysteria that threatened to burst out in laughter. She always said he was different. They joked time and time again about how they wished they were brother and sister, how people so often mistook them for that instead of pairing him and Sydney together. Now it seemed it was actually true.

A noise, the creak of the wood floor alerted her, but not in time. She looked up just in time to see Taylor snatch the notebook from her with a grin on his face. Oh Jesus!

"Why so serious?" he asked as he began to flip through it.

"No!" she cried urgently. "Give it back, Taylor.

Right now!"

He looked at her, his brows drawing together in a frown that suddenly reminded her so much of her father that she couldn't believe she'd never noticed before. She couldn't believe that everyone hadn't noticed and commented on it.

"No. I want to see what has you so bent out of shape that you're almost on the point of tears, for God's sake!"

"No, please don't read it!" she pleaded, but she could see she was already too late.

His frown deepened as he read the entries. His face paled and his hands shook.

"My mother and Uncle Phil?" His voice vibrated with revulsion. When he read the entries that discussed Helen's pregnancy, he slowly sat down in the chair on the opposite side of the desk. She could see the denial in his expression. How part of him wanted to pretend it wasn't there in black and white.

"She said I was premature," he stated hoarsely, "but it was all a lie."

"Taylor..." Annabel began, but in truth she wasn't sure what to say to him. He looked so crushed. But—oh my God—she had a brother. Not a cousin...a brother. She wanted to shout for joy, but she had to focus on what Taylor was going through.

"I always wondered why my father seemed so distant to me sometimes. Why he so obviously favored Sydney." Taylor's voice was choked. "And then there was the special interest that Uncle Phil took in me. Do you remember the day of your accident? Do you know Uncle Phil called me before he called anyone else?"

He looked so wounded. For once the smiles and the laughter had been washed from him as completely as a tidal wave sweeping away everything in its path, and she saw just how much this was messing with his head.

"Don't Taylor," she pleaded, unshed tears making her voice thick. She watched as his expression changed from the wounded, disbelief of shock into a tense, hard look.

"That bitch!" he snarled suddenly, slamming the journal down so hard on the surface of the desk that Annabel actually jumped in her chair. Taylor raised stormy blue eyes to her. "She knew! Your father knew. And I would bet George knew too! None of them said anything. Not a word, not in all these years. I have to go, Poppy. I have to go talk to them."

He stormed out of the office. She heard him take the stairs two at a time, followed by the sound of doors and drawers slamming. She put her head in her arms on the desk and cried. Why couldn't she just have trashed it all? If only she had just thrown it all out, Taylor could have gone on just as before. She hated to see him hurting. She would give up ever knowing he was her brother to save him that pain.

She had composed herself by the time he came back downstairs. He had a duffel bag thrown over his shoulder and was bouncing his car keys in one hand.

"Will you be all right on your own for a few days, Poppy?" He was as pale as she felt.

"Yes. Do what you need to do, Taylor."

He entered the room and bent down to kiss her on the cheek. "Please try to understand. I have to do this. I have to talk to her." He bent and put his hands on either side of the chair as he stared into her eyes. "As pissed as I am, I do realize something else about this. What I've always wished were true *is*...you are my sister. Not just the sister of my heart, but truly my sister. I love you, Annabel Lee."

She touched his cheek. "No matter what happens, Taylor, you know you can come back here. You know how much it means to me that you really

24

are my brother. I know you're angry. I know this sucks in just about every way it could for you. And I would spare you all of this if I had only known. But Taylor, this is the best birthday gift ever. Knowing I have a big brother and knowing it's you. It just doesn't get any better than that."

Taylor went down on his knees in front of her and wrapped his arms around her waist. She felt him swallow thickly as he laid his cheek next to hers. "Thanks, Poppy."

Chapter 3

She should have known her aunt wouldn't take the revelation of her secret lying down. And she should have known who her aunt would blame for it. Helen Stokes showed up early on the morning of Annabel's birthday looking like a madwoman. Things just went downhill from there.

"You silly little bitch!" Helen ranted, staring at Annabel with hate. "Couldn't you have just kept it to yourself? What would it have hurt? Do you know how many people's lives you've destroyed because you showed that journal to Taylor?"

The vitriol was one thing, but Helen so totally lost it she actually reached out and slapped Annabel before she spun on her heel and stormed out. The slap wouldn't have been such a big deal except Annabel was on her crutches in the doorway. Her balance was tenuous at best, and the force of the older woman's blow made her stagger. Before she could get her damaged legs working, she fell heavily against her hip, slamming against the hall tree before crumpling to the floor. She cried out in pain, but Helen was already slamming the door to her car and gunning the engine.

Taylor found her in the afternoon. Annabel had managed to lever herself onto the couch in the den, but now the muscles in her thighs were spastic and she couldn't get to her medication.

"Shit! Poppy!" Taylor exclaimed when he saw her.

"Please get my medicine!" she gasped.

He helped her take a couple of the valiums and

then began to work her legs, moving them as gently as he could. She cried with the pain.

"What the fuck happened?" he asked grimly. "It was my mother wasn't it? She said she was coming here, but I hoped it was just venting. Now you're laid up cramping and you've got a red mark on your cheek. What happened?"

"Nothing!" she gritted out. "I was stupid, and I fell."

As much as she hated her aunt, Annabel refused to drive an even larger wedge between Taylor and his mother. It was enough for her that she still had family. She looked at Taylor and tried to smile at him.

"Are you telling me the truth?" Taylor asked suspiciously.

"Yes. Leave it alone, Taylor." She watched a muscle in his jaw twitch.

"Are the spasms going away?"

"Yes. I love you; you know that, don't you?" Annabel hoped to distract him.

"I love you too, kiddo. Just relax. I'll bring you something to eat and drink. I guess you haven't had anything, right?" When she nodded in response, his lips tightened. "I'd like to stay here at the house with you, Poppy, if you don't mind. I told Mom and Da—George that I was moving out, so if you'd let me stay here you'd be doing me a huge favor."

She smiled tiredly at him. She had a feeling that his conversation with Aunt Helen and Uncle George had been a lot harsher than what he revealed. "You're my brother. Of course you can stay."

The valium began to kick in, making her sleepy.

He walked to the doorway that led to the kitchen. "By the way, happy twenty-first birthday, Popper. I guess the drink will be out of the question tonight, but we'll do it tomorrow—okay?"

"Sure."

****

Cayden sat on a rock out on the point. It was her birthday, his too. He'd never told her that they shared the same birthday. Wouldn't have made a difference. Twenty-four years old. Seven years since he had seen his parents. Seven years since he had talked to Bell. Damn! He was so tired of being alone.

Bell hadn't called to him, not yet, but he hoped she would. Right now though, he had a different mission. He was keeping an eye out for his family's yacht, the *Skerry*. He had missed his mother and father, and the need he felt to see them once again was nearly as strong as the need to see Bell, to talk to her, touch her, and take her in his arms. Just the contact.

There were so many nights he laid awake thinking about her, aching for her, and wondering what happened to her. He was never able to get any answers. Even the newspaper glossed over her injuries in its coverage of the rescue, simply stating that she would be going through rehabilitation at home. He even asked her cousin, but Taylor would tell him nothing, just that she was moving on with her life and he doubted she would be back.

Cayden's attention snapped back to the present as he saw the familiar outline of the *Skerry* approach in the distance. He pushed off the rock where he'd been basking in the sun and shot, torpedo-like toward the ship. Home. He could go home at last! Joy shot through his entire body in such a surge that he felt like he flew through the water.

He zipped in and out of the waves alongside the boat, hoping for a glimpse of his mother and father, but seeing nothing. With his attention distracted, he didn't notice his brother until Ciaran slammed into him from underneath.

You would never survive in the waters where I have been, weakling, his brother berated him. *You must be constantly on your guard, and you have always allowed yourself to be distracted.*

Leave off, Ciaran!

There were too many harsh words and actions between them for Cayden to forgive and forget. Even seven years couldn't erase that. Still, he followed his brother as they raced beside the *Skerry* while she turned into the harbor and lowered her anchor. As soon as Cayden transformed and started to climb the ladder at the stern, strong hands pulled him on board.

"My son! Damn, how you've grown."

Cayden looked into his father's eyes. They were the same height now. He saw the sheen of tears there and felt his own slide down his cheeks. He threw his arms around his father's neck and hugged him tightly. "Dad."

"Let me look at you." Carrick held him at arm's length. "God, how you've grown up. You used to be as lean as a barracuda. But you are worthy now of your Silkie heritage." His dad reached out and rubbed Cayden's beard stubbled cheek. "And what's this? That jaw could use a shave."

Carrick clapped him on the back. "Happy birthday, son. It's good to have you back. Go see your mother. She's been worried about you. She stayed below because she didn't want to embarrass you in front of the crew in case she got too emotional."

After pausing just long enough to pull on a pair of shorts, Cayden slapped his palms on top of the stair railings and simply slid down until his feet landed silently on the plush carpeting below. Catriona Clifton stood in the room that was her private retreat. When she turned and saw him, her hand went to her mouth and a soft gasp erupted. Tears already ran down her cheeks and she simply held her arms open to him.

"Momma!" He knew he should be stoic, should

let her see he was no longer a boy, but his deep voice suddenly thickened, and he choked with his own tears. "I've missed you so much!"

"Oh Cayden!" She couldn't say anything else. She just held him closely, but this time he was tall enough that it was she who had her face buried against his chest and not the opposite as it always was before. She cried and held him. He did the same, inhaling her familiar scent and reveling in the comfort her embrace still brought, even when he'd thought he had outgrown all that.

She finally patted his chest and leaned away from him. "What have you done with my little boy? You've turned into a man, Cayden. And I'm so, so proud of how you've done on your own."

"It wasn't always easy, Momma," he smiled slightly at her, but there was an edge of reserve he couldn't keep from his voice. "There were a lot of lonely, uneasy nights when I first left."

She stroked his cheek. "You were just a boy! I fought all I could, but they wouldn't listen."

Cayden smiled, trying his best to relieve the guilt he saw in her face. "It's all right, Momma. I'm all right and it's over now."

"Is it, Cayden?" his mother asked gently. "Is it really over?"

His eyes fell away from his mother's intense stare. He knew she meant Bell. "I don't know, Momma. She's back. It's the first summer she's been back since…since her accident."

"Have you seen her and talked to her?" his mother asked, curious now in a way that he found vaguely unsettling.

Caution made him careful with his response. "I saw her swimming with her cousin, but she hasn't seen me or called to me."

"And she appeared fine?" his mother asked, continuing with the gentle probing that Cayden found nonetheless disturbing.

"Yes, Momma. She's beautiful. I glimpsed her one evening at the Yacht Club as well. Annabel is even lovelier than she was seven years ago."

Her mother's expression was puzzled as if what she heard didn't quite fit with what she understood. She shook her head and smiled. "Then you wish to go to her?"

"If she calls me. Nothing would make me happier."

His mother hugged him again, and once more he caught just a glimpse of worry shadowing her dark green eyes. He wondered at it, but dismissed it in the joy of reuniting with his parents, and even Ciaran, after seven years of separation. His banishment was over, and he would allow nothing to cloud the happiness he felt. After seven years of loneliness, he was back with his family. The only thing that could make this moment better was to be able to hold Bell in his arms once again so he could reassure her of his love.

****

"I am not taking you to the Yacht Club to celebrate your belated birthday, Poppy." Taylor stated adamantly. "I know a great little dive in town along the waterfront where we can get buckets of oysters and clams, corn on the cob, some of the best chowder to ever touch your tongue, and the coldest pitchers of beer to wash it all down. Come on! Put on one of those cute little miniskirts and let's go."

Poppy punched his arm, only half-jokingly as they sat on the dock. "In case you hadn't noticed, Taylor, I quit wearing cute miniskirts about seven years ago when I quit having cute legs to show off under them. Never mind that they're downright indecent when you can't move your legs to keep people from getting an eyeful of everything under your skirt."

"Aw shit! I'm sorry, Poppy. But you've still got great legs. Put on some shorts. Hell, I don't care if you go naked!"

She laughed now. "That's because you're my brother."

"Well, you've got a great body, Poppy. You should show it off."

"Eww! I told you that seven years ago, and it still stands. It's even worse now, Taylor; you're my brother. You're not supposed to think I have a great body."

"I'm an attorney. I deal in facts. And that is a fact."

"Like I said...eww."

In the end, she dressed up and allowed him to take her into town. Figuring it would be easier to get in and out using her crutches, Annabel maneuvered through the tables until they sat near the back. She stuck the crutches on the floor under the table, where they would be out of the way. Before they even ordered, the waitress arrived with a cold pitcher of beer and two glasses.

Taylor grinned at Annabel and poured, tilting hers so that it had just enough head before he filled his own glass. After setting the pitcher down, he raised his glass and she did likewise. He tapped his beer against hers.

"Here's to being twenty-one and an absolute knock-out, even if you are my newly discovered kid sister."

They both laughed and drank. The music was loud and the crowd even noisier and Annabel loved it. She had never been in any place like it. Her father's idea of taking her out was usually to a restaurant with white-coated waiters and no prices on the menu. They would make small talk while they waited on precisely arranged plates of food. Here mounds of food appeared in just a few minutes.

Annabel and Taylor cracked shells and swallowed shellfish, chasing it down with beer. They chowed down on chowder and crunched their way through corn on the cob, all the while swallowing more beer. While Taylor might have been used to it, Annabel had to quit.

"I can't eat or drink another bite, Taylor," she giggled.

"Poppy," he said, tilting his head to the side. "Are you just ever so slightly shit-faced?"

"Plastered."

He actually looked repentant. "Oh lord. I'm sorry, kiddo. You wanna leave?"

She grinned. "Not a chance! But I think maybe something besides beer might be a good idea."

Taylor turned to the passing waitress to order Poppy a soft drink. When he didn't immediately turn around, Annabel turned her head to follow his gaze. A dark-haired guy who sat at the bar was glaring at them. As if becoming aware of her regard, he averted his face. But it was enough. Annabel stared for another moment, swallowed and then looked down again.

"Hey, Poppy," Taylor spoke absently. "Do you know the guy sitting at the end of the bar?"

She glanced up again. He still had his face averted, but the jaw… It couldn't be. It just couldn't be.

"I don't think so." But when she looked at the man sitting next to him, she felt all the color and animation leave her face. It was! "I know the man sitting next to him. It's Carrick Clifton."

She stole another glance and found herself staring into two sets of dark, hostile eyes. The third man wouldn't even look at her. Ciaran and Carrick stared at her and Taylor like they could easily kill them, but that wasn't what struck a blow to her very heart. The third man was Cayden. But this was a

Cayden she had never seen before. There was no longer any of the boy she remembered in him. At twenty-four, he looked like a man in his prime, and right now it appeared to be a very pissed prime.

"I think we should go, Poppy," Taylor said quietly. "I'm starting to feel like I'm going to have to step in and defend your honor. While I'd be happy to do that in the normal course of events, the odds right now are a little lopsided and not in my favor."

"No! I will not leave," she said. Pain and humiliation flooded her until she thought she would choke. "Do you think I want them to stare at me while I drag myself out of here? Do you think I want him to *see*?"

She stared down at the table, feeling all her earlier animation and sparkle drain away. Her hand clenched in a fist, the knuckles white. Taylor reached out and covered it with his own.

"Are you going to stay here all night then?"

"I don't know!" She looked up at Taylor, hating the pleading sound to her voice. "Please, Taylor, think of something!"

He stared at her intently. "I have an idea, Poppy, but it's certainly not going to help your community image."

"I don't care!" All she was after was escape. Ciaran and Carrick looked at her like they wanted to kill her, and Cayden wouldn't look at her at all. Like she wasn't there. And that told her everything she needed to know.

He leaned over and whispered in her ear, looking for the entire world as if they were simply sharing a good time. Taylor motioned to the waitress. When she came over he paid the tab and handed her another twenty.

"I need your help. While I'm getting my sister out of here, I want you to get her crutches from under the table and run them out back and around to the blue Miata parked in front. Throw them in behind the front seat, down on the floor where they can't be seen."

Annabel saw the sympathy on the waitress's face. It wasn't pity, that would have made her angry, just the understanding of one woman for another of the need to protect what self-esteem she had.

"Sure thing, honey. I can handle that." As she stood up, Annabel saw her glance casually around until she paused. She had spotted them. When the waitress turned back to her it was with a mixture of respect and puzzlement, as if to say...are you crazy? Avoiding *them?*

Taylor stood up and then bent at the waist. "Put your arm around my shoulder, Poppy, and smile. Remember, you're supposed to be a happy drunk. It's your birthday celebration."

She did what he instructed, relieved to feel his arm close around her waist, supporting most of her weight as he straightened back up. She giggled nervously and that at least was not faked. She had never felt more vulnerable, and she hated it. Damn her legs.

"Don't you dare let me fall, Taylor Stokes!" she hissed even as she laughed a little louder.

Taylor grinned at the group at the next table and laughed. "Sorry, my cousin's had a bit too much birthday celebration. Twenty-one you know!"

Everyone laughed, and Taylor began weaving his way out of the bar, Annabel vainly attempting to support her weight on her legs. As they passed near the Cliftons, she darted a quick glance up. Cayden looked away, his face flushed. Ciaran laughed, and Carrick's narrowed gaze held nothing but open contempt. As soon as the door shut behind them, Taylor swung her into his arms and hurried down the steps to the Miata. The waitress had just stowed the crutches and was heading around the back of the building.

"Thanks!" Taylor called out to her as he put Annabel in the passenger seat and buckled her in. Tears slipped down her cheeks. She tried to hide it, but the catch in her breathing gave her away.

"Don't, Poppy!" Taylor muttered. "They're not worth it. He's not worth it."

"He wouldn't even look at me," she said in a soft, barely audible whisper. "Take me home."

****

"Right off the top of my head I'd say your one true love hasn't spent seven years pining for you, bro!" There was a smirk on Ciaran's dark face.

Cayden spun on his brother, his eyes black with rage. "Shut the fuck up, Ciaran, before I take you apart right here!"

Ciaran's eyes narrowed. "Try it, weakling."

Carrick laid a restraining hand on each of his sons' shoulders. His grip was hard enough to remind them that he would and could still put a stop to anything they started. Cayden was the first to shake him off.

"I'm out of here."

Carrick looked into his elder son's eyes. "Let it die, Cayden. It's time to move on. She has."

Chapter 4

It was the middle of the night. Annabel felt like someone set up a drum line in her head. Upstairs, she heard Taylor softly snoring, but she was still wide awake. Big surprise there. With her mind going a million miles an hour and her temples pounding like she was banging her head against a wall, sleep was just a refuge to fantasize about, but nowhere near reality.

She sat up carefully and fumbled in the dark to find her crutches. She pulled herself up slowly and made her way through the kitchen out onto the porch and down the ramp. Slowly, carefully, she negotiated the slope down to the dock. When she finally reached the end, her breathing was harsh in the silence of the night.

It had always been the place she came to whenever her heart was heaviest. Here at the end of the dock, she could listen to the gentle lapping of the waves against the wood, feel the occasional bump as the *Revenge* brushed the dock while she bobbed on her moorings. She had come here when she was seven and her mother had just died. She had come here again when she was fourteen, hoping to find some answers to why her father would want to ship her off to Aunt Helen. Fate, God, sheer bad luck, whatever you wanted to call it, intervened that summer so that never happened. Instead, her life had turned into one long fucking nightmare, and she was still waiting to wake up. She supposed one good thing had come out of it. She discovered that she was indeed a lot tougher than she had thought in many ways. She also learned that some pain went too deep, that it never healed.

Now she was back again tonight, seven years later, because of that pain. Seven. Her life was ruled by that number. But where most people considered it lucky, she thought cynically, for her it was just the opposite. As she stared down into the water lapping at her toes, her gaze went to her legs. Taylor was right. You couldn't tell, just looking at her, that her legs were next to useless. Like right now, she couldn't even feel the water on her feet although logically, she saw it...saw that it lapped as gently against her as it did against the dock, yet she had no more feeling there than if she were the dock.

"I hate you!" she hissed at her feet. While she had regained a lot of feeling in her thighs, her feet continued to be numb. That inability to feel her feet remained one of her biggest stumbling blocks to training herself to walk. As she stared malevolently at her legs, the tears rolled slowly down her cheeks. One tear for her mother. A second tear for her father. A third tear for the events her father and Aunt Helen had set in motion. A fourth tear for Taylor, and a fifth one for Cayden. A sixth tear for what she had been and a seventh for the person she had become: a person she didn't much like, hardened by bitterness and cynicism. What she wouldn't give to get back that summer of her fourteenth year. Hell, she'd take back just one day; the day she'd capsized. But that was so not happening. If the last seven years had taught her nothing else, it was that you couldn't believe in miracles because they just weren't real.

Annabel dragged her hand across her eyes with sudden decision. Without bothering to remove the t-shirt she slept in, she dove off the end of the dock and swam out and away. At least here she felt at home, felt normal. She could pretend that nothing was different, that she was still strong and beautiful, able to swim and run and sail. To do all the things she had always loved doing. For a time at least she could forget the crutches that sat on the dock, could forget the wheelchair that sat ready for those times when her weakened limbs wouldn't tolerate her attempts to walk. And God! Tonight she needed to forget.

She swam along the shore, careful not to stray too far out. She had limits now, limits her body would make her only too aware of each and every time she tried to move beyond them. It was time to turn around. *Fool!* She was just asking to spend a day or two in bed at this rate.

"A little late for a swim, isn't it Annabel?"

The deep voice startled her. *Cay!* She floundered. Unable to effectively use her legs to tread water, she frantically scissored her arms to regain her equilibrium. Hard fingers closed around her upper arms. He grabbed her, holding her pressed against him while he stood, his feet firmly planted on the bottom of the bay.

"What the hell were you thinking? Out here swimming by yourself as drunk as you were earlier?"

"Leave me alone, Cayden!" she protested, arching away from him and pushing at him with her hands. Even as her mind panicked her body reacted to him, nipples hardened with desire and the ache of emptiness between her thighs. *No, not again!* At that moment she hated her body even more. Even in the darkness, she saw his nostrils flare as the scent of her arousal rose up to him. She didn't want this; it was too painful. He was in her past and he should stay there, not see her like she was, not see her as a cripple! "Go away!"

He swung her into his arms and walked toward the beach and out of the water with her.

"No!" She recognized the edge of hysteria

tightening her voice. "No! Take me back to the dock. Please!"

Cayden ignored her. As soon as they reached the sand, he set her on her feet and turned her loose. Annabel tried desperately to balance, but her legs were too weak and they buckled. He caught her as she fell and his expression was now even darker than before. She saw the fury in the lines bracketing his mouth, the way his lips thinned, and his brows drew together.

His voice dripped with contempt. "Your cousin got you so drunk you can't even stand up. And now you're out here swimming? Do you have a death wish, Bell?"

God yes! There had been so many times over the last seven years that she had begged to die.

"Take me back!" she pleaded desperately, not bothering to answer his question. Oh God. He couldn't find out. He couldn't *see!* "Take me back to the dock!" her voice rose as the bubble of hysteria worked its way to the surface, squirming and wiggling to break free so that she completely lost control.

****

Cayden watched her in confusion. She clung to him even as she yelled at him. It was almost as if she was afraid to turn him loose. He tried again to set her on her feet, but she clung to his arms until he pulled away. Maybe if he put some distance between them they could talk. They needed that. He needed that. But she fell to the sand, and this time she screamed.

"Get away from me! Go away Cayden! Go away! Do you think this is funny? Did you show up just to torment me?"

"But you called me," he whispered in a voice so quiet she couldn't hear.

Annabel was losing it. He could see the nearly

blind hysteria on her face, and she couldn't seem to stop it. Maybe it was the aftereffects of the alcohol, but he saw other things as well, fatigue and a heartbreaking look of humiliation that he would never have caused her. Crumpled as she was at his feet, for just a moment he wondered if she could even stand up. But he had seen her move in the water and in the restaurant. He bent toward her again, but before he could extend his hand, something slammed into him. He was knocked sideways by a Taylor he barely recognized. Her cousin was so furious the anger radiated off his body. Even as close as he knew Bell was to this cousin, it seemed all out of proportion.

"Get away from her, Clifton!"

Taylor turned back to Annabel and gently picked her up in his arms.

"It's okay, Poppy," he crooned. "It's okay."

She buried her face against his neck and clutched his shoulders. Cayden stared at them. Confusion mixed with jealousy and anger until he wasn't sure what emotion he felt.

"Take me home, Taylor!" she begged. "Get me away from him!"

Taylor stared at him, his eyes hard. "Keep the fuck away from her! Whatever was between you is over. You walked away from it seven years ago. So for God's sake leave her be! Hasn't she suffered enough for all of you?"

Cayden stood numbly watching the tall form of Taylor Stokes as he strode along the beach, effortlessly carrying Bell while she wept against him. He carried her away, up the steps until they disappeared at the top of the dune. He knew they were headed for the house. Did her cousin *live* there? Was there something he had missed or overlooked in learning about humans? Was that even allowed? His vivid imagination brought forth an image of Taylor parting her creamy thighs, stroking his fingers along the delicate skin of her core, the sex that he, Cayden, had denied himself, and his gut twisted.

The dominant male in him wanted to go after them. He'd waited seven fucking years to get her back! He wasn't walking away for any male. But then he saw her pale, stricken face and those wide, wounded blue eyes. He would kill himself before he harmed her. *Fuck!*

He ran back into the sea, intending to swim back to his boat. At the last minute, he turned and went to the dock. After levering himself up out of the water, he stalked toward the house.

Walked away? He had never walked away from her. He had been driven, pushed and kicked away. But hadn't he also been *pulled*, a small voice nagged. Hadn't his parents dragged him away just as fast as Phillip Barton drove him away?

"Damn!" he swore as he stubbed his toe hard on something lying in his way. Cayden looked down and saw he had kicked a metal crutch. His eyes shifted slowly, took in its twin and then the bar next to the ladder, obviously meant as an aid to help someone stand up. His expression changed as the pieces suddenly fell into place. He looked up at the end of the dock to the ramp that had been carefully constructed leading from the house down to the dock. His brows drew together as he continued to stare up at the house, and his mind balked at what his eyes showed him.

How quickly his parents had tried to get her off the boat seven years ago. How careful his mother had been to keep him away from hearing the medics assess her injuries. And his father? Carrick was livid when he found out Cayden tried to see her in the hospital.

"Whatever you think is between you and this girl, it can't be, Cayden. It can never be." Those were the

words his father had said when he bailed him out of jail and took him back to the *Skerry*. They had sailed for Scotland the next day.

And tonight, his father told him to let it die, to walk away because Bell had. He looked down at the crutches again and his eyes suddenly clouded with tears as he let himself feel the pain she felt right now. He opened himself to it, and it drove him to his knees. Annabel Barton had never walked away because she couldn't walk.

She couldn't walk, hadn't walked, since that day seven years ago when the boom on her skiff had cracked her spine, *and his parents knew it*. His hands shook before he clenched them into fists and jammed them in the pockets of his wet shorts.

Cayden ran back to where he'd beached the ski boat and scrambled on board. Paying no attention to the lateness of the hour, he fired the engine and shot out along the bay toward the *Skerry*. He tied the boat to the ship's stern and climbed to the upper deck where his parents' cabin was located. Without bothering to knock, Cayden shoved the door open.

He started to back hastily out when he heard the unmistakable sounds of lovers, the whispers, the grunts and moans. In the dim light he could see his father's form arched over his mother. God! He closed his eyes. Nobody wants to know the intimate details of their parents' sexual relationship.

Carrick rolled off Catriona with a snarl, tossing the covers up over her. She blinked and held them up in front of her as she came up on one elbow.

"Cayden?" She asked, puzzlement warring with growing concern in her expression.

"What the hell is the meaning of this Cayden?" His father thundered.

He stared at them with angry, accusing eyes. "You knew! All those years ago, you knew. And you said *nothing*?"

"Knew what, Cayden?" his father hissed as he stood up and grabbed a pair of shorts to pull on. "This is about that girl, isn't it? You went to her, didn't you? To Annabel Barton? Did we know she was damaged? Yes! We knew that, and knew we had to get you away before it was too late. You couldn't commit yourself to a woman who would only ever be half a woman. You need someone who can give you strong sons."

"I don't give a damn about that!" Cayden snapped. "Bell is my soul mate. Do you think I care if she can't give me sons?"

"Well you might not," Carrick retorted, "but I sure as hell do. You're my heir, Cayden. *You* must be the one to have sons to carry on our line, not Ciaran."

Catriona's eyes suddenly focused on a point over Cayden's shoulder, widening in shock.

"Ciaran!" she exclaimed, one of her hands stretching toward her younger son.

Cayden and Carrick both turned to see him standing in the doorway. His face was pale and his dark eyes were beyond furious. They looked dead. He stared at Cayden, and then his gaze turned to Carrick, glittering and filled with hate.

"The prodigal returns," he hissed, "and all is forgiven. I have spent seven years trying to please you, but it would never be enough, would it, Father? I was always second choice." With a look of contempt for both his parents, Ciaran turned on his heel.

"Ciaran!" Carrick called. "Wait!" he brushed past his elder son. Cayden let him go. He turned to his mother instead, his eyes filled with disillusionment.

"How could you?" he asked. "You knew how much she meant to me, how much we meant to each other. Yet you never said a word. Not then and not now."

"I only wanted what I thought was best for you, son. She was only going to bring you pain, and her father would never let you near her."

Cayden looked at his mother and shook his head slowly. "Well you have achieved one of your goals very successfully because she definitely doesn't want me near her. Unfortunately, she also called to me tonight. So now I must find a way to finish what started fourteen years ago, continued seven years ago, and has now begun again. Only now it's with a woman who went into hysterics when I came near her. Her cousin carried her away while she begged him to get her away from me.

"I won't leave her. I can't leave her. And now I have to make her mine, or die." He ignored the tears his mother shed. "So what have you really accomplished? You've driven Ciaran away. You've driven me away."

"Cayden," she pleaded. "Sleep on it. Let's talk about it in the morning. We can find a way to work it out…to help you."

Cayden laughed bitterly. "I got along for seven years without your help. I guess I can keep on."

"Cayden!" his mother cried. "No!"

"Goodbye, Mother."

Carrick stood on the deck, alone. Cayden could only surmise that Ciaran had left already.

"You're leaving." His father said it as a statement, not a question. He looked at his son and his face was suddenly bleak. "You're going to her, aren't you?"

"If she'll even have me. She's terrified of me for some reason, yet she called to me, so tradition says I must answer…"

"Or die trying," his father finished. He looked away for a moment, and his face suddenly twisted with pain. "I wish I'd killed her that day," he said softly. "God forgive me, I wish I'd killed her!"

Chapter 5

Tears rolled down her cheeks as Taylor put Annabel through the motion exercises the next morning. It was more than just physical exhaustion; she was mentally wiped out as well. He gave her valium when they were done. She welcomed the relaxation and the grogginess like an old friend. They were old friends. Seven years worth of friendship. Only Taylor had been her friend longer. As she popped the pill, she thought again about upping the dosage for a little chemical timeout, but the image of her father stopped her. She couldn't take that same way out.

"It's the last of the valium, Poppy," Taylor said. "I'll need to go to town to get it refilled. Do you want to stay in your bed, or what?"

She tried hard to focus on him. Stay in her bed all day? It was too much like the hospital. "The lounge on the porch would be nice. There's a good breeze and I can look at the water."

"Do you want your chair, or will you be all right until I get back?"

"I'll be fine. I left my crutches on the dock last night."

"Already got them," he grinned. "I woke up early."

Taylor brought her a book to read, but Annabel set it on her lap unopened. She barely spared him a wave as he took off in the Miata to get her meds. The distant sound of the water and the breeze gently blowing was peaceful. Just what she needed. Exhaustion made it impossible to focus. Combine that with the drugs, and she was soon sound asleep.

****

That was how Cayden found her. She looked like an angel dressed in a white sundress with her long hair in curls all around her face. He didn't want to frighten her again, so he simply sat in the chair nearest the lounge and waited. He studied her as she slept.

He hadn't gotten a good look at her while they were at Stan's and then it had been dark on the beach. Seven years had changed her. The fullness of face of her early teens had given way to finely molded features that would keep her beautiful for an eternity. Hers were no manufactured good looks that would fade with age. While her arms and shoulders appeared slender, he saw the muscle definition in them. His gaze wandered to her legs and he scowled. They looked normal. There was good muscle tone there, and he had seen her swimming. So why hadn't she been able to stand? Had it been just the alcohol after all? No, he had seen the crutches. His parents' reaction had confirmed it.

His gaze wandered back up to her face. Shadows. They lay like bruises beneath the half moons of her lashes. A faint hitch in her brows showed she spent a lot of time concentrating. He supposed she must. Her lashes fluttered open, and her mouth began to form a scream.

"No one will hear you, Bell," he interjected softly. "Your cousin is away. I made sure of that."

"Please leave." Her deep blue eyes begged with an intensity he could barely withstand.

"Not until you hear me out."

She turned her head away from him and stared out toward the sea, leaving him to look at the delicate line of her jaw where it blended into her throat.

"I didn't know, Bell." His voice was urgent.

"They took you away before I knew, and then no one would let me near you."

"Liar," she hissed, turning a face to him that was wild with hurt. "You left me just as soon as you found out I wouldn't be able to walk!"

"No!" He was horrified, but her expression showed she truly believed that. "Fuck! Someone *told* you that? Told you that I left because you were paralyzed?"

Her silence was all the answer he needed. Something cold settled around his heart. They had both been young and vulnerable and they'd been manipulated by the adults in their lives.

****

Annabel watched him. Cayden sat very still in the chair across from her, his hands gripping the arms until his knuckles showed white against his tan. His eyes were downcast, so she was unable to read his expression, but she could see the muscles clearly working in his jaw.

"Before they took you away," he said softly, "my mother let me come in to the cabin to say goodbye. Were you able to hear what I told you then?"

She lifted her chin and stared back out to sea again. Of course she remembered. She'd heard the words almost every night since then in her dreams, but she had long since stopped believing in the truth of them, and she hated the bitterness and cynicism that had filled the hole left behind by that betrayal.

"I love you Annabel Lee. That's what I told you."

Her mouth twisted. "You have a strange way of showing it."

"I also told you something else. I would come back to you again. No matter what."

The hurt broke through her wall of cynicism. She turned on him. "Then why did you leave?"

"I tried to see you in the hospital. Your father had me escorted out of the building the first time.

The second time, he had me arrested."

She stared at him. Her father? Had him arrested? It couldn't be true. "I don't believe you."

Cayden laughed bitterly. "And I now have no way to prove it, do I? Your father is dead, and my arrest was a juvenile offense, so my record is clear now. So where does that leave us my beautiful Annabel? My word against a dead man?"

"Nowhere. It leaves us nowhere. And I want you to go away."

Inside she was in turmoil. She didn't want to believe it, but somewhere deep inside there was a ring of truth to what he said that just hadn't been in her father's or her aunt's voices.

Now she could hardly bear to look at Cayden, and it wasn't because of the lies that had pulled them apart. He was so handsome. At seventeen, he'd captivated her teenage heart, but now he mesmerized her as a man. And he was once again trying to weave his way back into her life. What was worse was she knew she would let him if he were around very much. Just looking at him now stirred desires she'd thought were dead. Moisture flooded between her thighs along with an ache to feel him touch her there. She watched his nostrils flare and knew he had picked up her scent.

No. She wouldn't survive if he left again. She barely survived the last time. Everyone—doctors, nurses, and her father—thought her depression was because of her injuries, but the true source of her depression was Cayden, the boy who promised to love her, then left her alone when she needed him the most.

"Does your cousin live with you?" he asked out of the blue, his voice harsh. "Is that why you won't let me back in?"

She stared at him aghast. "You think I'm living with my cousin? You think Taylor is my *lover*?" Her voice started to rise. Anger broke through the fog of her medication. How could he always manage to wound her so easily? She wanted to get away from him, needed to get away, but she was trapped. Damn her legs! She had neither her crutches nor her wheelchair. It was suffocating, frustrating, and maddening.

"Bell..." Cayden's voice was meant to soothe, but she was in no mood for that.

"Get out. Get out of my house." She clenched her hands into fists in her lap, her rage all the greater because she felt so impotent. She knew she sounded hysterical, but she couldn't seem to stop it, and that made her even angrier.

Tires crunched on the gravel, and a moment later Taylor leaped up the front steps making a beeline for Cayden. The two men were of similar size, both powerfully and athletically built.

"I thought I told you last night to stay the fuck away from her," Taylor snarled. Without waiting for an answer, he swung his fist. There was a sharp smack as it connected solidly with Cayden's jaw. It could have been a rock. He simply shook his head and snarled as he came toward Taylor, his punch catching her brother in the gut so that the air whooshed out of his lungs.

They had both settled into fighting stances, warily circling, looking for an opening to land a punch or snag a leg.

"Stop it!" Annabel cried. "Stop it! Both of you!"

Neither man listened. The punches continued to fly. Somehow, both men ended up off the porch and in the front yard. Insults and threats flew back and forth nearly as fast as fists.

"I told you to stay away."

Punch.

"Me? You're the sick son of a bitch who's living with her."

Punch.

"I didn't fucking walk away and leave her."

Punch.

"You're her damn cousin, you sick shit."

Punch!

"Cousin, hell!"

Annabel couldn't take any more. She swung her legs off the lounge, realized her crutches were still inside, and dragged herself to the porch railing for support. Sweat popped out on her forehead as she rested most of her weight against her arms and slowly, painfully shuffled along until she reached the steps. Her breath came in gasps.

"Stop!" she cried hoarsely, but neither man could hear her. They were bloody by now. Taylor's nose was bleeding and Cayden's brow was split open.

Annabel stood at the top of the steps. There were only three of them, but it might as well be the top of a cliff for all of the ability she had to negotiate them. She looked at the two men still slugging away and then back down at the steps. This couldn't go on. She had to stop it. God, if only she could feel her feet. Clutching the railing tightly, she stepped down.

"Poppy! No!"

But Taylor's warning came too late. As her leg crumpled, she felt her weight shift forward even more and she lost her grip on the slick railing. Time slowed, making her aware of the sudden, heavy beat of her heart, the certain knowledge that she was helpless to stop what was happening. Rather than a sensation of falling, the stairs instead seemed to rise to meet her. In her mind, she could already feel the bite of the hard wood against her flesh, and she opened her mouth to scream. It died on her lips as strong arms abruptly caught her, holding her tightly.

"Bell! Are you all right? Are you hurt anywhere?"

Cayden's voice and hands shook as he held her close against him. Taylor was there next to her too. She looked between their two battered faces, and her anger dissolved into embarrassment. She had caused this. Her throat tightened. She wouldn't cry, damn it. She had shed too many tears over the years, and it would be just the final humiliation.

"Don't fight," she choked. "Please!"

She reached for Taylor. Her senses overwhelmed by Cayden's feel and smell; she needed the safety of her brother.

****

Cayden let her go, feeling a blow just as sharp as any that the other man landed. He looked at the two of them sadly. If Taylor was who she wanted, he wouldn't hurt her, not just to satisfy a tradition. What his own fate would be didn't matter, because without Bell, there was no reason to go on. He started to turn away, and then he felt her hand on his arm. He stopped his posture tight as he stared down at the long fingers curved around his forearm.

"He's my brother, Cayden, not my cousin."

"Huh?" A wild surge of hope raced through him. God, if he could only believe that.

"It's true," Taylor admitted.

"But..." Cayden looked at the two of them. Really looked. Once it was put into words, it was more than obvious. Their coloring was almost identical. Phillip Barton's coloring, not Helen or George Stokes' and when he looked at Taylor, he saw Barton clearly stamped on his features. He wanted to ask questions, but figured now was not the time.

"Please don't fight anymore." Annabel's voice interrupted the chaotic hopes swirling in his head. "Come into the house, so I can clean you both up. Please."

Cayden hung back as Taylor swung Bell into his arms. She looked at him over Taylor's shoulder, her expression wary and guarded. He had hoped to see love, but at this point, anything other than panic or fright was a gigantic step forward.

"Come in, Cayden. Let me at least get your face cleaned up. I wouldn't want your mother to be angry." With all that had happened to her, how could she be worried about that?

His mouth twisted. "You don't need to be concerned on that score."

Cayden followed them into the house. It hadn't changed much in seven years. Bare floors and comfortable furniture. A home, not a showplace.

"Do you want your crutches or your chair?" Taylor murmured, but Cay couldn't hear her reply.

"Go on in the kitchen," Taylor directed him. "We'll be back in a minute."

Cayden sat down, still looking around him curiously. Taylor came back first, but Bell was right behind him. *Jesus!* His breath caught and his chest tightened painfully. The chair made her paralysis real in a way it hadn't yet been. He had seen the crutches, but not her using them. He watched how easily she maneuvered the chair, the definition in her arm muscles now readily apparent as she deftly rolled through the kitchen. It was a part of her, and he knew his ability to accept it would determine what happened in their relationship.

****

She had a first aid kit balanced on her lap as she wheeled up to the table, pausing to set it on top. She glanced at Taylor and smiled. "Sorry, bro, guests first. Just pinch your nose together until I can get to you."

"Bud wud if ids broke?" Taylor whined.

She glowered at him. "Tough. I didn't tell you to start throwing punches over me. Do like I do. Take one of my valiums. Then you won't care."

She turned her attention to Cayden, trying to

avoid his gaze as she cleaned the cut just below his eyebrow. He winced, but continued to stare at her with his velvety eyes. Her hand trembled slightly, and she resented how it revealed her nervousness.

"This could really use a stitch, Cayden," she said softly.

"It will heal. Stick a butterfly bandage on it."

She nodded and found what she needed in the first aid kit.

"Could you move your chair closer?" She refused to meet his eyes as she made the request.

He slid forward, bracketing her legs with his own. She looked down at his knees. They were flush against the wheels of her chair. Heat shot through her. For just an instant she closed her eyes, imagining so many might-have-beens.

"You're more beautiful than ever, Bell," he whispered.

Her eyes snapped open as she dropped the box of bandages in her lap. "Don't, Cayden," she hissed. "Just don't."

He nodded, and winced at the movement. Annabel's mouth pressed into a thin line as she finished the bandage. She was now more aware of him than she'd ever been. If she reached out just a little bit, she could touch him, run her fingers down his chest and lower. As she noticed the bulge in his khakis, her eyes jerked back up to his face. Cayden stared steadily at her, not acknowledging in any way the erection tenting his pants. She felt Taylor watching both of them as he stood off to one side pinching his nostrils together. It made her feel awkward and stilted. Even Taylor must see what was going on. How could Cayden want her? Pity? But pity wouldn't give him a hard-on.

"You're going to have a black eye. Do you want to put some ice on it?"

"If you don't mind."

They could be strangers. Maybe it was better that way, but she so didn't want it to be.

She turned her head over her shoulder. "Would you get him a bag of ice, Taylor? Then I'll get to you and your nose."

While Cayden rested his head against the bag of ice, Annabel turned her attention to Taylor. His nose looked slightly swollen, but it didn't appear to be broken. She gently cleaned the blood off his face and stared at him. He, too, looked like he was getting a black eye.

"You're getting that look, Poppy," Taylor said cautiously. "Don't lecture."

She raised her brows and slapped the antiseptic wipe down on the table. At least this was ground she felt comfortable with.

"Lecture? Why would I lecture just because two big idiots start throwing punches at each other? Why would that be a thing to lecture about? All I'm going to do is get another bag of ice so you can put it over your eye. Then the two of you can commiserate together."

"And what will you be doing?" Taylor asked.

"In case it slipped your mind, Taylor, I was supposed to be resting. So if you don't mind handing over my painkillers, I'm going to take my lame, chemically addicted butt to bed and swallow enough pills to knock me out for the rest of the day."

Taylor dug in his pocket and tossed her the bottle which she caught in her right hand. This was her escape. Her way to evade whatever Cayden thought he still wanted. She looked at him for a long moment. Was it relief she felt or just regret? It would be better this way, she thought, and said quietly, "Goodbye, Cayden."

Annabel shut her mind, closed off her feelings and swallowed another valium before she rolled her chair next to her bed and set the brake. She grunted with the effort to scoot herself onto her narrow bed. As she finally lay back and stared at the ceiling unseeingly, her mouth twisted. She never wanted Cayden to see her like this. She hoped he understood her message. That this was goodbye.

****

The two men watched her roll out of the kitchen and then heard the door to her room click shut. Cayden felt Taylor watching him. He knew he must have a shocked look on his face. How the hell could he be anything but shocked? Seven years ago, the girl he had known had been vital, athletic and bubbling over with a willingness to experience everything life had to offer. Now she used a wheelchair to simply get around the house where she lived.

"You didn't know, did you?" Taylor's quiet voice interrupted his thoughts.

"No." Cayden's hand clenched in a fist on the table. "I tried to see her in the hospital and her father had me kicked out, then arrested when I tried again."

"I didn't know that," Taylor said. "But then, it seems there were a lot of things that Poppy and I didn't know."

Cayden looked over at him, at the blond streaked brown hair, the sapphire eyes. "You mean things like Phillip Barton being your father?"

Taylor snorted. "That would be the biggest one for me. It fucking sucks to find out at the age of twenty-three that you're the product of a one night fuck-fest between your mother and the man you thought was your uncle." His expression softened. "But one big benefit that's priceless? I got Poppy as a sister out of the deal. That makes up for a whole truckload of shit."

"You love her." Cayden envied Taylor that. It seemed so simple and straightforward for the other man.

"Yeah, I love her…like a sister, Cayden, but not any other way. She's always been like a kid sister to me, and it tore me up to see what you did to her seven years ago. You ripped her fucking heart out. The Poppy I knew died that summer, and I wanted to kill you then. Hell, there are plenty of days now when I still want to kill you!"

Cayden's free hand unclenched, but he continued to hold the ice to his eye with the other hand. "Fair enough. There are a few people I feel that same way about. You just don't happen to be one of them anymore."

"Why the change?"

Cayden shrugged. "You're not the fucking competition anymore. You're her brother. It takes you right out of the game."

Taylor crossed his arms across his chest and leaned back in his chair. "She'll never let you back in her life. And as long as she feels that way, I'll support her."

"I'll take my chances. I have to." Cayden stared down at his hand. There were so many things he could say. He could talk about how much he loved her, had always loved her, but that was such an easy word to throw around. "I can't live without her."

"You have for seven freaking years!" Taylor growled.

Cayden stared down at the back of his hand. "No. I haven't lived. I existed. Fucking existed was all I did. I went through the motions, doing the things I needed to do to get by without my family and without Bell, but I haven't lived." His hand curled up again into a fist and he swallowed thickly.

"What do you mean without your family?"

Cayden smiled distractedly. "My family's a little different. Actually, we're a lot different, and you wouldn't believe me if I told you. Anyway, after what happened to Bell, Poppy, I was brought before a Council of Lords and banished for seven years."

Taylor was looking at him as if he were insane. "Don't feed me a fucking load of bullshit, Clifton. I don't need it, and Poppy sure as hell doesn't."

Cayden stared at Taylor Stokes. "You know it just doesn't matter anymore. I'm a dead man if she won't accept me. I've already severed ties with my family over her. I might as well show you, because you won't believe me otherwise. Hell, no normal person would fucking believe it. You seem like a level-headed sort that won't go off the deep end when you see."

"I have no freaking clue what you're talking about, man," Taylor told him. "But it's just crazy sounding enough that I'm curious. I warn you though. You try to yank my chain or pull some crap over on Poppy, and I'll be all up in your shit."

Cayden looked over at the hall leading to Annabel's room. "Will she really sleep the rest of the day?"

Taylor followed his gaze. "Yeah. She's been doing too much, and her body can't take it. Last night was the final straw."

Cayden frowned. "I caused this?"

"In a roundabout way."

"You don't pull any punches, do you?" Taylor just arched a brow in response, so Cayden continued. "I just can't get it right. I've done nothing but fucking hurt her, and all I ever wanted was to love her. Ever since she was seven, there's never been anyone else for me."

"Since she was seven?"

Cayden put down the ice and looked at Taylor. His cut was healed and there was no black eye. As he expected, the other man's eyes widened in astonishment.

"Your eye! How the hell did you heal so fast?"

"It's part of who I am."

"You know, I'm in real need of whatever it is you're gonna tell me about yourself, because that is just some real out there shit that you can heal that fast. Just what the hell are you?"

Chapter 6

"It would be easier to show you, and then if you haven't completely freaked out, I can tell you."

Taylor lowered his own ice pack to reveal the beginnings of a real shiner. "All right."

Cayden glanced down the hall again. "We'll have to leave her and go someplace isolated."

"I can leave her a note. We'll take the *Revenge*. She won't mind."

Cayden began to have second thoughts as they sailed, but he needed an ally in the worst possible way, and if he was ever going to get through to Bell, he needed Taylor's help. Failure with her was not an option. No fucking way because if he failed, death awaited him. If he succeeded...well, he'd beg forgiveness of his king and the rest of the freaking Council of Lords. Even if they banished him again, at least he would have Bell. Taylor sailed toward Bell's cove. That was how Cayden always thought of it. It was where they'd shared their first kiss. Such innocence, it seemed so long ago. Now wasn't the time to think about it. Thinking of Bell always gave him the same reaction, and he didn't need to be sporting wood while he was trying to win Taylor over.

When they reached the cove, Taylor tossed the anchor over the side and then drew in the slack. He crossed his arms and looked at Cayden expectantly. "Okay. You've piqued my interest, Clifton. This had better be good."

Cayden smiled lazily and began to strip off his clothes. He glanced up and saw a flush on Taylor's cheeks.

"Whoa! You brought me out here to strip for me? Hey, I'm not really into that shit."

Cayden laughed. "Neither am I. But clothes just get in the way." He set his boxers off to the side and turned to look at Taylor. "Watch closely...and Taylor?"

"Yeah?"

"Whatever you think you're seeing? You really are seeing."

Cayden stood up on the gunwale, bent his knees slightly, and briefly touched the leather bracelet on his ankle before he leaped up and out to dive into the water. As his body twisted into the dive, Cayden morphed into a sleek, dark seal.

****

Taylor watched, his breath stopping, his eyes widening, and his mouth falling open.

"Oh shit! Holy fucking shit!" Taylor gasped. He rushed over to the edge of the *Revenge* and stared down into the cove. He must be hallucinating. Something was wrong with the aspirin Poppy gave him. Shit! Suddenly about twenty feet from him a seal popped to the surface, swam on its back and then dived below again. Taylor watched as the seal approached just below the surface and then transformed once again into Cayden Clifton's naked body.

Cayden surfaced and stared at Taylor warily. "Now you know."

"What the fuck are you?" Taylor asked faintly, flopping down on the seat.

Cayden levered back into the boat the leather bracelet once more around his ankle. "A Silkie."

Taylor blinked. "Poppy was into all that seal shit when she was a kid. If you're a Silkie, aren't you supposed to dance on the beach naked at midnight and seduce women?"

Cayden chuckled. "I have no doubt some of my ancestors have probably done just that. In fact, there's probably a few now who still do. Men, women, who cares? There's one of the lords on the council who will fuck anything that moves, anywhere, anytime. Hey, you have a towel?"

Taylor tilted his head. "Do it again."

Cayden scowled. "This is not Goddamn Sea World, Taylor! I showed you this to help you understand that things aren't as straightforward between Bell and me as they might appear. There's a whole lot of it that's just a royal pain in the ass."

"Yeah, but I'll bet there are some pretty cool perks too." Taylor flipped open a storage area under the seat and tossed Cayden a towel. Once he dried off, he hooked the towel around his hips and sat down next to Taylor.

"Is your whole family Silkies?" Taylor couldn't take his eyes off this altered reality of the Cayden he thought he knew. He felt an odd tug of familiarity, as if he should know this already.

Cayden nodded. "Our lineage goes back thousands of years. In our world my father, Carrick, is Lord Carrick over the Northwest Atlantic. I guess it would be kind of like being an Archduke or like that guy in Monaco."

"Prince Albert?"

"Yeah."

"So does that make you and your brother princes?"

Cayden shrugged it off. "It doesn't matter. I left."

"So explain to me how all this plays a role?"

Cayden stared at Taylor. "You don't think it will be enough of an issue for your sister that I can turn into a seal?"

"She doesn't know?" When Cayden shook his head, Taylor grinned, "Well I can see some potential problems, but then again, Poppy's always been fascinated by those cute little furry seals."

"Fuck you." Cayden snorted and leaned back against the stern. "There are a lot of problems, but let me give you the background. Do you know anything about Silkies other than the dancing at midnight and seducing women B.S.?"

"Not really."

"Well, we're basically the aquatic version of faeries and before you ask, not the kind in Key West looking for a new BF. The magic-making kind from legend. And at least part of what you know has some truth to it. We're attracted to humans. That is to say that some humans call to us. For some of us, it's a casual thing. Our job is to go make the human happy, and for most humans that means…"

"Sex," Taylor supplied with a grin.

"Right. So most of the time, the Silkie transforms, comes ashore, has a hot, steamy relationship with the human in need and then disappears. No harm, no foul, everybody's smiling."

"Why do I get the feeling that we're now getting to the 'but' and it's going to squarely involve Poppy?"

Cayden's face was totally serious as stared at Taylor. "She first called me when she was *seven*, Taylor. I wasn't even old enough to transform as easily as I do now. So I came to her only as a seal. No one but me could hear her."

Taylor's eyes widened. "Oh man! I remember that summer. Her mom died of cancer on Poppy's birthday."

"It's also my birthday. And she was devastated. She came down to the end of the dock and cried. It was her tears. Each time her tears called me. Seven tears."

"She told me that summer she made a friend, but when I teased her, she got mad and said I couldn't meet him because he was a seal. I thought she was lying."

Cayden shook his head. "We played all summer around the dock and farther up along the point. We even took naps next to each other. Because we were both so young, the Council of Lords let us be. After all, I would be prohibited from seeing her again for seven years."

"Why seven?"

Cayden shrugged. "Tradition. The Silkie like the number seven. In the past, when a Silkie impregnated a human, he had to wait seven years before coming back to claim the child. Once a human calls us, we have one season with them and then we must wait. If the human calls no other Silkie, then we're allowed to return again in seven years."

"When she was fourteen," Taylor said. "But this time you showed up as you, well as the human you."

Cayden smiled without humor. "And I also came with all the Silkie baggage that time around. I was under intense pressure to mate with her."

"You were supposed to fuck her? She was just fourteen!" Taylor snarled.

"In our world, she was old enough, and no one saw anything wrong with it. But I knew better. After hearing Poppy's call when we were nothing more than children, I spent the seven years after that studying humans, and I knew your customs were different. I also knew that even though she might look old enough to do it physically, she wasn't ready mentally or emotionally. I kept putting it off, making excuses, despite my promise to my father that I would do what I was supposed to. What tradition demanded. Then I fell in love, and by some miracle Poppy loved me back. Despite her father forbidding us from seeing each other, we found a way. We met secretly, but it was still so innocent. Too innocent for my heritage and too intense for hers."

"But the accident happened," Taylor interjected

quietly.

Cayden stared out into the cove and swallowed. His eyes narrowed as he remembered that night, and Taylor saw the sorrow limning his face, making him appear far older than twenty-four. "Yes. The accident. I failed her. When she needed me, I was gone. Her father was right. It was my fault, because if I hadn't left, if I hadn't been so proud that my father had asked me to come with him, to train to take over for him one day, then I would have been there. I could have fucking stopped her from sailing out into the sound that day. But I didn't. And when I failed her, I ended up failing my whole damn family. I couldn't fulfill what our traditions demanded. It didn't matter just how close we had come, just like it didn't matter what had happened to prevent it."

Cayden looked back at Taylor. "After your uncle...father had me arrested, my parents came and got me. We sailed immediately for the islands around Scotland where I was brought before the Council of Lords. They, including my father, heard my case and passed judgment. I was banished until my twenty-fourth birthday. I could have no contact with the Silkie. Even my own family."

Taylor stared at him. "But that was just two days ago. And last night, I saw you out with your father and your brother. Wait...I thought you said you couldn't come to Poppy unless she called. What about last night?"

"If you'll think about it, Taylor, I was watching you. I never made eye contact with Annabel, I never spoke to her."

"Then how are you here, now?"

Cayden swallowed again. "Last night after you got back, she came down to the dock and called to me. Seven tears, and to me each one reverberated as loudly in the water as a thunderclap echoing through the mountains. She doesn't realize that she's doing it. And I have no choice. I must come to her. God help me, Taylor. She may hate me, but I *can't* leave her."

"What happens if things don't work this time?" Taylor asked quietly.

Cayden's laugh was harsh. "I'll die."

"They'll kill you?"

"No. I'll die. My life will end. For me to live, I must fully mate with her or she must die."

"What?" Taylor's dark blue eyes narrowed chillingly. "You're not killing my sister, Cayden. I'll kill you before I let anything happen to her."

He looked at Taylor sadly. "Haven't you heard a word I've said? I could never kill Bell. She is my heart, my mate. Silkies may be into casual sex, but a mate is for life. She's mine. I would die before I hurt her again or let anyone else hurt her," he finished hardly.

Taylor stared at him. "Is someone threatening her?"

Cayden's expression shut down and he closed his mouth in a thin line. "I should go."

"Where? If you've cut off ties with your family, where are you living?"

Cayden shrugged. "What does it matter? I can morph into a seal so any beach will do."

"There is the little matter of clothing."

"I keep a stash around. And I'm buying a boat." Cayden stared at Taylor and said quietly, "I'm glad she has you, and I'm sorry about the eye and your nose."

He stood up, dropped the towel, and was over the side of the *Revenge* before Taylor could ask him anything else. And he still had a million questions. Like what had happened in less than twenty-four hours that Cayden had gone from going out for a beer with his dad to cutting off ties? Somehow, though, he knew it had to do with Poppy.

66

He pulled up anchor and sailed the *Revenge* back across the bay. He knew without having been told that what Cayden shared was done in confidence. Taylor grimaced. Besides, who would believe the guy was one of the seal people anyway, unless they saw it with their own eyes? After all, Silkies were a myth. Not people you lived around year in and year out. And Cayden had talked about Faeries like they were just as real. What the fuck was that? Suddenly Taylor was reassessing everything he had thought to be true for the past seven years.

He had no choice. He had to believe Cayden. He had seen with his own eyes the transformation from man to seal and back again. And having been shown that little brain-frying bit of information, he had no reason to doubt any part of his story. Even down to what happened after Poppy's accident. After all, he already knew his parents and Uncle Phil had lied. They'd lied to him for years. That left Cayden as the one who had told the truth, and risked revealing his family's secrets to do it. Pretty compelling evidence.

Damn. Somehow, he had to find a way to help Poppy and Cayden get together. And that would mean going against Poppy's wishes, but now that he knew the entire story, he found he didn't have a problem with that.

****

Cayden spent the rest of the day in the bay and the sound, swimming, hunting and ignoring the calls from his mother. She assaulted him with her telepathy. Of all things, why did he have to have a mother who could project her thoughts? After being inundated all afternoon, he finally responded.

Leave me alone. If you ever want to see me again, you've got to give me space now.

Silence. It was what he'd fucking wanted, but it felt so lonely.

Seven years he'd spent longing for his family, longing for Bell, and he'd already screwed everything up. Cayden swiveled and twisted in and out of rocks and junk scattered along the sea floor. He narrowly slipped through a gap in a fishing net that was tangled on part of an old ship's hull and silently took himself to task. He knew better. The ocean was unforgiving to those who made mistakes. Distraction was deadly above and below the surface. On that point, Ciaran was absolutely correct.

Chapter 7

Taylor was very close-mouthed about his conversation with Cayden, but Annabel sensed a real change had taken place. Yet every time she tried to broach the subject, Taylor turned it away. Apparently even her brother wasn't immune to Cayden's magic. He left for the weekend, saying vaguely that he'd promised Sydney he would visit his toddler nephew, Thomas Remington Hensley, IV or little I.V. as Taylor had taken to calling him behind Sydney's back.

So here Annabel now sat, her legs hanging limply over the end of the dock. She had wheeled down in the chair, and although she didn't look forward to the return trip, she knew she could do it, as long as she was careful not to overtax herself. She stared down at the water with equal parts longing and trepidation. She needed to swim, needed the water to help her exercise her legs, especially with Taylor not there to help.

A sudden splash a few feet away made her look up. A harbor seal had its head poked out of the water watching her. Annabel suddenly had the strangest feeling as she stared at the seal.

She vividly remembered the summer, fourteen years ago, when she had laughed and played with another seal. *Whiskers.* Her best friend. She smiled sadly as she looked at this seal. It ducked below the surface. Then just a few seconds later, it reappeared, closer this time.

Now she swallowed nervously. No way could she get away if it decided to approach her. She braced her hands, intending to move herself back slowly when the seal suddenly rolled over onto its side and flapped one of its flippers at her. Annabel's eyes widened and she couldn't help herself, she giggled. The seal rolled onto its back and clapped both flippers together. She caught her breath.

Whiskers had done that! Surely not. Surely this couldn't be the same seal?

She stared into the seal's dark, liquid eyes. It swam closer, bigger than she remembered and she drew back. As she stared into its dark eyes again, an odd compulsion made her whisper, "Whiskers?" And then she felt immediately silly for having done so.

The seal gently nudged her feet, startling a cry from Annabel partly because she couldn't feel its touch, only see it. At her cry, the large animal ducked under the water then surfaced several feet away with an athletic, graceful flip. It surfaced again and made a soft growling noise, almost like a purr. Some of the tension eased from her. Once again it approached, this time stopping right at her feet where it began to blow bubbles.

"Oh! It *is* you." Annabel laughed. Then her laughter turned to tears and Whiskers nudged her feet again. She wiped her face and pulled her t-shirt over her head. She scooted her body to the very end of the dock and levered herself down into the water. She must have lost her mind, she thought. What were the odds that this really was the seal from so long ago? Almost non-existent. But when he came back again and gently bumped her, blowing bubbles around her, she was convinced. She laughed out loud and struck out swimming, moving her body in the modified dolphin kick that she was able to make her legs do.

The seal stayed right by her side, turning when she turned, and when she paused to rest, hovering close enough that she could hang onto him for support. She stroked his sleek head. Somehow he sensed that she had different needs now than she had when she was little.

All too soon, she turned regretfully back to the dock. Fatigue drained her reserves. She touched the seal's head.

"I have to go. I shouldn't have stayed as long as I did."

He blew bubbles at her. When she reached the ladder at the dock, she hooked her hands as high as she could reach and pulled up until she could lock her legs in place and reach up again. She got to the top and twisted. Whiskers had disappeared. Annabel grabbed her towel and blotted herself dry. The muscles in her arms trembled. She looked over her shoulder at the ramp up to the house. It looked a lot longer than it had earlier.

She would just rest a while. Then she would be ready to tackle it. After a new coating of sunscreen, she rolled over onto her stomach and put her head in her arms. It felt good to lie here with the warmth of the dock below her, the sun on her back, and the gentle lapping of the water. She had forgotten how wonderful it was, how it always restored her, and realized that in trying to blot out the heart-wrenching events of seven years ago, she had also blotted out the heart-warming ones.

Maybe she should keep the house. She could live here year round. She mentally shook her head. What was she thinking? She couldn't drive. She needed help with the sailboat. Summer maybe, but there was no way she could live here in winter. No. She would have to go back to the city, find a place there with good accessibility. She had already pretty much decided she would take a year off from school. She could always finish next year.

****

"Bell?" Cayden's voice was quiet, with an edge of

wary reserve.

She rolled over and pushed herself to a sitting position. "What are you doing here, Cayden?" she asked, equally wary.

He glanced away and then back to her again. "Taylor said he was going to be away this weekend, and he asked me to just drop by and check on you."

Annabel grimaced. "Checking to make sure the cripple doesn't do anything she shouldn't?"

Cayden scowled. "He worries about you. Is that so wrong?"

Annabel brushed her hair behind one ear. "No. I'm sorry. Look, I'm fine so you don't need to hang around like some babysitter."

He arched a brow at her. "Trying to get rid of me?"

She tilted her head, and for just a second it reminded him forcibly of Taylor. How had the entire world not realized the relationship between those two?

"Yes, Cayden. I am. I was never the picture of grace before my accident. Now, even less so. I have to get in my chair and get up that ramp. It's not pretty. I don't need an audience. So go away."

His mouth tightened. "I could help."

She glared at him. "I don't need your damn help! I've fought for seven years to get where I am now. Where were you then?" She brushed a hand across her face, obviously fighting for calm. "I'm sorry. That was uncalled for."

"I'm here now, Bell."

She looked up at him, so far above her. His eyes were dark and sincere. So handsome it made her heart ache. She swallowed convulsively. Conceding anything made her feel weak, something she'd sworn she'd never be again.

"Wait for me at the end of the dock. You can push me up the ramp."

He nodded and turned his back on her to walk that way. After gathering her towel, her MP3 player, and the rest of her belongings and shoving them in the bag on the back of her chair, Annabel maneuvered around so she could use the bar next to her chair to pull herself up. She sat for a moment with her head bowed after getting herself into the chair, more tired than she wanted to admit. Expertly, she turned the chair and began rolling up the dock to where Cayden waited for her.

He leaned casually against one of the posts, but straightened away when she approached. His feet were bare, and it suddenly dawned on her that she had never seen him wear a pair of shoes. He had beautiful feet, long and arched. The rest of him had been just as beautiful. Was it still? As if he realized where her thoughts were going, he smiled slowly, but instead of embarrassing her, she found herself smiling back.

"Here, Let me," he said quietly and began pushing her up the ramp from the dock to the house. "Were you really going to be able to do this by yourself?" he asked curiously.

"I would have had to take some breaks."

He didn't reply, but she felt his disapproval flowing over her in waves. Annabel dismissed it. She had more important concerns at the moment; chief among them was the ominous tightening of the muscles in her thighs. Oh God! All she needed right now was to start having muscle spasms, and if her thighs were already tightening, chances were other parts of her were already going into spasm and she just couldn't feel it.

She tried to keep her tone casual. "If you don't mind just pushing me on into the kitchen, I won't impose on you anymore."

He chuckled. "Trying to get rid of me again?" He paused to get the door and turned to glance down at her. His brows drew together. "Is something wrong?"

She gritted her teeth. "No. I'm fine."

He stood uncertainly in the kitchen. "Well. Okay. If you need anything, you can call the Yacht Club Marina. I'm usually around there in the evenings."

"Fine. You really don't need to worry, though." *Go. Just go before I embarrass myself!*

Cayden blinked like something had startled him, and then he turned to leave. As soon as he was out the door, Annabel scrambled to get to her valium. She twisted the cap and tapped two pills into the palm of her hand, throwing them in her mouth and dry swallowing. The first spasms hit as she turned to wheel out of the kitchen and she choked back a cry of pain. If she could just get to her bed and get in it, she could live with it until the drugs kicked in.

****

Cayden stood outside, staring back at the house. He had heard her thought! What was she worried would embarrass her? He wanted to go back inside. He opened his mind, trying to feel her, sense what was going through her head, but the only thing he could feel was tightness and pain. He grimaced as it rolled through him. Spasms? Was that what was going on? He sprinted back up the steps and into the house, through the kitchen and down the short hall. She had already managed to slide onto her bed, but her face was contorted with pain.

She opened her eyes as he slipped into her room and her face flushed. "Go away, Cayden!" she cried, but there was no real conviction in her voice, just a weariness and the pain that never seemed to quite leave it.

"I can't leave you like this, Bell," he said quietly, urgently. "Tell me what I can do to help."

She hesitated, but pain contorted her

expression, driving her like a demon. "My leg muscles are cramping," she admitted. "They need to be massaged and moved. I've taken some valium, but it hasn't had a chance to kick in yet."

He stepped forward and began to gently massage her legs with her instructions guiding him. After a few minutes, he felt her start to relax.

"Better?" he murmured.

Her eyes drooped. "Mmm."

"What about your thigh muscles? Do I need to massage them?"

"I—if you don't mind."

Cayden watched her changing expression, ignoring his own physical discomfort. As the hard knots of muscle in her leg relaxed, the tension in her face eased. He just hoped like hell she didn't open her eyes to see the effect this was having on him. Far from relaxing for him, his cock was painfully aroused. He was starved for her! It would be so easy to touch the soft folds between her thighs. Even now the tantalizing aroma that was uniquely hers filled his nostrils and made his cock twitch with longing. All he had to do was slide his hand just a little higher...

"All right now?" he asked, trying to keep the tension out of his voice.

"Umm," she breathed softly, and he realized she had gone to sleep.

Cayden escaped out onto the porch overlooking the dock. With a frustrated groan, he unzipped his pants and pulled his stiff, swollen cock out. His fingers brushed over the engorged head. As he began to stroke his aching shaft, hoping for relief, his mind went back to the first time he'd really been alone with her, when he was sure there were no prying eyes. It was right there on that dock. He'd found her after a fight with her father.

"Bell?" he'd asked softly. "What's the matter?"

She looked around but saw no boat.

"How did you get here?"

He sat down next to her and took her hand. "I brought the boat, but I hauled in farther up the beach."

"He doesn't want me to see you anymore!" she whispered.

Cayden felt like he'd been punched.

"Why?"

Poppy looked at him, her chin trembling. "It's my Aunt Helen's fault! She told him people were talking about us. I have to go with him to the city for a couple of days."

Cayden had turned toward her and pulled her over until his arms went round her. "Oh, Bell, don't cry. You'll be back, won't you?"

"Yes, but I don't want to go," she confessed. "I want to be with you."

She threw her arms around his neck and buried her face against his throat. Cayden breathed in the flowery scent of her hair and felt her lithe body nestle against him. He was careful to keep his hands on her back and her shoulders. Friends. Though he knew it would land him in a world of hurt, he'd promised himself he wouldn't touch her. Not until they were both ready.

Over the years, his feelings for her had grown stronger and stronger. The spark that reignited the very first time he saw her again now raged. A heat that threatened to engulf what few good intentions he still had. He moved his hand so he could put it underneath her chin and tilt her face up to his.

Their lips met, and this time the kiss was not quick. It was not light. Their inexperience made it tentative to begin with, but the passion on both sides was as intense as it was innocent. His body was telling him how much he wanted her, while his mind kept reminding him of his promises.

"Bell!"

It was a whisper against her mouth. A protest. It held the knowledge that they needed to stop, even as his body ached, letting him know just how much he wanted to continue.

"Please!" she pleaded.

He nibbled at her lips and her mouth parted for him. Cayden groaned. He felt her heat, and smelled her scent. The Silkie in him knew he could take her, wanted to take her. He knew if he touched her now she would be moist and ready for him. His body ached, crying out for the release only she could give him.

"No!" he said harshly and tore his mouth away from her. "Oh Bell, not like this! Not when you're upset and angry with your dad! Not here! Not on the end of the dock!"

He buried his face against her hair.

"I love you," he whispered.

"Then why wait?" Poppy pleaded. "When we both feel the same way?"

Cayden set her away from him, just enough to prevent them touching one another as anything more than the friends they had been as children. He had to be sensible, yet in the back of his mind was always the reminder that he was supposed to mate with her. It was his destiny, but not hers. Not until she was older.

"Not yet, Bell. I want it to be right for both of us."

She stuck her lower lip out, and her mutinous look suddenly made him chuckle.

"What's so funny?"

"Nothing." He said and then added with real feeling. "Trust me on that. I think we could both use some cooling off. Wanna go for a swim?"

"I don't have a suit."

"Just skinny dip."

"I thought we were being restrained and mature."

"Then don't look. I won't if you won't."

She tilted her head to look up at him. "Turn your back then."

When he had turned away, he heard the rustle of her clothing and then a splash as she dove off the end of the dock. He turned to see her t-shirt and the tiny piece of cloth that passed for her underwear. He picked it up, but nervousness and uncertainty made him drop it as if he had picked up a hot potato.

Seven years later, Cayden thought disgustedly, he was still just as overcome by the scent of her, and now he stood here like a hormone-crazed adolescent getting his rocks off just thinking about Bell. That night, he'd been a virgin who hadn't known what to do or how to handle it, and the truth was things weren't much different now. He could still smell the sweet fragrance of her sex. His fingers worked his cock from the shaft to the head. Would she still smell as sweet? As he fantasized about burying his face between her thighs, his cock jerked and his come spurted on the ground again and again until his nuts felt drained. He gasped for breath and then shut his eyes. He needed to be inside her and soon. He'd already waited a lifetime.

****

Annabel wheeled back down to the dock the next day around lunchtime. It probably wasn't the smartest thing to do with Taylor still gone, but she wanted to see if Whiskers would come back again. When she didn't see him, she felt a vague sense of disappointment. Still, now that she was down here, she needed to swim, just not as much as she had yesterday. She slipped off her shirt and eased down into the water. She played for a little while and then took a deep breath, before diving down where she could skim along the bottom using her arms and her dolphin kick.

Holding her breath for a long time was the one thing she had learned from Cayden seven years ago. As she explored the bottom for a couple of minutes, she moved forward a few more feet and then saw a sleek body moving lazily toward her. She smiled, and the seal swimming toward her barrel-rolled and moved supplely around her body in the lightest of caresses, blowing bubbles at her as he passed. Annabel giggled and then had to surface, gasping for air.

Whiskers came up next to her and she reached out to stroke his sleek fur. His nose nudged her cheek. Annabel laughed and slid her hands along his body, her fingers stroking the back of his head and then running along his powerful flippers. As her hands moved back up to the spot where his flippers joined his body, the seal moved his tail and sent them forward. She held on, laughing as they moved through the water. When he started to move too quickly, she let go and he slowed down and came back, blowing bubbles in a circle around her from her feet up to her face.

"Silly," she murmured softly. "Not so fast. You scared me." He offered himself again for another ride, and this time she stretched out along his back, her legs floating on other side of his long body. They bobbed through the water, her laughter floating up carefree and easy.

****

Taylor watched from the top of the dune. He was alarmed at first, but then quickly realized what he was seeing. What on earth was Cayden thinking? Had he told her? He began to walk slowly down the ramp, watching his sister and the animation on her face. It had been so long since he'd seen her so carefree, and he realized that Cayden was giving her a freedom of movement she had lost since her accident. Although she was much more mobile in the water, she still had limitations and those limitations were even greater on land.

When he set foot on the dock, the seal suddenly stopped and growled. He swam close to the ladder and then ducked away from Annabel and was gone. She looked after him, disappointment plain on her face, and grabbed the ladder.

"You scared him, Taylor!" she complained as she pulled herself up to the dock.

Obviously she didn't realize who her seal friend really was. "Poppy! What are you thinking? Don't you know seals can be very dangerous?"

She laughed. "Not him. That's Whiskers. I used to play with him when I was just a little girl!"

"Well, how do you know it's him? What if it were some other seal?" Taylor immediately thought of Cayden's brother or father. "How could you tell before it was too late?"

Poppy hesitated. "I don't know."

Chapter 8

Cayden came by that evening. When Annabel excused herself to make coffee, Taylor waited only until the door shut behind her. He turned to Cayden and demanded, "That was some shit this afternoon? Does she know it was you?"

"No, she doesn't know it was me," Cayden replied. "I just thought it would be a way to keep an eye on her, make sure she doesn't overextend herself. Although I didn't do too well yesterday."

Taylor frowned, his protective urges instantly on alert. "What do you mean?"

"She was exhausted when she got out of the water. I let her sleep for a while and then used the clothes I stashed in the *Revenge* to return in human form. I had to help her back to the house and then massage her legs. She cramped. Does that happen a lot?"

"It's pretty common. There's a very fine line between enough exercise and too much exercise. It can also be a sign of other problems like bladder infections, but she has feeling almost everywhere but her feet, even if she doesn't have muscle control, so that's normally not an issue. Her mobility isn't as good. Especially in her right leg." Taylor paused. "Look, I can see the benefits to you swimming with her as a seal, but what if it's not you who shows up? How would she know?"

Cayden's eyes narrowed on Taylor before he looked up and out across the bay.

"I see your point. I'll admit it's hard to tell us apart in seal form, unless you're one of us or a real seal. Still, she seems to know."

Taylor raised his brows. "I don't need maybes, Clifton. Is there a reason to be concerned for her safety?"

Cayden stared at him. "Yes. That's one of the reasons I've been hanging around as soon as I know she's in the water. My father...well, I think he was just shooting off his mouth, but he said he wished he'd killed her all those years ago."

Annabel came back through the screen door. Her sapphire eyes went from one man to the other. "You two aren't arguing again, are you?"

Taylor laughed. "No. We've buried the hatchet and not in each other's heads."

She smiled. "Coffee's ready. Do you want to bring it out on the porch or drink it inside?"

Taylor stood. "I'll put it on a tray and bring it out here." He needed time to let what Cayden said sink into his head. His father had threatened her?

****

Taylor's departure left Cayden and Annabel alone together. She pleated the material of her skirt with trembling fingers. He couldn't take his eyes off the small, nervous movement. He cleared his throat.

"Are you feeling better today?" he asked stiltedly. *God!* She was so fragile. He wanted to hold her close and never let her go. But he knew she would hate for him to hover over her like that.

"Yes, thank you. I—I'm sorry I wasn't better company last night."

"That's okay."

The silence stretched.

"Would you...?" he began.

"We can't..." she began at the same time.

They both stopped. Cayden motioned to her. "Ladies first."

"We can't keep on like this, Cayden." Her mouth trembled.

"You want me to leave?" His gut twisted. Christ, please say no.

"Yes. No!" She bit her lower lip and swallowed. He could see the pulse beating in the hollow of her throat. "I'm afraid to let you back in my life," she whispered. "I'm afraid that if you leave me again... it was so hard last time. I—I can't go through that again."

He reached over and took her hand in his. "Unless you tell me to leave, I'm not going anywhere, Bell. I swear that to you. There's a lot we need to talk about. Things I need to explain." He stopped and simply stared at her. "May I take you out sailing tomorrow? Could we try to make a new start?"

She looked at her hand in his and her eyes scanned his face to read his expression. Cayden returned her gaze, hiding nothing from her. Finally, she said firmly. "Yes. Yes, I'd like that."

The weight of the world had just lifted off his shoulders. "Great! I have my own boat. She's not as big as the *Revenge*."

Annabel laughed. "It doesn't matter. I could pack a lunch."

Taylor came out just then carrying the coffee tray. "Making plans?"

Cayden nodded.

"That's good," Taylor remarked. "I forgot to tell you, Poppy. I have to run into the city tomorrow to get some paperwork completed. You know, I'll be starting at the firm the first of August, and they want to get some of the insurance and benefits paperwork out of the way so I can hit the ground running."

"Cayden's taking me sailing." She offered.

"Great!" Taylor said. "Make a day of it. Are you taking the *Revenge*?"

"No. I bought a boat," Cayden clarified. "She's a little smaller and older. I've been fixing her up as I paid for her."

"I'd like to see her sometime. I did that with my first dinghy and really learned a lot. Poppy even helped. Do you remember that summer? You were eleven or twelve, I think."

"That was the summer I went back to the city looking like an Appaloosa from all the paint spots."

Cayden hated to leave. He enjoyed their company, especially now that Bell was smiling and looking happier, but if he was going to have her on board, he wanted to make sure the *Belle* was as spotless and neat as she could be. If Annabel were to get around the boat, there could be nothing out of place that might cause her to fall or get hurt. He looked at her as he finished his coffee. She was so damn pretty it made his heart ache and his cock throb just to look at her. He wanted things to be like they were. He wanted to hold her and touch her. He wanted to make love to her until she fell to pieces in his arms.

He set his cup down with a definite click.

"I better get going. I'll pick you up around ten. Is that okay, Bell?"

"Yes. Good night, Cayden."

He returned her smile, shook hands with Taylor and then disappeared into the darkness.

****

Annabel couldn't do anything right the next morning. She spilled her pills in her lap, burned her fingers on the toaster and added too much coffee to the coffeemaker so that their morning brew looked and tasted more like sludge. Taylor just laughed, which made her mad.

"It's just Cayden, Poppy!" Taylor teased.

"I know you're a guy, but have you looked at him?" she demanded. "He's gorgeous! And even though I keep telling myself that it's Cayden, the boy I loved seven years ago, he's different!"

"How?" Taylor demanded as he helped her through some motion exercises.

"He's bigger and older."

"Poppy—you're older too, even if you aren't much bigger."

"He's harder."

"What do you mean 'harder'?" Taylor drawled, pausing in manipulating her leg.

Annabel rolled her eyes. "Not that way...tougher. He's changed. There used to be something so sweet about him."

Her brother held her leg up carefully flexing and extending her foot. "He's had to be tough, Poppy. There are things...well, he needs to tell you. But I think the Cayden you knew and loved is still there. You just have to find him."

Annabel turned her face away and stared at the picture that was sitting on her bedside table. It was a shot of Taylor and her taken the day they competed in the regatta that summer she was fourteen. Her mouth twisted. Those days were gone.

Taylor paused in the act of picking up her other leg. "What is it, Poppy? Something's still bothering you."

She looked at him knowing she could do nothing to hide the uncertainty and defensiveness in her eyes. "Why?" she whispered. "He could have anyone, Taylor. Why would he want me," she gestured at her legs, "like this?"

He set her leg down and sat on the edge of the bed. With one arm braced by her head, he leaned closer to her. "Because I keep telling you, kiddo, you're beautiful and sexy. He wanted you seven years ago, and he still does. 'Love is not love which alters when it alteration finds.' Shakespeare— Sonnet 116. If I thought for a minute that he loved you any less because of 'this' as you keep saying, I would never have let him back through the door."

He stroked her hair off her face. "I have to go so I can get into the city. Keep an open mind, Poppy. Trust him."

She grimaced. "That is not an easy task, Taylor. I've had damn little to trust in for most of my life."

She worked on packing a lunch in the big cooler Taylor had brought out of the pantry for her. In an odd way, it helped to calm her, so that when she heard Cayden's knock she was able to smile fairly normally as she went to the door. He was dressed in long khaki slacks, a light blue polo shirt and deck shoes.

She giggled.

"What's so funny?" Cayden asked looking down, obviously wondering if he had spilled something on himself.

"You have shoes on. I don't think I've ever seen you with shoes."

Cayden grinned and then looked at her sundress and sandals and the thick braid of her hair. "You look beautiful, Bell," he told her. "Are you ready?"

She swallowed. "Will I need my chair? I thought if we were just going sailing, I could leave it and use the crutches."

"I wanted to take you to your cove. I thought we could swim and eat lunch there."

She tilted her head quizzically. "My cove?"

Cayden flushed a little bit. "It's how I always think of it...Bell's Cove."

"Then I'll use the crutches. If you'll take the cooler and my backpack, I'll follow you down." She hoped that if he was in front of her, he wouldn't have as much time to notice how ungainly she was. No matter how she went about it, there was simply no getting around the fact that for her walking was work, and not very pretty work at that.

He took the backpack from her, slung it over one shoulder and then hefted the cooler.

"I'll meet you down at the bottom." She watched him easily negotiate what was a struggle for her each and every time she wanted to get to the water.

****

Cayden knew what she was up to, and did his best to allow her some privacy. But he also knew that if they were going to make a relationship work, the issue of her paralysis would have to be dealt with head on. There could be no hiding. He would not spend his entire life walking in front of her so she could save face. He wanted her beside him. Once on board the *Belle*, he stowed the cooler and backpack and busied himself with getting out lifejackets and checking the wind.

Cayden turned just in time to lift her over the gunwale and set her in the stern. Remembering the conversation he'd overheard when she was out with Taylor, he handed her a lifejacket and put on his own. He was rewarded with a smile that almost made him forget what he was doing. He blinked and hopped up onto the dock to untie before jumping down next to her.

"Ready?"

Annabel watched him as they cut through the water toward the cove. He was a good sailor, more cautious than Taylor had ever been. She wondered if some of that was because she was on board. It reassured her, comforted her. She liked the way the wind ruffled his dark hair, and the way his eyes crinkled as he looked up at the sail. He turned once and caught her looking at him. She blushed. He smiled.

A thousand things still needed to be said, but she had no idea where to even begin. When he grinned, she saw a shadow, a memory of the Cayden she had known seven years ago, but they had both changed so much and she just didn't know how they would find their way back to what they had shared, or if they even could. Seven years was a long time. Things changed. People changed. They weren't kids any longer, and she knew that opened up a whole new area in their relationship. But they had been such close friends then.

Annabel turned her face into the wind and smiled as she remembered how they played together that summer when she was fourteen to his seventeen. She had spotted him on the beach the morning after a storm and thought he was dead, but she'd found out pretty quickly he was anything but!

Poppy ran forward and knelt down next to a boy who appeared to be about her Cousin Taylor's age. He was beautiful. Her hands shook as she reached out to touch him, half afraid she would feel that same coolness and lifelessness she had felt with her mother. His skin was cool, but it still had the resilience of living flesh, and she blushed at having touched his bare skin.

"Hey!" she called again, more softly this time. "Are you okay?"

That was stupid. Of course he wasn't. She saw the scrapes on his forehead, his shoulder, and his legs. He must have been caught in the storm. Had he been on a boat? She searched the shore but saw no wreckage. She shook him slightly. His wet hair was long, thick, and straight. Although olive tinted, his skin was still pale.

As she looked at him, she saw nothing obviously broken. His arms and legs were long and straight. She swallowed again and felt her face heat with a blush she couldn't control. He wore only a pair of cutoffs. Like hers, they hung low on his hips. She stared at the smooth skin of his stomach and chest. Just a faint line of dark hair arrowed down his chest. His muscles were well defined. Probably a jock, she thought, and that put him way out of her league. She was so not the cheerleader type.

When her gaze returned to his face, she found him looking at her out of velvety brown eyes, thickly lashed and somewhat dazed. Poppy jerked back so quickly she overbalanced and plopped onto her bottom on the wet sand. Great! That was sure to make a good impression. Somehow, her klutziness hadn't turned him off.

They were nearly inseparable until Aunt Helen spread her poison. She'd dropped hints to Annabel's father that people were talking about how much time she spent with Cay. Just the thing guaranteed to grate with a father already concerned that Cayden was too old for her. Annabel now knew just how much from his journal entry the night of their argument. Her father had taken her into the city to try to get her away from Cayden.

Dear Em,

I wish you were here. Our little girl is growing up too fast for me. She's been hanging around a boy. A young man, really. They spend all their time together. Helen says something's going on, and tonight, while we were at the apartment, Poppy admitted kissing him. She swears nothing else has happened.

But what if she's lying? Just the thought of him touching her...my baby. God. You would know how to handle this, Em, but I just feel like a boat adrift at sea. The look on her face when I asked her if she'd had sex with him!

I don't see any other way than to simply forbid him to see her again...

As she looked at Cayden's hands on the wheel, she remembered the way he had held her and comforted her, and her lips parted. Her father might have forbidden them to see each other, but that hadn't kept them apart. They'd snuck out at night. Annabel shook her head. Cay could have taken advantage of that. She had suffered from such a crush back then, but he had always been so careful. That attraction still had the power to heat her blood and make her heart pound, and that scared her more than anything else.

He turned his head and caught her look. There was an instant answering flare of heat in his dark gaze, and she began to wonder exactly how the day would end. She vividly remembered her last trip with him here. His mother had packed a hamper for him. He had snuck her out at night after her father was asleep and they'd sailed here. Her eyes drifted to the beach as she remembered biting into the peach she'd found in the basket.

It was incredibly tender and juicy. Some of the juice ran down her chin and dripped onto her fingers. She laughed as she demolished the rest of it, but when her eyes met Cayden's, his velvety gaze was intent, staring at her mouth. He leaned toward her and softly kissed her lips, and then he did something that nearly made her faint. His tongue darted out to lick the juice from her chin. He captured her hand in his wrist and sucked the juice from her fingers.

Poppy's heart pounded erratically and her breath gasped between her parted lips when he finished. She was both thrilled and frightened by what she felt. She moaned softly. "Cay!"

His fingers traced the line of the peach juice, tickling her neck until they paused at the hollow of her throat.

"Bell." His voice was an agonized whisper of sound in the dark stillness of the cove.

Poppy breathed so quickly now she was afraid she would pass out. Would this finally be the time when he took things farther? Did she really even want him to?

He kissed her and rubbed her shoulders with his broad palms. Slowly, shyly, she touched his chest with fingers that trembled. Her heart pounded so hard she knew he must hear. "There's plenty of time, Bell," he murmured against her mouth. "We have all the time in the world. I won't do anything to hurt you."

But in the first flush of sexual arousal, slowly was not what she wanted.

"Don't you want to?" she asked, afraid that he hesitated because he didn't feel that way.

Cayden chuckled and rolled onto his back. "It's practically all I think about, Bell." He heaved a sigh. "But I don't want to feel like your dad was right about me. Like the only reason I want to be around you is for that." He rolled toward her again and stared down at her in the darkness. "It's so much more."

Poppy touched his cheek. "For me too. While Daddy and I were arguing, I told him I love you, and he told me I was too young, and I didn't know what love meant. But I do Cayden."

Back in the present, Annabel closed her eyes against the powerful memory. She had wanted so much more. As she'd gotten older and realized how much she'd lost, she had fantasized how differently the night might have been. How differently she wished it had been?

In her dreams, the grown up Cayden would lean down and kiss her. "Let me at least do something for you. Okay? I won't hurt you, I promise, and you can tell me to stop any time you want."

He would slowly remove her bikini. When he'd bared her breasts, he would lower his head to kiss and suckle them until she moaned softly, her hands fisting in his hair. While he continued to caress her, his hands would move lower, sliding her bottoms down. He would slip them from her. When she started to cover her mound with her hands, he would shake his head.

"No, Bell. You're beautiful."

He'd hold her wrists to her sides as he lowered his head and kiss down over her belly. He would pause for a moment at her navel to tease it with the tip of his tongue. Her trembling legs would fall apart and his hands would part them farther. He'd look up and they'd simply stare at one another for a long moment before he would lower his face between her thighs...

It wasn't what had really happened. As always, Cayden had been the perfect gentleman. A few kisses, some tender touches and then he had gruffly insisted they go swimming because after all they had all the time in the world. And what a cruel joke that had turned out to be.

They had lost so much since that night. She wanted it back. Was it too much to ask?

Cayden reduced sail as they entered the cove, guiding them as close to shore as he dared before dropping anchor.

"Do you want to swim first, or would you like to just sit and talk for a while?"

She looked up into his face, seeing the steady warmth in his brown eyes. "Talk," she murmured softly. They had to start somewhere.

He took off his lifejacket and helped her with hers. "Are you comfortable enough?"

"Yes."

"I remember the last time we were here. I asked you that same thing...if you wanted to swim or talk. You picked swim. Do you remember that night?"

She blushed and nodded. Oh she remembered it all right, in fact had relived it and built it to such a fantasy that she knew her sex would be dripping wet.

"You had a picnic basket your mom packed with the juiciest peaches."

"Mmm." Cayden closed his eyes, a smile playing around the corners of his firm mouth. "I also remember licking the peach juice off your chin, and wishing I could lick a few other things as well." He opened his eyes and looked straight into her face, grinning wickedly as he saw her blush. His expression turned abruptly serious again. "I loved you then, Bell. I told you so that night. Nothing has changed. I still love you."

She stared down at her hands. "Everything has changed, Cayden. I'm not the same person I was then. I was young and thought I had the whole world at my feet, but the accident changed that. As much as I might want it, I...I don't think I can be the woman you need. Look at you! You're so vital and I am..."

"Still the woman I love." He sat at her feet and took her hands in his own. "Nothing changed that, Bell. Nothing. Please don't try to save me from myself. Too many people have already tried." He pressed her hands to his face and then turned them over to press kisses in each of her palms. "You're all I've ever wanted. All I ever will want."

She yanked her hands away and covered her face. "Then why didn't you come back?" she demanded in a choked voice. She was afraid that pain would shatter her into pieces. "I needed you so much after the accident. I hated what happened to me! I hated that I drove you away."

"No! You never drove me away." He was beside her in an instant, pulling her into his arms, and onto his lap, cradling her, rocking her. "Oh Annabel, don't ever think you drove me away. If I could have been there, I would have been."

Sincerity shone from his dark eyes. She clutched at his shirtfront. "Then why weren't you?"

He held her and she heard the uneven thud of his heart, the harsh, shaky sound of his breathing. She took some comfort in the fact that he was as torn up as she was at the moment. He buried his face in her hair while one of his hands cupped the back of her head.

"There are things... things about my family that I can't tell you right now. I had to go with them. I didn't have a choice." He held her away from him and stared into her face. "I had broken rules, traditions that our family—our extended family—takes very seriously. I was punished."

She looked at him in confusion. What he said made no sense to her. "You mean like grounded? I don't understand."

Cayden looked away. "The heads of our family sent me away. You would call it being banished."

Annabel pushed at him, straining away from him until he set her on the seat. "Don't *fuck* with my head, Cayden! You sound like you just stepped out of some bad medieval movie!"

He raked a hand through his hair, his own temper rising. "That just about sums it up! You have no idea what my family is really like! I was sent away for seven years! Had I even attempted to contact you, I was afraid of what would happen to me and to you. I saw my family for the first time since then on the day of my birthday...your birthday. Yes, that's right. We even share the same goddamn birthday! The night after you begged Taylor to get you away from me, I argued with my mother and father over you, and I haven't seen them since then. They knew what had happened to you, and they never told me because they knew if they did, they would never get me away from you!"

Cayden stopped, his hand shielded his eyes from her view, but the muscles in his jaw and throat worked spasmodically. He was teetering on the edge every bit as much as she was. She still wasn't sure how his family could wield such power, but she could see how upset he was.

"Don't." she whispered shakily. "Please don't,

Cayden! I...I'm not worth it."

"Fuck that!" He slid down onto his knees in front of her, his eyes tortured. "Don't say that. Don't *ever* say that. I loved you then, Bell and I love you now. I never stopped loving you. I need you, sweetheart."

He grabbed her and pulled her into his arms, his mouth searching and finding hers with a hunger that had only grown in the seven years since their separation. Her mouth opened to him and he plunged in, deepening their kiss as his hands roved over her restlessly.

"I dreamed of you. For seven years, all I wanted was to touch you and kiss you again," he declared.

His mouth covered hers once more, his fingers trailing down the column of her throat and brushing lightly, delicately against her breast. His body quivered with need.

"Cay." Her fingers twined in his hair pulling him closer. She clung to him, molding herself to his body.

"I want to make love to you, Bell. Completely, so there's no doubt that you're mine. I've waited seven years for this moment."

He had waited? She drew back to look at him, searching his passion-filled expression. "You've never?"

He shook his head. "Have you?"

She smiled at him. "Men haven't exactly lined up at the door to take me out. A wheelchair and crutches have a rather ardor-dampening effect."

He touched her cheek and swallowed. "Don't belittle yourself, Bell. It's certainly not dampening mine in the least."

They stared at each other, face to face, their fingers stroking cheeks, touching lips, and caressing jaws.

"May I take you below?" he asked softly.

"Yes."

His eyes traveled the length of her body. "Can

you? I mean, is there any problem? I won't hurt you, will I?"

His concern warmed her. She tilted her head and touched his cheek again. "It's never really come up before. I don't think it's a problem, and I have feeling...there."

She stopped and blushed. Cayden groaned and slid his arms behind her back and under her legs before he lifted her and carried her down into the small cabin. After setting her on the bed in the bow, he unzipped her sundress and slid it from her shoulders. His eyes darkened even more when he unveiled the curves of her breasts.

"Lie back," he whispered. His hands tender and his eyes intense as he slid the dress from her and then gently loosened her sandals. He cupped her feet in his large hands, brushing his thumbs over the arches. She lay on the bed clad only in a wisp of white lace. Shyness overwhelmed her and she fought not to cover herself from his heated gaze because she could certainly see the effect she had on him.

"You're so damn beautiful, Bell," he breathed. Hunger burned in his dark eyes.

After laying her legs down carefully on the bed, he touched her breast with the tip of his fingertip and then let his fingers trail across her stomach to rest lightly against the lace covering her. She sucked in her breath and he smiled ever so slightly before he looked up into her eyes again. As she watched, he pulled his shirt over his head to reveal a chest lightly covered with dark hair that disappeared in a thin line beneath the waistband of his khakis. Seeing her intense stare, he smiled slowly and wickedly and smoothed his hand down over his rounded pecs and ripped stomach to the waistband of his pants.

Annabel swallowed as her eyes focused on the bulge in the front of his slacks. She vividly remembered how large he was from the peeking she'd done when they were teenagers. He slid his belt off, but as his hands went to the button at his waistband, she begged nervously, "Wait! Can we...could we just kiss for a while?"

He smiled and stretched out beside her, his hands cradling her. "Whatever you want. Whenever you're ready."

She kissed him again, moaning softly as the hair on his chest tickled her breasts. His leg eased between her thighs, rubbing gently against her until she felt her breath quicken at the sensations he created. When his fingers slid beneath the lace to play with her clitoris and stroke along the smooth wet folds of her sex, she whimpered at the exquisite sensation.

"Okay?" he asked.

"Oh, yes! More Cay."

"Tell me if anything I do hurts you."

Her head fell back against the pillows. "The only thing that would hurt right now is if you stopped."

He chuckled softly as his lips slipped down her throat and over her chest until he took one of her nipples into his mouth, teasing it into a hard peak. The pull of his suckling tugged all the way down to her aching sex. He eased her panties down and away, standing briefly to strip his khakis and shorts off. She looked at him and swallowed. His cock was long and thick, so hard that it touched his stomach, a drop of fluid already leaking from the swollen red head of it.

"I won't do anything you don't want me to, Bell," he promised her.

They both lost themselves in sensations, touching and caressing each other as the boat rocked gently in the water, the sound of it lapping against the outside of the hull. His breathing roughened, but his hands were exquisitely gentle and careful as he parted her thighs and ran his fingers up the soft flesh on the insides. "Can you feel this?"

Oh God! She could and it nearly made her sob out loud with gratitude.

"Yes, Cay!" she cried softly as he touched her again. She saw the way he struggled to control himself, to go slowly. "I don't want to wait any longer. Please."

"I want to make sure you're ready." His expression was intense, his jaw hard and his nostrils flared. His dark eyes met hers for just an instant before he lowered his face between her legs and used the flat of his tongue to lick from the opening of her vagina up to her clit where he stopped to suck lightly. She arched against his mouth. "That's it, baby," he crooned and slipped two fingers into her tight passage. Her juices made a soft sucking noise as he teased her by flicking his fingers back and forth inside her. With his free hand he spread her legs apart in preparation for him.

His eyes searched hers hungrily as he positioned himself between her thighs. "I'm afraid I'll hurt you," he whispered softly. "I can stand anything but that, Bell."

"I won't break." She watched him take hold of his thick cock and he began to slowly rub the head of it up and down her slick lips. His big body shuddered.

"You're so wet for me. Are you ready, darling?"

At her nod, he pushed forward, his breathing ragged, until he met resistance, and his breath went as still as his body.

"Are you all right?"

"Yes."

He lowered his mouth to hers, kissing her hungrily as he thrust forward. She cried out softly and he stilled once more.

"Did I hurt you?"

She shook her head. What did it matter if she had felt a momentary sting?

"I can feel you," she said wonderingly. "I can feel you inside me!"

She closed her eyes and sobbed.

"Bell? What is it? What's wrong?" He was instantly concerned that he had done something to hurt her, but even his concern was losing ground to the amazing sensation of feeling his cock so tightly sheathed inside her. She was like a hot, wet glove around his pulsing shaft, nothing at all like the hand he'd made do with when he thought about her.

She touched his cheek, tears running from her eyes into her hairline. "Nothing! Absolutely nothing! I can feel you moving inside me."

He smiled at her in relief and then gasped as his balls tightened. He could feel the rush of his oncoming orgasm and knew there was nothing he could do to stop it. Not this time.

"I'm sorry!" he muttered. "I wanted this first time to be so good, but I've imagined this for so long and I can't. Wait. Any. Longer."

He thrust in and out of her, his hands cupping her hips. It was so hard to hold back when she was wrapped so tightly around him. It was a sensation he'd only fantasized about. While the rest of the Silkie males might have been fucking since puberty, he'd always known Annabel Barton was the only woman he would love, but his fantasies never prepared him for the reality of what it was like to have his cock buried balls deep inside of her. His groan of completion mingled with her cry of pleasure. Cayden lowered his head next to hers and whispered in her ear. "I'm so sorry, Bell. I didn't know how it would be, how it would feel once I was all the way in. I'll make next time better for you, I promise."

She turned her face to his and touched his

cheek. "That you want a next time is enough."

He smiled at her, pulling her on top of him as he rolled onto his back. "Oh, God! A next time and a next time and a time after that, until you tell me you don't want me anymore."

She smiled. "That will never happen."

They slept, curled together on the wide bunk and rocked by the gentle waves. Cayden sheltered her with his big body, pulling her close, his arms twined protectively around her. Sometime later, he whispered, "Eat or Swim?"

"Swim."

He grinned wickedly at her as he turned her to face him. "With suits or without?"

"Without."

"Right answer." He growled against her ear and then lifted her in his arms and carried her up top.

"Set me down on the stern," she murmured. "I can get in from there."

"I'm going to get our stuff to shore and I'll join you."

He had anchored shallow enough that he could stand. Holding the blanket and towels over his head in one arm, he used the other to float the cooler to shore. Annabel couldn't help but watch as he emerged from the water, sleek and graceful with his powerful butt and thighs. He truly had the body of a swimmer, all long smoothly defined muscles. His calves were shapely, narrowing down to strong ankles. Her eyes widened as she noticed he still wore the same leather anklet he'd had all those years ago. After setting everything down, he turned and caught her staring at him. He grinned and ran back into the water, leaping into a smooth dive as he swam toward her.

She took a deep breath and dove below the surface, opening her eyes as she headed down to the bottom, gliding along, her fingers touching sand and rocks and shells. As he dove down, she used her stronger leg to push off and shoot toward the top, undulating her body in a dolphin kick that brought her laughingly back up into the sunlight. He surfaced next to her.

His expression was curious. "How do you have so much mobility in the water?"

She smiled. "It supports a lot of my weight for one thing, but I've also learned how to use other muscles in my body to make up for my legs. Most of my kick comes from my stomach and lower back."

He floated next to her and blew bubbles at her before he raised his head. "Mmm. Sex muscles."

"What?" She spluttered

"Some of the same muscles you use for sex. Trust me, Bell, watching you swim is an erotic experience. Wanna feel?"

When she reached out and circled his erection, he groaned. Then she startled him even more by sinking underwater and taking him into her mouth. While she sucked him, her hand caressed his butt. He pulled her up, wrapped her legs around his waist and slipped his cock inside her. He continued to tread water while he gently thrust in and out of her, but when they were both ready to finish, he guided them to water shallow enough that he could stand. While his hands supported her ass and her thighs, he drove himself in and out of her until his hips jerked as he pumped his semen in her in several bursts.

They played, diving and chasing each other. Cayden was amazed at how well she still moved through the water, using her arms and her body to twist away, as graceful as she had ever been even before the accident, but he watched her carefully because he knew she tired more easily. As soon as he saw it, he swam over to her.

"Put your arms on my shoulders, darling. You

can ride on my back and I'll give you a piggyback ride onto the beach. How does that sound?"

"Like a wonderful idea." She kissed him. "I love you, Cay."

He closed his eyes for just a second to savor it. Seven years he had dreamed of hearing her say those words. His mate. No matter what anyone said. She would be his mate.

They ate and made love again. This time Cayden held himself back long enough to pleasure her with his mouth and tongue. He turned her over on her belly, moving her until her bottom was up in the air. He kissed his way down her spine to the scars at the small of her back.

"Do they hurt? The scars?"

"No. Not anymore."

His eyes drifted over the smooth, round cheeks of her ass, and he felt his cock go instantly hard again. She was beautiful from any angle, but seeing her positioned as the Silkie traditionally made love was almost more than he could stand. He gently spread her to prepare her for his entry.

"What are you doing?" She whispered over his shoulder.

"Loving you, darling. Just a different position. He teased her moist sex with his fingers, slipping inside her to stroke. She sobbed his name. The Silkie in him growled with satisfaction.

"You like that?" He murmured as he kissed the smooth globe of her butt cheek. "I want to hear you scream when you come for me, love. I want to feel you tighten on my finger."

"Cay!" she gasped and pushed back against his hands. He bent over and softly bit her on the ass. With a scream she climaxed, gasping his name as her hands curled into the blanket underneath her. He pulled his fingers out and guided his cock into her pulsating core. He groaned when he joined his body to hers.

She still sobbed with pleasure.

"Oh Cay, I never dreamed. More, please, more."

He braced his hands on the ground on either side of her and thrust his cock back and forth until he climaxed deep inside her once more.

With both of them sated, they fell next to each other and slept. As the afternoon shadows lengthened, he touched her cheek tenderly. "I should get you back," he murmured softly. "I don't want Taylor at my throat again for tiring you out, or wondering if I've abducted you."

He gave her a piggy back ride out to the boat, helping her on board, and wrapping her snugly in a towel before he went back to get the rest of their things. When he saw how tired she was, he helped her dress and pulled back the covers on the bunk.

"Lie down and rest, Bell. Do you need your medicine?"

"I don't want it Cay. It makes me sluggish."

In the end, he persuaded her to take it, afraid that if she didn't she would endure more of the painful spasms he had seen the other night. Once she settled down, he stroked her hair and went back up on deck to haul in the anchor and unfurl the sail. In just a few minutes, the *Belle* had come about and was headed out of the cove. Bell's cove. The place where he'd first kissed her and the place where he'd finally mated with her. He whispered a spell learned from his mother when he was still young, spreading protection over the cove and making it visible only to the Silkie and their friends. Now it was truly Bell's cove. Cayden smiled and lifted his face to the breeze. After seven years of grayness, he reveled in the late afternoon sun, and felt hope and power flow through him.

Chapter 9

So he'd finally done it. Ciaran watched the *Belle* pass by and followed from a distance. Cayden had finally fucked his human. He'd heard them on the boat, saw them on the beach, and felt a searing shaft of jealousy and anger at his elder brother that he took out on the Silkie maid who'd followed him. Part of him was grateful for her presence. She wasn't looking for a long-term relationship. It was simply late in the mating season and she was horny. He obliged her, taking his anger at his brother and parents out by being rough with her. He'd gotten over his teenage crush on Annabel Barton. She'd been one hot teenager seven years ago, but who wanted a cripple for God's sake? His resentment of Cayden hardened. All his elder brother had to do was crook a finger and he had their parents fawning over him and the human begging him to fuck her.

Ciaran spent most of his time in seal form these days, ignoring the calls from Catriona to come home. He felt a blinding hatred for his parents, but in particular his father. He would have his revenge, and then he would take over Carrick's position even if he had to fight Cayden to do it. There was only a year separating them and Ciaran had always had the size advantage over his brother. They'd fought often enough seven years ago. Ciaran had started most of those battles, egging his brother on over his little human.

He thought several times about just forgetting all about it and heading south again. He could just forget the pain then, the betrayal. How could his father so easily discount the last seven years when Ciaran had worked so hard to be the perfect son?

If he just left, he could put it behind him. Start over. He had enjoyed his time with the South American Clan when he was a teenager. They were far more easygoing, far more open and relaxed in their mating relationships and that appealed to Ciaran. There were always females, human and Silkie, hungry for fucking.

He pushed aside the female he'd just taken and dove back into the bay. He could go south, but bitterness ate at him, bitterness and a need for revenge. One thing was sure. His family would not continue to overlook him.

****

Catriona Clifton stood on the bow of the *Skerry* and let the wind ruffle her dark auburn hair. She had been uneasy and upset ever since her sons left. As much as she would never admit it aloud, though, it was Cayden about whom she was really concerned. Ciaran would always look out for Ciaran first until the time came when he found his own mate. That was his way, but she knew her elder son would sacrifice his own life to protect Annabel Barton. It had been that way since they were just children, and nothing had changed that.

But something else had changed. She felt all day long that his relationship with the human was transitioning. Something monumental was taking place, and it only increased her uneasiness. Had Cayden finally joined with her?

Catriona shivered. She feared Carrick's reaction should he find out. He was incensed that Cayden still wanted the girl. It was more than her disability. Somewhere along the line, he had begun to blame Annabel Barton for everything that had transpired. Cayden's banishment, his falling out with them again and leaving.

It was hard sometimes not to blame her. Yet Catriona still remembered that first summer. She had watched the two of them together, both so young. Even then there was a connection between them that was magical. After all, wasn't magic what they were all about? And that was one reason why King Riordan had allowed them to simply be. He understood the magic, although much of that seemed to have evaporated in recent years. Humans dismissed it as ordinary superstitions, their lives now ruled by technology. Plain and simple, people just didn't believe anymore, but it was hard not to when you saw Cayden and Annabel. They were magic.

"Why are you here so pensive, my love?" Carrick murmured in her ear.

"I was thinking of Cayden," she said turning in his arms and resting her cheek against his chest.

"He has joined himself to her," Carrick stated. At his wife's look of surprise he rolled his eyes. "Even I, dimwitted, emotional telepath that I am, can sense that sort of monumental shift."

Carrick turned away to stare off toward the point where the Barton house stood. Catriona felt how livid he was that Cayden had mated with the girl. She had always been able to read him when he was angry, and right now he believed Annabel had taken his son away from him, and he saw no way their relationship could come to a happy ending, but somehow it would have to end.

"Carrick," his wife said softly. "It's done now. It had to be done this time. Perhaps since it is, you might convince him to come back. Perhaps now he will be free of her."

He arched one dark brow at her. "Do you truly believe that?"

She turned away dispiritedly. "No. It was never just sex with the two of them."

Just a month ago, she looked forward to seeing her son again after being apart from him for seven years. He had grown into such a fine man, but he had also grown into an independent man, accustomed to going his own way without consulting anyone else. And Cayden had drawn his own conclusions about everything that had occurred since Annabel Barton's accident. While the facts as he surmised them might be correct, he didn't fully understand all the motives behind them.

"He will come back," Carrick Clifton said. He stared out again at the house on the point. Catriona gazed at her husband sadly.

"Getting rid of her won't bring him back," she said.

Carrick's dark gaze turned on her. "Stop reading me."

She smiled. "Stop broadcasting."

****

Cayden sailed the *Belle* home that night with a smile on his face. In fact, he found it difficult not to smile. The day was perfect. She was perfect. The entire fucking universe was perfect. He knew Bell planned to swim in the morning, and he decided he would visit her again as Whiskers. He smiled at the absurdity of the name.

He knew he should tell her. Taylor already knew, and she needed to know as well, but he was reluctant to throw too much at her at once. She had already been through so much between the deaths of her parents and the accident. He wanted to marry her, and he knew that would open up additional problems.

Yes, there had been marriages between Silkies and humans in the past, but it was usually between human males and Silkie females. None of the stories had happy endings. Cayden was determined things would be different with Bell and him. They would

107

find a way.

In his heart, though, he knew the sacrifice would have to be his. She could not live in the ocean, nor even spend the amount of time in the water that his family did, and they lived like humans much more of the time than most of the Silkie. He would be the one who would have to change...and he would. There was nothing for him now with his family. He turned his back on them. Cayden stared down at the leather anklet before his eyes lifted once again to the water. He would find a way to fit his life with hers, even if it meant giving up his pelt.

****

Annabel sat at the end of the dock the next morning lost in thought. She half hoped Cayden would show up, but he hadn't promised. She knew he worked jobs around the Yacht Club and sometimes crewed for various boats.

She fingered the gold necklace around her throat. She had thought a lot about what Taylor said about being able to tell Whiskers apart from other seals. It was a very real danger. There was no way she could get away from a different seal. She fingered the necklace again. It was something her father gave her for her fourteenth birthday. It was a longer, thicker chain than she was used to. Long enough to put on a seal? Would he even let her?

A splash startled her, and she looked up to see Whiskers waving a flipper at her. Annabel laughed and pushed off into the water, absurdly happy to see her friend again. He nuzzled her cheek and blew bubbles at her before flipping away and somersaulting through the air. When he approached her again, he hovered nearby to signal to her to grab hold of his flippers. Annabel rode on his back, momentarily reminded of her time with Cayden yesterday. She blushed and shook her head.

She stroked the top of the seal's sleek skull a

few minutes later. She had moved into the shallows to relax and he lay next to her, his head resting on her lap.

"My brother, the one who scared you the other day, seems to think I need some way to tell you apart from other seals." She took the chain from around her neck, studied it and then looked at the seal. "I wonder if you would…"

His nose touched the chain and then he looked up at her. Annabel held it out and gently slipped it over his head. When he simply nuzzled her again and put his head back on her lap, she smiled and once more glided her hand along his sleek fur. She hoped the chain would stay, that it wouldn't be a danger for him.

After a few more minutes, she gently pushed him away. "I have to go. Taylor's taking me into the city today to visit my doctor." She trailed her hand through the shallow water. "I hate these visits. The doctor just spouts the same platitudes about how I'm making excellent progress, but we both know I haven't progressed." She looked down bitterly at her feet, still hidden by the gently lapping water in the cove. "After seven years, this is as good as it gets."

She thought about her limitations, something she tried not to do because it became too real. She would much rather focus on everything she could do, but her time with Cayden, while beautiful, reminded her of everything she'd lost, and suddenly she was crying. Whiskers made a low clicking sound in his throat and nudged her with his nose.

"I'm not usually like this. It's just…there's this wonderful man. He's argued with his family over me, and I don't want that. I don't want to come between them. It's wrong. Family is important. He doesn't seem to realize…maybe because he still has a family. I wish I could tell him how many times I now wish I could go back and say something different or do something different if it would just bring my dad back. I'm afraid he'll hate me if I tell him."

Annabel looked into the seal's dark, liquid eyes and laughed even as the tears rolled down her face.

"I have truly lost my mind. I'm here talking to a seal." She pushed on Whiskers again and slowly swam toward the ladder on the dock. He hovered nearby, not even leaving after she pulled herself out of the water.

Annabel toweled herself off with a vengeance. She really did hate going to the doctor. What was the point? He and his smiling nurses just said the same thing over and over. How it was a miracle she had as much feeling as she did. She must keep doing her exercises and pushing herself to do more. She grabbed her crutches and set them next to the bar before pulling herself up. When she tripped and fell halfway down the dock, Whiskers raised such a ruckus in the water that Taylor came out of the house. She groaned in frustration as she saw him come tearing down the dune and onto the dock.

"Poppy! Are you all right?"

She jerked away from him, her face a mask of anger and frustration.

"I hate this! I hate my body. I hate my *life*. I wish I had died in that accident."

He tried comforting her, but she swung her fists at him, knowing, even as she did it that she was being childish. Taylor blocked her blows, his expression as distraught as hers. He finally pinned her arms to her sides.

"Stop it! You don't mean that and you know it."

She leaned her head against his chest. "I do," she said tiredly. "The only place I feel alive is in the water. I hate having to come back on land. I wish I were a seal, like Whiskers. I wish I were anything but me."

****

Taylor looked sadly down into the water at the seal staring up at them. He saw the glint of gold around the animal's neck and realized that Poppy had found a way to help tell him apart from the other seals. Their eyes held for a moment and Taylor mouthed, *she needs you*. He thought he received a nod in response, and then the seal was gone.

"I'm sorry, Taylor," she choked. "I'm sorry."

"Poppy, shh." Taylor held her for a couple of minutes and folded her close against him. "Let me look at you to make sure you're all right."

She kept her face averted as he straightened her legs, checking them to see if she had hurt or scraped herself anyplace where she couldn't feel it to tell him. He started to scoop her up, but she turned back to him then, her expression closed and reserved.

"Don't pick me up. I'll walk."

She did let him help her to her feet, and Taylor stayed beside her as she laboriously worked her way back up to the house. He could feel the anger and frustration still running high in her and wondered now at his having mouthed to Cayden that she needed him. As emotionally wound up as she was, that might be a mistake.

As if he conjured him just thinking about him, Cayden stepped off the porch, wearing, Taylor noted, clothes he'd obviously grabbed out of Taylor's bedroom. Seeing the glint of gold at Cayden's throat, Taylor made a face at him and gestured to his neck. Cayden's fingers touched the chain before he hurriedly removed it and shoved it in his pocket.

Annabel looked up just then. "Cay? What are you doing here?" She sounded faintly breathless.

He smiled his devastating smile at her. "I couldn't stay away, Bell."

She leaned on her crutches. "I have to go in to the city to the doctor."

He came forward to touch her cheek. "Is

111

something wrong? I didn't hurt you, did I?"

She flushed, and Taylor looked sharply between the two of them.

"No. Oh no. It's just a regular visit." She looked around in confusion. "How did you get here?"

Taylor, who stood behind Annabel, arched a brow at Cayden, curious to see how he would get out of this.

"I was over at the Yacht Club and had a friend run me by. I thought maybe we could go to lunch, but I see this is a bad time."

"I'll run in and start getting ready, Poppy," Taylor said. "You and Cayden can talk a bit."
****

As soon as Taylor left, Cayden stepped forward and bent to kiss her lingeringly on the lips. She leaned against him, and he caught her firmly by the elbows, lifting her toward him so he could better access her mouth.

"Let's go up on the porch," she breathed shakily, her fall and her outburst forgotten in the wake of his kisses.

"Hold onto your crutches," he told her and swung her up into his arms.

"Cay!" she hissed at him, "Put me down! I can walk."

He grinned at her. "I know, but I just like having you close. How long will it take Taylor to get ready?"

She giggled. "He likes a long shower."

He sat down on the lounge and arranged her on his lap before once again molding his mouth to hers. "We can do this, right?" he murmured against her lips.

"Kiss? Yes."

His hand wandered under her T-shirt to her bikini-clad breast. "And this?"

"Uh-huh."

112

He began nibbling along her neck. "What about this?"

"Oh, yes." She forgot about what happened down on the dock.

Now his hand slipped seductively over the skin of her stomach and his fingers beneath the elastic of her bikini bottom. She gasped as his fingers slid between her legs and stroked her clit. "Do we have time for this?"

There was a distinct chuckle in his voice now, but she was too turned on to notice.

"Oh, yes."

He turned her quickly to straddle his lap and his hand returned to touching her, a finger pressing into the moist center of her. As his lips nibbled near her ear, he whispered softly. "I want you, Bell. Can you feel?"

His free hand cupped her bottom and brought her closer against him.

"Yes."

He eased her away. "But we don't have time now. You have to get ready."

"Cay!" she complained. "Surely you don't mean to stop right now?"

He smiled gently, though his breathing was ragged and his cock was plainly outlined against the taut material of his slacks. "Yes. That's exactly what I mean to do. I will not have your brother catch me on your front porch fucking as much as I might like to spend the rest of the day with you doing just that." He moved her again so she sat crosswise on his lap. "Can I come by tonight? I'll bring the *Belle*. We can go out for a late night sail. Maybe go back to your cove."

She hugged him close to her. "I'd like that."

He smiled and winked at her. "Up you go, then. Go see your doctor and be sure to tell him that some things work very, very well."

Annabel laughed. "Don't tempt me!"

He set her on her feet and then waved goodbye.

"Where are you going?" she called after him.

"Back to town."

"Don't you need a ride?"

He waggled his brows at her. "No. I have my own ways of getting there."

Chapter 10

"The shore seems to agree with you Annabel. You are significantly stronger than you were, and we were already amazed at how much mobility you have achieved..." blah, blah, blah. It was nothing more than white noise anymore.

Her eyes glazed over as she listened to the same speech again...keep doing your exercises and pushing your limits. It's a miracle how far you've come. Who knows what else you might be able to achieve...

"What about sex?"

This time she caught Dr. Gorski off guard.

"What?" His eyes blinked owlishly behind his wire-rimmed spectacles.

"Is it okay to have sex?" She rephrased her question and enunciated carefully as if speaking to a slightly deaf old man.

"Well, yes. You should take all the same precautions as any other female against STD's and pregnancy."

She continued to regard him frankly. "Would there be problems if I were to get pregnant?"

His Adam's apple bobbed. "Not necessarily. You would be considered more high risk than other women."

"You mean women who can actually walk instead of shuffling along with most of their weight balanced on some damn crutches?"

"Miss Barton," he began severely, but Annabel cut him off with a chopping motion of her hand.

"Look, doctor, it's been seven years since that

boom cracked my skull and broke my back. Every time I come here I listen to the same speech about what a miracle I am and how I should keep doing my exercises. But the bottom line is it's not going to get any better than where I am right now, is it?"

He looked at her steadily. His Adam's apple bobbed a couple of times. "No. The chances of you making any significant progress beyond where you are right now are almost non-existent without some major medical breakthrough in repairing spinal cord injuries. Even then, you were injured so many years ago you would be an unlikely candidate for surgery."

Her lips twisted into more of a grimace than a smile.

"Then I guess I should thank God that I have control of my bladder, my bowels, and that I can actually feel my lover fuck me."

Gorski's eyes widened even more. "Really, I don't..."

"Need to know all about that sex part? Good. Suits me. I have to tell you, you are right about one thing. The shore does agree with me, so if you'll recommend a doctor out that way, it will save me a trip all the way to the city just to be told to keep doing my exercises."

When she met Taylor in the waiting room she actually grinned. That had felt good. She had continued to see the doctor that her father took her to following the accident, but she'd never liked the man. She was fed up with hearing the same platitudes visit after visit.

"Let's go, Taylor. Cayden's taking me out for a sail this evening."

Her brother glanced through the receptionist's window and Bell followed his gaze. The doctor was in conference with one of the nurses. He was gesticulating in a manner that showed his agitation.

"Poppy," Taylor asked slowly. "What did you

do?"

"I asked him if it was okay to have sex and told him I wouldn't be coming back here."

Taylor choked and coughed. His blue eyes shifted to the doctor and nurse again. The pair stared out at her brother and her. Taylor clasped her arm at the elbow.

"Let's go, Poppy! I want to get you home before you decide to lay it out there for everyone."

He had driven her dad's Volvo. The Miata might be great to tool around the beach in, but it left something to be desired when it came to any kind of longer trips. It was late afternoon by the time they reached the blue house on the point. Taylor shook her.

"I'm sorry. I must have fallen asleep on the way."

"Let me take you inside."

She batted at his hands, but Taylor ignored her protests, carried her inside the house, and set her on her bed.

"I'll bring you a valium; then you need to lie down and rest for a while so you'll have enough reserves for your evening with Cayden."

****

He sat with her until she fell asleep. When her lids began to droop, Taylor studied the faint shadows beneath her lids and he sighed. She put up such a tough front, and she was tough, mentally and emotionally, but her physical reserves were nearly nonexistent.

She slept through the afternoon. Taylor woke her around six when he started dinner so she could get ready. When Cayden showed up just a short time later, Taylor had him join him in the kitchen.

"She's getting ready, Cayden. It will take her a little while. Would you like some dinner? I was just going to throw some fish on the grill."

"Sure. I love fish," he added with a chuckle.

Taylor turned from where he was shucking corn.

"Speaking of your liking of fish.... When are you planning on telling Poppy about your alter ego, Whiskers?"

Cayden flushed. "Soon."

"She won't freak out. She's tougher than you think. She's had to be."

"I have a sneaking suspicion, from the name of her old boat and all the seal figures she had in her room seven years ago..."

"You were in her room seven years ago?"

"Once. Anyway, I suspect she knows a lot more Silkie myths than you. I want her to understand I'm not leaving her, no matter what, before I tell her. We do have a reputation for loving and leaving."

"Are you having sex with my sister?" Taylor inquired, one brow arched.

Cayden frowned, his dark eyes suddenly remote. "I'm not going to answer that, Taylor. That's something between Bell and me."

"Fair enough," Taylor responded and then added, "Just don't hurt her."

****

Annabel entered the kitchen then and smiled at both of them. She used the wheelchair tonight, a sign of just how exhausting a day it had been, but she smiled brightly at both men. Cayden smiled back, and leaned over to kiss her softly on the cheek.

"You look lovely, baby. I like that shade of blue with your eyes."

He didn't look half bad himself. Her gaze roved over the polo shirt and jeans he wore this evening. His feet, she noticed, were once again bare. It made her smile. He made her smile. In fact, just looking at him made everything heat until she felt like she was melting from her head down to her toes. And she couldn't wait to be alone with him, but Cayden insisted on helping clean up the kitchen with Taylor before he wheeled Annabel down the ramp to the *Belle*.

"There's not much wind tonight," she commented eyeing the clear sky as they stopped next to his boat. "Should we make other plans?"

Cayden smiled at her. "We'll be fine. I had plenty of wind on the way over." He helped her on board and set her crutches next to her. "Do you want me to bring the chair, too, or leave it here on the dock for when we get back?"

"Leave it. I can't use it on the boat anyway."

He cast off and hopped onto the deck, turning on the motor to take them out away from shore and into the bay. As he set out, he paused to lean down where she sat and kiss her lingeringly. In the evening light, she caught just a glint of gold around his neck right before his mouth touched hers and made her forget everything else.

He was right about the wind. When they got out into the bay, it picked up just enough to fill the sail. Annabel lifted her face, enjoying the feel of the warm wind and salt air. It cleared away the aftereffects of having to go into the city and erased the memory of her visit to the doctor. Her eyes turned to Cayden, watching as the wind ruffled his hair and molded his polo shirt against the muscles in his chest. He was so incredibly handsome; it made her feel guilty that he was out with her. He should have some leggy blonde on his arm, headed out for a night of dancing.

He turned to look at her and must have caught something in her expression. His brows drew together.

"Bell? Is something wrong? You're not uncomfortable, are you?"

"No." She didn't elaborate, unwilling to let him see where her thoughts had taken her. "I guess I'm just a little moody after visiting the doctor today."

There. That was generic enough that it should satisfy him.

"What did he say?"

She grimaced. "What a miracle it was that I had as much mobility as I did. That I should keep doing my exercises and pushing myself... blah, blah, blah." She paused and then plowed resolutely onward. "I also got him to finally admit that this is about as good as it gets, that after seven years, there won't be any more significant improvement."

She stared at him. It was time to get it out in the open. "You could do so much better than me, Cayden," she whispered. "You should find someone else."

"No," he declared, his tone leaving no doubt of his conviction. "We've been through this, Bell."

He turned the boat into the cove and reduced sail, once again anchoring in almost the same spot as before. He joined her, sitting down next to her and putting an arm around her shoulders before pulling her close against his ribs. "Now, why don't you tell me exactly why you're pushing me away?"

"I'm a burden, Cayden. While I can do a lot of things for myself, there are times when I need help with just common everyday tasks. You should find someone who can fully share your love of the sea, someone who can then turn around and walk on shore with you, but that's never going to be me."

His fingers tilted her chin up and his mouth touched her forehead, her eyes, her nose and finally her lips. "I want *you*. I love *you*. It is *you* I can't live without. As long as you breathe, as long as I breathe, there can be no one else. I don't give a damn if you walk, wheel, or crawl just as long as you stay with me."

She rested her head against his chest. How could she make him understand? "I want you to be happy, Cayden. I want you to find someone your family can be happy with. I don't want to be a wedge between you."

Cayden smiled somewhat sadly. "There was already a wedge driven right through my family in the form of my brother, Bell. His jealousy has haunted us both. Hell, that summer seven years ago, my parents sent him away it was so bad."

"Why?"

Cayden sighed. "The night we were on the dock and then went skinny dipping, you remember?" At her nod he continued. "Ciaran watched the whole thing. We had a terrible fight the next day, and when my father got to the bottom of it, he sent Ciaran to visit some relatives for the rest of the summer."

So his parents had encouraged Cayden to begin with. It was only after her accident that his parents and her father had united to keep them apart.

His fingers stroked her hair. "Do you want to swim or talk for a while?"

"Let's swim. Being in the water at least gives me the illusion of being whole."

He arched a brow at her "With or without suits?"

She laughed and for an answer began removing her clothing right there on deck.

His dark eyes burned. "Oh that is so the right answer, baby."

Being with him was certainly making her a whole lot less self-conscious about her body. And as soon as she got a glimpse of his tight, muscular ass again, she felt her pussy begin to weep. She could almost feel him slipping inside of her, filling her... and oh God! She wanted him.

The water was cool but not cold against her skin as she slipped over the edge. Cayden dove over her head, arcing out over the water and then down. He must have circled under the water because he resurfaced next to her, blowing bubbles at her as he did. Annabel laughed at the tickling sensation along her sensitive skin. His hands followed, skimming over her before he leaned in and quickly kissed her.

She noticed again the faint glint of gold at his neck and reached out to touch the chain there curiously. "I had a chain just like that," she laughed. "My father gave it to me. I've never noticed you wearing one before."

Cayden touched the chain. "Mine was a gift too."

He was relieved when she didn't pursue the subject, instead striking out across the cove with smooth, powerful strokes. He watched her, wondering how she could view herself as anything less than whole when she was far more fluid and graceful in the water than almost any human he had ever seen. Even now. Surely there was some Silkie magic somewhere that could heal her and make her whole in her own eyes. He thought of his mother. She would know. She had more magic than anyone he knew. He would swallow his fucking pride if it meant helping Bell. He had to. She was his mate.

He followed her, diving under the surface, his vision unhampered by the dark. His beautiful Annabel Lee. Her hair flowed out behind her like a silk curtain, alternately revealing and concealing the slender curves of her body. She mesmerized and bewitched him until sometimes he felt like an addict in need of a fix. He hadn't realized how truly starved he was until she came back into his life. And right now, his cock was letting him know in no uncertain terms what it wanted.

Kicking to the surface once more, he shook his head, spraying drops of water around him. She paused, dunking her head to get her hair out of her eyes, and then she surfaced next to him.

"Put your arms on my shoulders," he told her. "I can tread water for both of us and give you a rest."

She smiled gratefully. "It's much easier to keep myself afloat with my arms in the salt water than it is in a pool. That was the only place I had to swim in the city and at school."

"Are you going back?" he asked. "To school, I mean."

"Not this year. I want to take a break."

"Stay with me," Cayden whispered softly. "Here. I don't think I can let you go again."

She twined her arms around his neck. "I don't want to talk about the future tonight, Cay. I just want to feel."

He kissed her then. It started off softly, but quickly deepened. He was so close to coming he could already feel his sac tightening in anticipation. When their mouths broke apart, they were both breathless.

"Hang on!" he instructed as he turned to swim strongly back toward the *Belle*. When they reached the ladder and he would have helped her up, she stopped him.

"Can we stay in the water, Cay? I feel so much more coordinated here."

"Whatever you want, Bell. I'll do whatever you want."

She touched him then, her hand circling his thick shaft and caressing him until he groaned and kissed her again, his mouth slanting over hers passionately. His sensitive fingers caressed her cheek and the column of her throat before gliding along the deceptively fragile line of her shoulder. He touched her breasts, gently kneading them before lowering his mouth to tug at her dusky nipples. Annabel moaned. Encouraged by her response, he let one hand drift down across the smooth, taut line of her ribcage, the narrowness of her waist, and the trembling muscles of her abdomen until he stroked her between the legs. In addition to the moistness from the water, he felt the slick juices of her cunt and he nearly orgasmed on the spot.

"Cay!" She undulated against him, shivering with need at the feelings his stroking fingers ignited. He flicked her clit lightly and rapidly until she whimpered in his arms. Every nerve ending tingled with awareness of him.

"That's it, my darling Bell," he crooned in her ear. "You're so damn sweet. Come for me before I fuck that tight pussy of yours. It's all I can think about. Is that bad?"

She laughed in relief. "I hope not. Because if it is, then we're both in trouble."

He chuckled low in his throat and wrapped her legs around his waist, stroking the sleek muscles that embraced him. "Can you hold on to me with your thighs?"

"Yes," she responded breathlessly.

He kneaded her thigh once more and went back to kissing her. While her arms were hooked around his neck, he had one hand hanging on to the *Belle's* ladder and the other wrapped around her back supporting her. Her hand slid down again, over his chest and down his stomach. He trembled as she fondled him, cupping his testicles and stroking the rampant thrust of his cock.

"Easy, Bell!" he whispered hoarsely. "Not too fast or I'll come on you instead of inside you."

"I don't want to wait," she breathed against his lips, and pressed herself against him. Grabbing his penis, she guided him between her legs. He groaned and sheathed himself inside her with one sharp thrust forward.

"Hang on," he growled, bracing his feet against the back of the boat as he pumped powerfully into her, keeping one hand on her hip to help hold her in place. Despite the passion clouding his senses, he made sure he supported her and kept her from hitting against the boat. She gasped his name against his lips and her head dropped back. In the moonlight, he watched waves of pleasure wash through her. Both of his hands bracketed her hips as he plunged into her tight core once more. His head dropped next to hers as he cried out and came inside her.

"Oh my!" she laughed as she continued to cling to him.

"You can say that again." He kissed the end of her nose. They stayed that way for several minutes while their breathing and their heart rates settled down. "Let's get you back on the boat and dried off before you get too chilled."

He had just boosted her over the *Belle's* stern when something slammed into him, making his head whip forward so that his forehead struck the boat with a sharp crack.

"Shit!" he exclaimed, an explosion of pain fogging his brain.

"Cayden? What is it? What's wrong?" Bell's anxious face appeared over the edge of the boat.

"Get back, Bell!" he ordered. Still half-dazed, he spun around to see Ciaran turning to make another pass at him. Cayden snarled. Logically he knew he needed to transform, he could never fight him off in human form.

"Cay! Watch out!" Bell yelled right before Ciaran slammed into him again. Cayden's thigh hit the propeller on the small motor. Pain sliced through him, but he ignored it. He had to protect her, and he could only do that if he transformed. He stared up at Bell, his dark eyes pain-filled and pleading.

"Whatever you see, Bell," he gasped, "remember I love you!"

He ducked under the water and shifted into his seal form, at once feeling power flow through him despite his injuries.

****

Annabel thought she was going to faint. She turned and slumped down inside the boat for a minute and shook her head. She must be hallucinating! She would have sworn she just saw Cayden turn into a seal! That wasn't possible. Was it? She twisted back around and peered over the edge of the boat again, now hearing two seals as their fight continued above and below water. She remembered the glint of gold around Cayden's neck, and suddenly it all fell into place.

Whiskers. Cayden. They were the same. She watched in fascinated horror. Silkies. They were Silkies! But that was just a myth, a fantasy. Not something that was real. Yet the proof was fighting right in front of her. She had loved seals since she was a little girl and had read every bit of lore she could find. As a child, she fantasized that Whiskers was a Silkie. At the time she had longed for him to turn into a boy who would take her away from her mother's death and her father's grieving. As an adult another part of her was furiously angry that he'd kept it hidden from her.

"Stop!" she yelled at them, but to no avail. Who was it? Another seal? But she had never known them to be aggressive toward humans without provocation. Was it his father? Oh God, not that. She shook her head. Not Carrick. He would never battle his own son as if he wanted to kill him. His brother. It had to be Ciaran. Hadn't Cayden said they had often fought? The fighting continued, teeth ripping at one another and bodies slamming together, it moved from the water onto the edge of the beach. Even in the dark, she saw that Cayden was not moving as fast as Ciaran, and she knew he must be hurt. Cayden was also not as large as his younger brother, and the weight and size differences took their toll, in addition to the injuries he'd already received before he shifted.

They weren't paying any attention to her. She had to get help from somewhere. The radio. She'd seen the antenna and knew the transmitter must be down in the cabin. Bell grabbed her crutches and dragged her uncooperative body below to the radio there. She fumbled with it for a minute and then turned it on, praying she would find the right frequency that someone would answer.

"This is the *Belle* calling the *Skerry*." She waited for a few seconds and when she got no reply she went to the next frequency and repeated herself. On the fifth try she finally heard a response.

"This is the *Skerry*, go ahead *Belle*."

"I need to speak to Carrick Clifton."

The voice on the other end was cold. "Speaking. Who is this?"

"Annabel Barton…"

"I have nothing to say to you."

"Please! Listen!"

She spoke to dead air. "Aargh. Pig-headed seal."

That left only her. Her hand trembled as she clipped the microphone back on the side of the radio.

****

Cayden was weakening. He felt his strength wane each time Ciaran slammed into him. He knew he had lost a lot of blood, mainly from the propeller cut he'd suffered before he transformed.

Stop Ciaran. I have done nothing to you. Stop.

Nothing? You've taken my place, the place I earned *after your banishment.*

I don't want it. You can have it. I won't fight you!

I don't believe you. Fight or die, Cayden.

Cayden struggled to defend himself, but wouldn't strike back at his brother. Whatever it was Ciaran wanted, he could have it. All Cayden wanted was to protect Bell.

Fight! Damn you, Cayden.

No.

He would not fight his brother, only try to defend himself. As Ciaran continued to press his attack, Cayden's strength waned.

****

If Carrick or no one from the *Skerry* would help, then she would stop this on her own. Annabel frantically lurched through the cabin until she located the compartment that held Cayden's emergency kit. She found a flare gun and two flares. The snarls and the slamming of the two male seals against each other continued, the sounds echoing through the cove. With her breath coming in sobs, she dragged herself back up on deck. She saw one seal standing over a form that appeared human and very still. Oh God! Had he killed him?

"No!" She screamed. She jammed a flare into the gun and raised it toward the remaining seal. "Get away from him, Ciaran. Get away or I'll shoot!"

The seal hesitated a moment, his sleek head swiveling between Cayden's limp body and the flare gun she held steadily on him, and then he threw himself into the dark water. While the threat to Cayden might be history, now Annabel faced a different and even more frightening dilemma as she stared at the expanse of water that separated them. She had no idea where Ciaran had disappeared. It never occurred to her that he might try to board the boat. He was interested in Cayden, not her.

Her eyes shifted. Cayden lay so still. He needed help. She couldn't bring the *Belle* closer for fear of beaching or capsizing her, and she saw no way of getting him on board. She would have to go to him. She would have to risk being in the water with Ciaran.

Annabel was in agony. She wanted to get to Cayden quickly, but she also knew she could make only one trip. She did not have the strength to go back and forth. She found the small inflatable life raft, released the inflation trigger and then put it over the side of the *Belle*. Then she went through the boat, methodically locating everything she thought she might need before tossing it into the raft. She went below one more time and tried the radio again. Someone had to answer. They had to.

"This is the *Belle* calling the *Skerry*. Over."

She waited. No answer. God. She was afraid to call the Coast Guard because of what she now knew Cayden and his family to be. They would want to take him to a hospital and then what if he turned into a seal again? She would try one more time, but longer than that she couldn't wait. God! Cayden could be bleeding to death for all she knew.

"Please," she begged on the same frequency she'd made contact before. "This is the *Belle* calling the *Skerry*. If you can hear me, we're anchored in the cove approximately ten miles northwest of Barton's point. Please answer. Cayden needs your help," her voice broke on a sob. "Please help him. Over."

No answer. For just a moment, she let her shoulders slump wearily, but she couldn't afford to wait any longer.

Annabel gathered their clothing and tossed it onto the raft. Finally, she grabbed the spear gun she had found and headed for the stern. She had loaded it and checked the CO_2 cylinder. If Ciaran came after her, she would have to use it. If it didn't stop him, it might at least slow him down. She had to get to Cayden. And she wouldn't let his brother stop her. She slipped into the water, the spear gun on a wrist tether, and swam around to the raft. As much as she tried, she couldn't stop the nervousness that made her whole body quake. Her eyes darted around her and then again to the distance between the boat and the sand where Cayden lay so still. If Ciaran attacked her the way he had Cayden, he would kill her unless she could shoot him first. She untied the raft, pushing it along by butting it with her head while she swam.

Ahead of her, on the shore, Cayden lay so still she wondered if she would find him alive.

Chapter 11

Despite having turned the volume down on the radio, Carrick Clifton heard Annabel Barton's second call. He scowled at the radio, stubborn pride holding him rigid. The girl was the source of all the problems they had, and if Cayden had trouble now... well then it was no more than he'd asked for walking out on his own flesh and blood to tie himself to a cripple.

A slight sound behind him made him turn. Catriona stood in the doorway to the bridge, staring at him in disillusionment. He had seen the disappointment on her face ever since Ciaran and Cayden left. His chest tightened.

"Are you going to answer her?" Catriona asked. Her beautiful face was pale and showed the ravages of recent events in the hollowness of her cheeks and the circles under her eyes. She tried almost non-stop to reach out with her thoughts to both her sons, but they had closed their minds to her. The efforts had taken a toll.

"He made his bed; let him lie in it."

Catriona stared at him. "What's happened to you Carrick? What's happened to the man I have loved since I was just a girl? When did you harden your heart so?"

"That girl has been nothing but trouble for all of us!" he thundered. "I will not talk to her."

Catriona moved to his side and laid her hand on his arm. "Didn't you hear her, Carrick? She's telling you Cayden needs our help. Think. Do you think he would have put her on the radio, knowing how you feel about her, if there was any way *he* could talk? Think, Carrick. Don't let your anger cloud your judgment so that you spend the rest of your life in regret."

He stared at the radio.

"Please, Carrick," Catriona pleaded. "He hasn't answered me telepathically, but I just have a feeling something is wrong. Please, my love, I beg of you. If you won't do it for him, then for me."

Carrick snatched the microphone. "*Belle*, this is the *Skerry*. Go ahead."

There was no answer.

"*Belle*, this is the *Skerry*. Go ahead."

Dead air.

Carrick hung up the microphone and raked his fingers through his long hair. "She gave an approximate position with her last transmission."

"Do you remember what that was?"

He shook his head.

****

Annabel panted with the effort of pulling both herself and the raft from the water. Cayden still had not moved. As soon as she was sure she had the raft far enough up the sand so it wouldn't float away, she turned her attention to him. She checked to make sure he still breathed and then checked his pulse. Both were strong but slightly elevated. She sobbed with relief and closed her eyes for just a moment to steady herself so she could get to work.

She had dragged the emergency kit with her. Fumbling around inside, she located a flashlight and turned it on to begin checking his injuries. There was a large bump and bruise on his forehead along with numerous cuts and scrapes on his arms, shoulders and torso, but the real damage was to his thigh. She gasped as she saw the gaping wound, still slowly seeping blood. It needed stitching.

"Cayden?" she called softly, her voice thick with

tears and shaky with fright. "Cay? Please, answer me, Cay. Wake up, baby, please!"

No response. Everything around them was silent. There was no one, no one at all to help. She stuck the flashlight between her teeth and gathered swabs to clean the wound. It was her or no one. So if she didn't clean his wound, it wouldn't get done. It didn't matter how tired she was. After cleaning the cut, Annabel searched for butterfly bandages. They would have to do until he could get it sutured correctly. She surveyed what she had done and checked him again for any other injuries, but she couldn't see any. He felt cold, and he was still lying partially in the water of the cove. She had to move him.

For just a moment, her composure crumbled again. She couldn't do it. She was exhausted and her muscles already trembled with fatigue. It was too much. She covered her face with her hands as she shivered in the cooling night air. In that moment, she hated the weakened body she had been left with seven years ago, hated herself for having put Cayden in harm's way because she was so helpless. Her head fell forward, but then she saw his pale, still face.

This man loved her. He was willing to give up even his own family to be with her. He deserved better than her giving up on him because she was a little tired. Annabel tied a rope around his waist and made a loop on the other end which she slipped over one shoulder. Slowly, laboriously, she crawled up the beach. She struggled to find purchase in the sand as she dug her elbows in and dragged not only her body, but his as well. The rope bit into her shoulder, abrading her flesh.

Annabel lost all track of time as she focused on getting him away from the water. Her breath came in painful gasps and sweat poured from her body, but she had done it. He was clear of the rising tide.

Still, she couldn't rest yet. She had to get him covered. By the time she had pulled a blanket over him, she could do nothing else, not even cover herself. She had pushed her fragile body beyond the limits of its endurance and there was simply nothing left. She fell to her side next to him and fainted.

****

Carrick Clifton stared at his wife. He had been so angry hearing the girl's voice he paid little attention to what she actually said. He struggled now to remember.

"It was a cove ten miles from Barton's point." He swallowed. "I don't remember the direction. Can't you tune into him?"

"No. He's shut his mind to me, Carrick. Try the radio again. I'll get on the phone and try her house to see if someone answers."

A quarter of an hour later, they were still no nearer locating them. The options were narrowing. The Coast Guard would be a last resort, because if Cayden had been unable to come to the radio, there was always a possibility it was because he wasn't in human form.

Carrick looked at his wife, hating the heavy, haunted look in her eyes. He pulled her into a snug embrace. "We'll find them, Cat. I promise."

His mind flashed back to seven years ago. That time it had been Cayden he'd tried to comfort as they searched churning seas for Annabel and her boat. Carrick knew he would have to bury his animosity toward the girl, at least temporarily, so he could find his son and discover what had happened. But later? Later, once things were all right, he would find a way to separate them. He had to for the sake of his son. Right now, though, he had to come up with a plan. He stroked Cat's long red hair as he thought.

"Let's take the ski boat," Carrick finally said. "We'll go to the Barton's house. Maybe by the time we get there, someone will be home. Maybe Annabel and Cayden will already be there. Even if they aren't, we'll need to use the house as a base and set up search quadrants."

He woke the skipper and left instructions for him to move the *Skerry* closer to Barton's Point. In the meantime, Carrick helped Catriona into the ski boat and then gunned the engine as he turned to head toward the Barton's dock. There was little talking to be done over the roar of the engines but he felt his wife's worry reach out to him, and sensed her once again sending out calls to Cayden. It took them another quarter hour to reach the dock below the big blue house that belonged to the Bartons.

As they pulled up to the dock and Carrick jumped up to tie a line, Catriona spoke. "There's a light on downstairs. Let's both go up."

****

Taylor heard the pounding. He'd gotten home a half hour earlier, tired after an evening at one of the bars in town. His best friend, Geoff Sanderson had come down for the weekend. They'd both had plenty to drink, and through the evening, it had become obvious to him that Geoff was very unhappy with the job he'd taken at a major law firm.

When he returned home and saw Poppy hadn't yet returned, he didn't think much of it. She was out with Cayden no doubt having a wonderful time. So he'd stripped down to his boxers and crawled into bed. Now, hearing the pounding this late at night, he was instantly alert, and his heart pounded an equal tattoo with the knocking on the door. He jerked on a pair of shorts, grabbed a shirt and his shoes and started down the steps.

"I'm coming."

The last people he expected to see when he opened the door were Carrick and Catriona Clifton, especially after what Cayden told him about the split with his family. The very next thing that struck him was something was terribly wrong. Taylor swallowed and felt the blood drain from his face.

"What's wrong? Is it Cayden? Poppy?"

"May we come in?" Catriona asked. "You're her cousin aren't you? Taylor?"

He flushed. If there was something really wrong, he didn't want there to be any lies. "I'm her half-brother. It's a long story and it doesn't matter right now. What's going on?"

"Do you know where they were going? We got a call from Annabel about an hour ago over the radio. She said Cayden needed help."

Taylor blinked and ran his fingers through his hair. "They didn't say, but it's probably to the place Cayden calls Bell's Cove."

"How far is that from here?" Carrick asked tensely.

"About ten miles, I guess. Ten miles northwest of here."

Taylor watched as the big male scowled.

"That's got to be it. That's the place."

"If there's anything wrong I'd like to go with you. Poppy may need some specialized help."

Carrick looked like he was about to protest, but Catriona laid a hand on his arm to silence him. "Of course you must come, Taylor. If there's anything you think she might need, you should bring that, too."

"Cat," Carrick began warningly, "What if..."

Taylor sensed the tension between the two of them, and guessing its cause, he looked at them. Hell, even as intimidating as Carrick Clifton was, he knew he had to admit to what he already knew about Cayden and their whole family, especially if Cay and Poppy were in some sort of trouble. "If...um...if it's about what you are..."

Carrick's dark eyes narrowed dangerously.

"What do you mean 'what we are'?"

Taylor swallowed nervously before the older man's stare, but continued on, resolutely. "I know."

"What do you know?" Catriona asked softly, gently.

Taylor's eyes flicked from her to her husband and back to her again. "I know you're different...um...that you're Silkies."

Carrick swore. His dark eyes almost black with fury. "What the hell is the world coming to when we allow humans to know our true identity?" He shook his head in disgust. "Let's go!" he snarled.

****

The sound of a boat engine woke her. Annabel struggled to sit up, her hands automatically fumbling in the dark until her sensitive fingers located the spear gun's slender profile. The lights of a smaller craft glimmered in the distance as it came into the cove. She scooted over to Cayden until she leaned across his muscular body protectively, covering as much of it as she could with her own slender frame. The night air had cooled and she shivered again, only just now realizing she was still nude, her body covered in sand. Her leg muscles screamed with pain, but she ignored it as she tried to see through the dark.

"Cayden?"

Annabel heard the deep voice, but wasn't sure if it was Carrick or Ciaran. She sobbed and brought the spear gun up in front of her.

"Go away, Ciaran." she cried. "Don't come near us. If you do, I swear I'll shoot."

"Poppy!" Taylor called out to her. "It's me and Cayden's parents!"

She sucked in a sobbing breath of relief and dropped the spear gun. Knowing help had arrived, she finally allowed herself to feel the fatigue and pain that wracked her body. "Taylor?" her voice broke. "Please help! You have to help Cayden. Please."

She could see them now from the lights of their boat. Time sped up. While Catriona guided the boat in until its bow scraped and wedged against the sand, Carrick and Taylor vaulted over the sides and sprinted on to shore. She looked at Cayden's father pleadingly.

"Help him! Please. I didn't know what else to do. Please help him."

Taylor threw a blanket over her shoulders and scooped her up in his arms. "Shh, Poppy. Don't talk right now. Are you cramping?"

"Yes." She spoke through gritted teeth.

Carrick examined Cayden. He turned his sharp, suspicious gaze on Annabel Barton. "What happened here?"

"Ciaran..."

"You want me to believe Ciaran, *my son*, is responsible for this?"

She nodded.

"Carrick!" Catriona interrupted. "We need to get him back to the *Skerry*. You can find out how it happened later."

As Annabel felt Catriona's gentle hands, she stared up into sharp green eyes that glowed with respect.

"I see what you did for my son," the woman whispered to her. "Thank you."

"I want to be near him," Annabel murmured.

"Cat! You can't..." Carrick protested.

"She's too weak..." Taylor said at the same time.

"Leave them be." Catriona's voice was firm.

Annabel smiled and let her eyes drift shut.

It was Catriona who began to efficiently direct everything once they pulled up to the *Skerry*, insisting that Taylor bring Annabel on board. While Carrick assessed the damage to Cayden, his wife ran a warm bath for Annabel. Bell watched them all in a daze.

"Put her in," Catriona told Taylor. "Did you bring medicine for her?"

Taylor nodded. In the light in the luxury bathroom, the bumps and scrapes on her body were clearly visible. "I brought painkillers. Poppy? Are you hurt? Did the bast… Ciaran… hurt you too?"

She turned glazed eyes away from the scrapes and bruises she had no idea how she'd gotten and looked at Taylor. What? Before she could even try to formulate an answer, she cried out in pain as a cramp knotted her leg muscles. Taylor shook out a couple of valiums and shoved them in her mouth before reaching for a glass of water to help her wash them down.

"Swallow, Poppy."

****

He looked from his sister to Catriona Clifton.

"Don't let her stay in the tub. She needs to be moved, her muscles are beginning to spasm. If you can get her something to wear I can handle her. You can go to Cayden."

She nodded gratefully and hurried to clean Poppy up. Taylor stepped out of the cabin and onto the deck. With his hands braced on the *Skerry's* deck rail, he let his shoulders slump. He had feared something like this. Her body could only take so much, and she refused to acknowledge it.

He squeezed his eyes shut and clenched the rail until his hands hurt. He loved her, but in this he felt so helpless to stop any of it. All he could do was clean up the damage.

When Taylor returned, his sister lay on the bed in the cabin clad in silky pajamas, her face twisted in pain. Catriona touched Poppy's forehead soothingly.

"We owe her, Taylor. Even in the dark, I could

139

see what she accomplished. Anything you need, you have only to ask!"

Taylor nodded and turned his attention to his sister. He hardened his ears to her cries as he forced her spastic muscles to move. Even so, his expression reflected almost as much pain as hers at what he had to do if she was to avoid a permanent setback.

When she swore at him, he clenched his teeth. He knew she didn't really mean the words she hurled at him. Still...it hurt.

Chapter 12

Cayden surfaced slowly. Vague memories assaulted him as he did so. The shock on Bell's face, the slicing pain of the propeller against his leg right before he morphed. The bitter brutal assault from Ciaran. And again Bell's voice right before he passed out on the beach with Ciaran paused above him. Was he dead? Had his brother killed him?

He groaned with pain as he opened his eyes, and then groaned again as he recognized the interior of the *Skerry*. What the fuck? How had he gotten here? Sure as shit Ciaran didn't bring him.

"Oh Cayden! Thank God!" It was his mother's melodic voice. Twisting his head ever so slightly and ignoring the pain that throbbed in his forehead like the incessant beat of some heavy metal garage band, he gazed uncomprehendingly at her face. He felt a surge of the love he had tried to deny, but still, her face was not the one he longed…no…needed…to see.

"Bell." His voice was little more than a hoarse croak.

"She's sleeping in a guest cabin."

Part of him relaxed. She was here. On board the *Skerry*. They were both really here. He started to sit up but a wave of dizziness made his head swim and his stomach turn.

"Not so fast, Cayden," his mother soothed. "It's been two days since you arrived."

Worry over Bell exploded like a flash bulb in his brain. From the light coming in the windows, he knew it was well past the time of day she was normally up and about. Was something wrong?

"Bell," he tried again. "Is she...?"

His mother touched his shoulder and gently but firmly pushed him back against the covers.

"She's an amazing young woman, Cayden. She still won't talk about what happened, but I saw what she did. Somehow, she loaded the life raft with everything she needed and got it and herself to shore. She even dragged you up out of the water, cleaned and treated your wounds, and when we first arrived, she was shielding you and had a spear gun pointed at us."

Cayden listened to what his mother told him with horror. Fuck! He knew how very little it really took to overtax Bell. What his mother just described was so far beyond Bell's physical capacity it bordered on the unbelievable. If she had truly done all that, there was no telling what harm she had done to herself.

This time he sat up again, fighting the dizziness and nausea and swinging his legs off the bed. "I must see her."

"Cayden, she's resting and you should be too."

He turned his velvety eyes, so like his father's, on her. "Please, Momma. Just for a moment so I'll know she's all right. If Ciaran touched her..." he let the sentence dangle in the air. He would kill him. While he might not fight his brother on his own behalf, when it came to Bell, all bets were off.

Although the surface wounds he'd received had healed, his thigh was still mending, and the blow to the head had slowed his recovery and left him dizzy. His mother would have to help him, but go to Bell he would, even if he had to crawl there.

He sat down in the chair next to her bed, his body shaking with weakness he despised. She looked pale and her face was lined with pain.

"Taylor has been moving her," Catriona said tensely, "but she screams with the pain. Is it always like that?"

Cayden picked up Bell's hand and held it against his cheek. He closed his eyes and swallowed thickly as he listened to his mother. He needed to talk to Taylor. His fears grew that she had somehow injured herself or that Ciaran had injured her in some way. He stared into her pale face. "I love you, Bell," he whispered quietly. "I have always loved you. I will always love you. It doesn't matter what I am."

"She knows?" his mother asked.

"I had to change in front of her when Ciaran came after me."

"But you had already told her brother. Why not her?"

Cayden closed his eyes, pain searing his heart. "I was a coward."

Bell's eyes fluttered open. They were glazed from the valium. Her fingers touched his beard-shadowed cheek. "Cay!"

"Oh baby," he sighed. "What have you done to yourself?"

"He hurt you," she whispered. "I made him leave, though."

He covered her hand with his large palm. "How?"

"The flare gun. I told him I would shoot him." She shuddered.

"What did he do?" Cayden knew Ciaran's temper, his unpredictability.

"He left, but you were on the shore and I was on the boat. I didn't know where he was, so I loaded everything I needed on the raft and found the spear gun before I pushed everything over to you. I knew I would have to kill him if he came after me like he did you. Even a fraction of what I saw him do to you would have killed me."

He could imagine the terror she felt. Even fully

mobile, she would have been no match for Ciaran either as a human or especially in his seal form. His throat tightened as he looked at her. It had taken an incredible amount of bravery and love to get into that water in the dark and come to him.

Cayden touched her. "My beautiful, brave Bell."

A fat tear welled in her eye and rolled down her cheek. "I didn't feel brave. I was so scared. I called, but no one would help, so I had to do it. There was no one else. I couldn't leave you there. I love you. I— I thought you were dead. I thought he'd killed you." Her voice broke.

"Even knowing what I am you still came?" There was a world of uncertainty in Cayden's voice.

She smiled, her eyes starting to droop. "You're Whiskers, my very best friend."

He wiped the tear from her cheek and simply stared at her. His head ached abominably, but he didn't want to leave her. Catriona touched his arm.

"She's asleep, son," his mother said quietly.

"I want to stay."

****

In the end, Catriona and Taylor moved a comfortable chair and stool next to the bed so that Cayden could keep his leg propped up. She had seen that stubborn look before. It was one that Carrick was a past master at, and it appeared Cayden had inherited it. When she came in later to look in on them, they were both asleep, Cayden's hand lightly holding Annabel's fingers. She sighed as she looked at them. They had already been through so much, but she knew it wasn't over yet. Not by a long shot. Catriona had seen the light of battle in her husband's eyes. He was still determined to keep the two of them apart, and the fact that he owed Cayden's life to Annabel wouldn't make one bit of difference.

Those were almost the same thoughts going

through Carrick's mind. It was one of those times when his inclinations as a father were at odds with his responsibilities as head of the clan. As a father, he saw the way Cayden and Annabel looked at each other. He wasn't an unfeeling man, or even a cold one. He still remembered what it was like when he first fell in love with Cat. But he had a duty to the clan, as did Cayden. With Ciaran now so obviously beyond redemption, Cayden could not be allowed to abandon his duty as the elder son who would one day be lord. He must bring forth heirs. Strong Silkie children to rule future generations. It was one thing to dally with a human, it was another to actually mate for life with one. His greatest fear was that he might be too late on that score. Many Silkies never mated, but among the ruling class, it was much more common. When it happened, it was for life and sometimes beyond.

Carrick stepped out onto the deck. The *Skerry* was now anchored just offshore from Barton's Point. He would stay there until he could find some way to get Annabel Barton off his ship and keep Cayden on it.

"He won't leave her," Cat said softly just behind him. "We must find some way around this, Carrick, around this custom that requires the Silkie Lords to take Silkie wives. Does Cayden even know of it?"

"No," Carrick admitted. "I never thought it would be an issue, and after his banishment seven years ago, I thought this whole relationship with the human would be a thing of the past."

"Can't you appeal to the Council? Your father was able to get an exemption for me."

"That was different. Even though you were not a Silkie, you were also not human."

"Human...Faerie, what does it matter? I was a land dweller just like Annabel."

"But the Faeries are cousins, still of our broader

world with an even greater understanding of magic than ours, so the match in some respects was desirable. She is a human with not only human limitations, but limits even most humans don't have."

Catriona stared out at where the *Belle* once again bobbed at the Barton's dock. "I can see her memories, you know."

Carrick turned his head abruptly to stare at his wife. "She allows you?"

"I don't know if she is even aware she's doing it. They are foggy, but I wonder how much of that might be the drugs she takes for the pain. Her brother says he's never seen her this fragile since just shortly after the accident."

"That's exactly what I mean," Carrick cut in. "She's too weak...even for a human!"

Cat tilted her head to one side as she looked at him in astonishment. "Do you even think about what you say? Honestly, Carrick, what she did that night would have been tough even for an able-bodied person. And few people, man or woman, would have had the nerve to get into that dark water not knowing where Ciaran might be lurking. Yet she did. Barely able to use her legs at all, she still got into that water and pushed that loaded raft over so she could take care of our son. Did you not see that she had even managed to move him away from the water?

"Imagine that Carrick! On land, with little or no use of her legs, she managed to drag him up the beach and out of the water. She must have crawled on her stomach, with only her arms to pull her."

"Enough!" Carrick thundered. He didn't want to picture it. He didn't want to feel any kind of empathy with Annabel Barton. Yes, he owed her a debt for saving his son, but that still did not make her a suitable mate. In their world, she would not have survived the accident seven years ago, but more than anything else, she was human.

****

Annabel dragged her mind out of the valium fog it wallowed in. She needed to wake up, needed to move. It was one of those moments where she still had the dream, the illusion of mobility. At the waking edge of these drug-induced rests, she always had the feeling, the fantasy, that she would wake up, swing her legs over the edge of the bed, and run to the kitchen like she used to.

Reality hit though as soon as she attempted to sit up, when her legs refused to move, refused to support her weight. The reality was she could never keep up with Cayden. Her body still felt like she had been rolled over by a freight train. And if she had doubts about her ability to be with him when she thought he was only human, now she knew there was no possibility whatsoever.

She could not survive in their world. She would never be one of them. Always on the sideline, always partially paralyzed, that's what awaited her. Ciaran's attack had made one thing more than plain. She must end this relationship for Cayden's sake as much as her own. He would always be thrust into the role of protecting her because she couldn't protect herself. She grasped the edge of the bed with her hand and used it to help her roll onto her side.

That was when she saw Cayden. He smiled at her, his velvety brown eyes warm and tender. There was so much love shining there that she began to have second thoughts about what she would do. So much love radiated from him that it started to fill her with the idea that together they could do anything, overcome any obstacle.

She would give them both the gift of today, and she would do her best to make sure it was the best day that it could be. But then she hardened her heart. Tomorrow she would put her plan into action and ensure Cayden's future, but for that she would need help. And she knew exactly where she would go.

"Good morning, sleepyhead," he said softly.

Her eyes darted to the windows, and she saw that the sun was just beginning to rise above the water.

"How long have we been here?"

"It's the third day."

Her eyes took in the fading bruise on his forehead. "How are you?"

"Almost healed. Still a bit of a limp, but that should be gone. We heal quickly."

Could she use their differences as a way to drive a wedge between them? Part of her even felt a twinge of jealousy at his ability to heal. What would have become of her seven years ago had she been a Silkie? Would she be able to walk now? Annabel didn't want to go down that road. It was pointless. She was human. A very limited human. And the only thing she would do by continuing to hang onto him was to drag Cayden down.

"Do you think you can get up today?"

Honestly? No. Still, she would do it. She had to. She had to make this day seem like it was normal, that everything was all right, just as it had been. She would do it for herself as much as for him, a gift she could remember when she was gone. And the time to do that had to be soon. She was here with his family. More importantly, he was here with his family. Now was the time for her to disappear, while he was back with them.

She nodded. "I'd like that."

"Taylor brought your chair. The *Skerry* is big enough you can use it to get around most places. We even have an elevator so you can get to different decks."

Annabel smiled at his enthusiasm. It was obvious, no matter the problems with his family right now, that he regarded the ship as his home.

"I'd like to go up, out in the sunshine, and feel the breeze."

"Do you need help getting dressed?" He paused and smiled slowly, sensuously. "I'd be happy to assist."

Her nipples hardened and she felt the instant surge of wetness between her thighs. One more time. Even as battered as she still felt, she needed to feel him make love to her one more time. She glanced meaningfully at the door. He chuckled and then crossed over to shut it and lock it. Cayden lost no time stretching out beside her on the bed. His hands roamed everywhere, touching, caressing, exploring, and teasing her sensitive skin. As his fingers slipped along her slick pink pussy, she looked up into his dark gaze with alarm.

"What about your parents?" she whispered.

"They went ashore for supplies, and they dropped Taylor off at the house. Other than crew, we're alone."

She snuggled into his embrace, reveling in the feel of his strong arms holding her body and his breath ruffling her hair. She closed her eyes momentarily in pain, but this time it was a pain of the heart, not her battered body. Leaving him would be like killing half of herself. He turned her so she faced him. She dropped her gaze to hide her expression and instead ran her fingers lightly over his pecs and their covering of crisp, springy hair.

She teased the hard, flat nipples. With her mouth, she traced the line of his collar bone and touched her lips to the strong muscles of his throat. As much as he wanted to touch her, she wanted to memorize every line and bulge of his taut muscles.

"I've missed you," he told her. "And right now,

all I can think of is sliding my cock into the tight, hot core of you. Touch me there, Bell. Feel how I want you!"

Her hand slid down over the hot rigid bulge in the front of his shorts, touching him through the cloth until she sighed impatiently and used her other hand to release the button at his waist. Inch by inch, she slowly slid the zipper down, the rasping sound it made as erotic as a caress. As her hand curled around his thick, pulsing shaft, he gasped and his eyes turned slumberous. Heat burned through her core and she thought for a moment she would climax just from knowing how much her touch affected him. Her eyes swept down to the glistening, swollen head of his penis.

"I want to taste you, Cayden."

"Oh fuck yes!" He moved up to a half sitting position where she could easily reach him with her mouth. She captured the bobbing length of his hard-on and brought the tip to her mouth. "That's it, Bell," he groaned. 'Yes, suck it for me."

Her lips slid down over him and she used her tongue to tease the ridge just behind the head of his cock. When he groaned, she shifted to take him deeper while her hand curved around the base of his shaft, caressing it and his ball sac. He teased one of her cloth-covered nipples with one hand while he used the other to hold her head in place so he could fuck her mouth.

"That's it," his hoarse voice encouraged her. His own hands were busy, sliding the silky pajama shirt off her shoulders as he released the buttons. When he had her breasts bared, he eased his penis from her mouth and teasingly slapped the hard buttons of her nipples with its rigid length.

She cried out. "Yes. Rub it between them, Cayden."

She loved the intensity of his expression as he

pushed her back against the bed and slid down, positioning his cock between her breasts and squeezing them up and around his shaft. Slowly, teasingly, he pumped his penis back and forth. His breathing was ragged, but then so was hers as she stared unblinkingly at the head of his cock moving in and out between the creamy globes. The sight was incredibly erotic.

"If I turn around baby," he groaned, "can you suck me while I taste your pretty pussy?"

The heavy throb at her core grew to an outright ache. "Yes, Cay. Taste me."

He straddled her face, before she felt his lips slowly kiss down to her belly and then further, taking the pajama bottoms with him until he stripped them from her and tossed them aside. Her pulse beat and she cried out again as his fingers slid over her swollen vulva, stroking her lightly and rhythmically. Their breathing accelerated. He parted her thighs with his hands and she felt the soft rasp of his cheek as he lowered his face between her legs. Palms cupped her bottom and lifted her so he had better access and then his lips and tongue explored her. The flicking back and forth over her hypersensitive flesh sent her careening upward, gasping even as she took his cock deep into her mouth.

Her climax came upon her like a wave crashing into shore and she cried out as her hands rubbed his hot shaft. "I love you! Oh Cay! I love you so much!"

As she lay back, limp in the afterglow, the aches and pains she still felt receded into nothingness. He stood next to the bed and smiled down at her. She watched him, love swelling her heart.

How was it possible for anyone to be so beautiful and intimidating at the same time? He was all gorgeous, hard, and fully aroused masculinity. Annabel pushed herself into a sitting position with her legs hanging off the side of the bed, and stretched out her hand to him. He needed no other invitation as he stepped toward her.

She circled her hand around his cock and began sliding it slowly up and down his shaft, her eyes watching the blissful expression on his face as he tilted his head back. Thinking of how he had touched her, she bent her head forward and once more took him into her mouth. When he shuddered and groaned, she grew bolder kneading his muscular ass with her fingers. His hands trembled as he stroked her hair back from her face. She continued until he was nearly incoherent.

"Let me love you, Bell," he moaned, pushing her back. Still standing next to the bed, he raised her legs high and guided himself into her tight, slick opening. "That's it baby. That's it."

He thrust in and out of her in a slow, sensuous rhythm, stroking until he was balls deep in her and then slowly almost all the way out. The sensations he created sent her desire rocketing upwards until she gasped and whimpered with pleasure, begging him to finish. At last, he shifted her so that he knelt over her, his weight braced on his forearms as he drove into her.

He cradled her in his arms afterward, smoothing her hair from her face and pressing kisses against the top of her head where she rested against him. She rested her cheek against the hard plane of his chest, not wanting him to see what her face might reveal about her thoughts.

****

For his part, Cayden had never felt so content. For the first time in a long while, he began to think that things might work out for everyone. His mate. His instincts made him want to do everything he could for her, but he forced himself to temper that with her need for independence. Still, he helped her bathe and dress and then they went up and out on the deck.

He couldn't take his eyes off her as she lifted her face to the sun and the wind. She was so much a part of the sea, he thought, more even than she knew, and he wondered, not for the first time, if the magic of the Silkie Lords could help her. In some ways, she was more Silkie than some of his own clan.

"Marry me," he said softly, his eyes warm and compelling as he leaned against the deck railing and gazed at her face. "Marry me, Bell."

She stared back, her brow furrowed. "How can that be, Cayden? You're a Silkie and I'm human."

He smiled at her. "I'm a man now. I'm a man on land, and I don't spend all my time in the sea. In fact, it seems I spend less and less."

"Because of me?" she asked in a whisper.

"Some," he admitted, "but our life has become more and more one that is lived out of the water. Don't think, Bell. Say yes."

She stared out over the sea and for just a moment, he thought he saw a flicker of grief so profound it made his heart hurt with the pain of it, but then when he looked at her again, it was gone.

"I must think about it, Cayden," she said softly. "Please understand. The days when I could make impulsive decisions are over. There are so many things I have to consider." She smiled at him. "Can you give me some time?"

He leaned down and kissed her on the forehead. "Take as much time as you need, my love." He bent then and waved his hand across his ankle so that the leather anklet released. He wrapped it around her ankle, kissed her foot and smiled at her. "Keep it safe for me."

****

Annabel stared at the anklet until tears blurred

153

her vision. He had given her his pelt. He couldn't shift without it. He had given her a present seven years ago, symbolic of this very thing. A stuffed seal toy she still had. She just hadn't realized it at the time. It was after her father sent Cayden away and told him not to come back. Had he somehow known what Cayden was? She shook her head as she remembered that night and Cayden's gift. It was the last time they were together before the storm and the accident. A lifetime ago now, or so it seemed...

Poppy was having the most incredible dream. She was on a sunlit beach with warm, white sand. No one else was there except Cayden. They lay together in the shade of a palm tree, their bodies pressed next to each other. She could feel every inch of his hard, muscular body as it wrapped around her, locking her in a cocoon of warmth and safety. He always made her feel safe.

"Cay," she murmured softly.

"I'm here, my beautiful Bell."

She started to roll over to go back to her dream when she realized the arms around her were real. Her eyes snapped open and she stared into warm, laughing brown irises.

"How? What?" He put a finger over her lips and grinned.

"I snuck in."

"Oh God, Cay! Daddy will kill you...us...if he catches you in here!"

Cayden stroked her cheek. "He's sound asleep. Snoring. Mouth open. I could drop flies in there and he wouldn't notice."

Poppy giggled. "Stop, Cayden! That is so wrong. You need to be more respectful.... He is my dad!"

"Sorry," he chuckled and dropped a kiss on the end of her nose. "I decided to sneak in because you looked so tired when you got home from the city."

"You've been here that long?" It warmed her,

made her feel...loved.

"Yes. I've thought about you all day long. I couldn't wait. Here, I brought you this." He reached behind him and handed her a little stuffed seal. "I figured since your boat is the Silkie you must like u...seals."

She framed his lean cheeks with her hands and leaned closer to press her lips against his. She was tentative at first, but as she felt his response and heard his groan, she wrapped her arms around his neck. With his free hand he skimmed his way down along her arm to the curve of her waist and out again along the flare of her hip. She had kicked the covers off earlier, and as his hand continued down, he encountered the smooth, bare skin of her legs.

"What do you have on under that T-shirt, Bell?" he groaned against her mouth.

"Underwear."

His whole body shuddered, but his hands were gentle as he set her away from him.

"I have to stop," he choked out, and he took his hand away from her.

"No, Cay!" She pleaded, her hand skimming the sensitive skin of his chest. He shivered at her touch, but when she would have gone farther, he eased away and stood up, putting half the distance of the room between them.

She looked over into his passion glazed eyes. "I want you to stay."

He trembled, twisting away from her as he fisted his hands in the pockets of his shorts.

"I can't. Things would get out of hand. I won't do it, Bell."

"Don't you want to? Other people our age do it."

"You're different. Special." He raked his hands through his hair. "It wouldn't be right."

"It's me, isn't it? You think I'm just a kid too, just like my dad does." She bit her lip, felt tears well in *her eyes. After her arguments with her father, she'd wanted Cayden to hold her, kiss her, and touch her. Instead he just kept saying he couldn't!*

"Don't say that! We're both young! Neither one of us are ready for this. It doesn't mean we can't be together down the road from now. What if I got you pregnant just like your dad worried might happen? You're fourteen, Bell!" He stared at her miserably. "I have to go. I want to touch you too much. This was so not a good idea."

Before she could say anything else, he was gone. She ran to the window and watched him fly down the dune and disappear along the beach...

It was the last time she remembered seeing him. Two days later she had taken her boat out in a storm and paid the price for her foolishness. She stared at the anklet he'd wrapped around her leg, and her resolve hardened. She would not keep him from what he was. He needed a woman who could share every part of his life, and stand proudly next to him. Not sit in a wheelchair.

Chapter 13

The day was glorious. Carrick and Catriona didn't return until close to dusk. They tried to talk Taylor into joining them, but he reluctantly begged off saying he had promised to attend a dinner at the Yacht Club. Dinner on the *Skerry*, although an informal affair, was still served by a quiet and efficient crew. Annabel wondered if these people were human or also Silkie like Cayden and his family. In looking at them, though, she knew it didn't matter. They would not help her. The only one who would become her ally in this plan to leave Cayden was the man seated across from her, the Silkie Lord himself.

She looked up and caught him watching her. She stared back at him, wishing she could find some way to let him know that she wished to speak to him. Her glance skittered to Catriona, but Annabel swiftly dropped her eyes and closed her thoughts off.

Cayden's mother saw far too much. As a teenager meeting Catriona for the first time, Annabel had gotten a small glimpse into just how perceptive Cayden's mother was. She had sensed Annabel's fears for her father...fears that ultimately became reality.

No, that couldn't be her source of help. Catriona would sense how much Bell truly did not want to do the very thing she was compelled to do. Instead, she focused her thoughts on Cayden's father.

I need to speak with you.

Carrick looked up at Cat, but when he saw she was saying something to Cayden, he turned his gaze instead to Annabel. His eyes widened slightly and then narrowed speculatively. She stared at him. Had he heard her? She had never thought of herself as telepathic, but these Silkies seemed to hear her.

"I see you're finished, Bell," Carrick said quietly. "Would you like to join me on deck for a few minutes? I'd like to speak with you, if you don't mind."

She nodded and smiled faintly, ignoring the quick, suspicious looks Catriona and Cayden shot Carrick. The older man politely came around the table and pushed her wheelchair out to the bow where she knew they would still be visible to Cayden and his mother. Annabel had sensed their fears that Carrick might harm her. In fact, both of them had been very careful never to leave her alone with Carrick.

He turned when they reached the bow and crossed his arms over his chest.

"You wished to speak to me?"

She looked up at him in surprise. "You heard me? I didn't know if it would work with you like it does with your wife."

"You are a very surprising human, Annabel Barton, very surprising indeed."

"But you still don't like me."

"I wouldn't say that. I just don't think you are a suitable mate for my son. He has a position he must fill in our clan. You cannot be a part of that."

Relief washed through her, and she smiled sadly. He looked surprised when she murmured, "Then that is at least something you and I agree on."

"Pardon me?" Carrick's astonishment was plain to see.

She blinked away the tears that threatened. "Your son has asked me to marry him. I don't think he will take no for an answer."

"I cannot let such a marriage take place,"

Carrick began stiffly. "Tradition frowns on it, but for someone like Cayden, my eldest and my heir, marriage to a human is forbidden."

"Then perhaps we can work out an arrangement. Would you be willing to help me get away?"

Carrick arched a dark brow, trying hard to hide his surprise. "What do you mean get away?"

She picked her chin up and faced him bravely. "Like I said, I don't think Cayden will accept my refusal. So I need to disappear. Go someplace where he can't find me. It's the only way for him to move on with his life."

Carrick tilted his head, reminding her for a minute so strongly of Cayden that she nearly lost control of her emotions and began weeping.

"You mention my son moving on with his life. What about you? I notice you don't say anything about your life."

She gestured to her legs and her chair. "What life? This is all I will ever have. And it will never be everything that Cayden should have in a mate. Please say you'll help me!"

He looked at her now with grudging respect. "I've misjudged you." Slowly he inclined his head. "I will help you in whatever way you ask, to the best of my ability. I find I owe you first for my son's life, and now for the sacrifice you make so willingly for him."

"Then I'll collect, and we'll call it even, my lord. I put off giving Cayden an answer to his proposal, but I can't do that for long. I can't stay here, and I can't go back to the city. He'll look for me there."

"We have a small house we haven't used since we got the *Skerry*. It's along the Connecticut shore, and not too far by boat. I could offer you that as a place to stay until you decided what you wished to do."

Annabel met Carrick's eyes without flinching.

While she didn't see actual liking in his eyes, she did see the glint of respect. "I'd like that. You don't have to, but if you could help me get there, I'd be grateful."

"How soon do you wish to go?"

Never. "Tomorrow or the day after," she looked away from him out to sea again. "I don't want to drag this out. It would be too hard," she whispered.

"We'll plan on day after tomorrow. That will give us both a chance to figure out how to make things work."

"This feels strange," Annabel said gazing into eyes that were both wise and cunning. "We should be enemies, yet both of us see that my being with Cayden is not what's best for him, so instead we're allies. I would never have guessed it would turn out like this."

Carrick's mouth lifted in a half smile. "I would echo that sentiment. I quite liked you as a girl."

She tilted her head. "Just never as the girl for your son."

Carrick held out his hand and she put hers in it. He smiled at her and squeezed it gently. They received some strange looks from both Cayden and Catriona the rest of the evening. It was obvious they had come to some understanding and no one wanted to question Carrick's apparent change of heart about Bell.

Getting Cayden and his mother off the *Skerry* for the day proved far easier than either Carrick or Annabel could have foreseen. The two announced the following morning that they were headed into the city for the day. Catriona wanted to do some shopping and Cayden had agreed to accompany her.

Annabel wished she would have had at least one more day with Cayden, one more day to build memories to last the rest of her life, but it was not to be. There was simply no way that she and Carrick could allow such an opportunity to pass.

"Will you miss me?" Cayden asked softly, his brown eyes twinkling wickedly.

For eternity. She touched his lean cheek with a gentle finger. "I already do."

"You could come with us," he offered.

She shook her head. "No. There are things I still need to get done at the house. I'll spend the day working there."

And so it was arranged. Cayden dropped her off at the house before he and Catriona took the launch to the Yacht Club to pick up the car. Annabel kissed him lingeringly when he dropped her at the house. He smiled at her in a slightly bemused way.

"If you keep that up, I'll have to stay so we can fuck until we both pass out from it," he whispered in her ear and then kissed her nose. "I'll see you this afternoon, Beautiful Bell," he told her reassuringly.

"I know." She watched him turn and head to the door. "I love you, Cay."

He turned and grinned. "I love you, too."

She was okay until she heard the boat engine start once more, and then she lost it. Taylor had gone sailing with friends, so she was in the house alone, crying as if her heart would break. At least this time she'd been able to say goodbye. Seven years ago, she'd just thought he'd left her...

After Cayden rejected her offer to spend the night with her, he hadn't shown up the next night. When he was also a no-show the second night, Poppy's grief turned to anger. At least he could have told her he was dumping her instead of just disappearing. She thought they were friends. He said he loved her! Was he really so fickle that he would just disappear without even a word to her?

She asked her father again the following morning if she could take the Silkie *out. This time he said yes.*

"Thanks, Daddy."

Her dad squeezed her tightly for a moment, his blue eyes searching her face. "I love you, Poppy, you know that. I only want what's best for you, even if it doesn't seem like it to you right now. There are just some things...some things I can't explain to you."

Poppy packed a lunch and some water and then headed out into the sound. Most of the time she kept the dinghy in the quieter waters of the bay, but today she wanted a challenge to help get her mind off Cayden. The sound was rough and the wind strong. It was exactly what she needed. But Poppy realized as soon as she turned for home that she had made a mistake from the very beginning. When she set out, she headed upwind to practice tacking, but now she was faced with sailing downwind on the way home, and conditions were a lot tougher to handle. She had spent a fair amount of time practicing sailing in conditions where the boat was heeling while she was with Taylor, but now she was on her own, and she felt overwhelmed and exhausted.

The other problem she had to contend with was the amount of wind. The Silkie *heeled so sharply that Poppy leaned out the port side as much as she dared without a harness to help balance the boat, and the waves were brutal. She knew she needed to reduce sail, but the size of the waves made her afraid she'd lose control of the boat.*

Poppy tried to remember everything she'd learned about conditions like this. She knew she needed to secure the boom before she began reducing sail. God! If she only had one of those newer boats that would do it automatically!

Calm down! She told herself that over and over, but her hands still shook, making it almost impossible to work. How could she have been so stupid? Why had she gone out without looking at the weather? And to go out into the sound! Her father and Cayden were right. She was an ignorant, irresponsible child!

Just please, please let me get through this!

At last, she managed to reduce sail enough that she felt the Silkie *would be okay. She had just untied the boom again so she could get back to work when a sudden gust of wind ripped it out of her hands.*

It swung wildly away from her and just as she leaped up to catch the rope it came flying back, catching her along the side of the head. Time slowed as she felt the crack against her skull and then the sensation of being lifted by the sheer force of it. Her body flew, arcing up into the air when the boom delivered one more blow, catching her across the back of her hips as it sent her over the edge of the Silkie *and then down, down into the rolling, roiling waves of the sound. As consciousness faded, she saw another wave catch her dinghy broadside, capsizing it.*

Annabel had known nothing of the search for her or how Cayden and Carrick had gone into the water and pulled her broken body out of it. She had been spared all of that, and when she had finally woken up seven years ago, Cayden had simply been gone and she had been left with a broken body and a shattered life.

She had cried then like she did now. But tears, even ones that rip a world apart, don't last forever. When she was through, she went into the bathroom and ran a washcloth under the cold water so she could wipe her face. She dared not look at her reflection, knowing she would see swollen, red-rimmed eyes and blotchy cheeks. Instead, she packed everything she knew she'd need and had the cases waiting when Carrick arrived an hour later.

He stared at her pale, averted face.

"I'll take your bags down to the ski boat and then come back to help you."

She stuck her chin up. "If you can get the bags, I can get myself down to the dock."

His eyes narrowed and then he nodded his head. When he picked the cases up, he paused to look back at her. "You're doing the right thing, you know."

"I know," she choked, "but it hurts like hell."

A few minutes later, he lifted her onto the boat and then carefully stowed her chair below along with her crutches and her bags. Carrick glanced over at her to see she had buckled up her life vest and was staring resolutely away from the *Skerry*.

"Ready?" he inquired gently.

"Yes."

He untied and fired the engines before pushing the throttle forward. As they moved away from shore, he turned to look at her. "You are doing the right thing. Don't doubt it."

Yeah. Sure. It was the right thing to do. Cayden needed someone who could stand proudly at his side and that was something she would never be able to do.

****

Cayden glanced at his mother as they rode in the back of the limo Catriona had hired to take them into the city.

"I just don't see why we need to go all the way to New York to buy this ring, Momma."

"We're not buying a ring, Cayden. We're going to my safe deposit box there so I can get my mother's ring. It's perfect for Annabel."

He smiled and squeezed her hand. "Thanks. You've been wonderful about this since you brought us back to the *Skerry*."

She glanced at Cayden softly. "There are hurdles you will have to face, Cayden, objections you will have to overcome, but seeing how she was willing to risk her life for you made me reconsider things. I want you to be happy, and I will do everything I can to help."

"I just don't understand why Dad wouldn't just tell me about the marriage prohibition," Cayden began, a hard edge in his voice.

"Don't be too harsh on him, Cayden," Catriona said. "You're his heir, and for all that he is your father, he's also bound as a Silkie Lord to uphold the traditions that have kept the Silkie strong for generations. We face critical times, one of which is a shortage of females for mating, and ultimately that may help you."

Cayden looked at his mother curiously. "She is my mate as much as you are his. You were not a Silkie. You've told me that before, but you are now. How did that happen?"

Catriona smiled sadly. "Carrick and I had our own set of troubles, Cayden. It wasn't easy. You're right, I was not a Silkie. My family is descended from the Faerie folk, so the Council gave us a choice. We could choose to live as Faeries or as Silkie but not both."

"So you made the sacrifice, naturally," Cayden said with an edge of bitterness he couldn't keep out of his voice.

"Son," Catriona said softly, "it was no sacrifice. It was a choice I had to force Carrick to accept. You claim to be Annabel's mate, so then you understand how it feels when you perceive any obstacle to you being with her. He was ready to give up everything. I couldn't let him do that, so I let the sea take me."

Cayden looked at his mother, puzzled by her almost pained expression. "What do you mean you 'let the sea take' you?"

"I drowned."

"What!"

"I walked into the water and swam out to sea. I never intended to come back."

"But how?"

Catriona's dark green eyes took on a faraway look. "Carrick brought me back. I was all but dead when he shared his breath with me, and eventually the Council of Lords took pity on us both. Although by then, they didn't need to."

"Why was that?"

Catriona's eyes sparkled. "Magic, Cayden. In sharing his breath with me, Carrick changed me. When he brought me back from the brink of death, I was no longer a Faerie. I had become a Silkie."

Cayden turned away from his mother's face and stared out the window, a frown marring his broad forehead. His mother had nearly died to become a Silkie? He could not ask such a thing of Annabel. He didn't even want her to know of it. Bell would try to do something similar; he knew it. But she was not strong enough for that.

He turned back to his mother. "Please don't tell Bell that story. I could never ask that of her, but she would want to try it. I know her. There must be another way. I'm afraid she's not that strong, Momma."

Catriona smiled at him. "Perhaps not, but perhaps you also underestimate her. She is a very determined young woman, and she was a very determined young girl."

****

Carrick kept glancing at Annabel Barton's profile as they traveled along the sound up the coast. There was a determined tilt to her chin and the set of her shoulders, but on those occasions when their eyes met, he saw the depth of the grief in her eyes. He had to look away from it because it reminded him too forcefully of the way Catriona had looked right before... No, he wouldn't think of that. He was on the other side of the issue this time and he had to do what was best for his son. Carrick forced himself to keep his attention on guiding the big ski boat on its

166

way to the house in Connecticut.

He had called last night to have the house opened up and aired out, so he knew it would be ready for her when she arrived. He had even hired a crew to complete the necessary ramps for her to get in and out of the house. Those would be done when they arrived. Additional modifications would take longer, but Carrick was more than willing to make them. He owed Annabel Barton and he knew it.

He owed her for saving Cayden's life, and now he owed her for giving that life back to the Silkie.

****

The farther they traveled away from Cayden and Barton's Point, the more Annabel tried to gather the shreds of her determination around her. She was doing the right thing. She kept telling herself that, but her conviction lessened. Instead, she felt some of the despair she was sure her father must have felt at losing her mother. She had packed some of his journals, hoping she could find insight there into how he survived, because even though he had eventually succumbed to that despair, somehow he carried on for fourteen years.

Maybe she could find something that would make it worthwhile for her to continue to live.

The house sat in a sheltered cove. It was smaller than Barton's Point. She was glad about that. She waited patiently while Carrick Clifton tied up to the dock, and then retrieved her chair. As he set her in it, she glanced up and saw the obviously new ramps leading up to the house from the dock. Her eyes widened.

"You had this built just since last night?"

"Yes," the older man said quietly. "I know how much you like the sea, Annabel. I didn't want you to feel you couldn't get to it."

She stared down at her hands, fighting to control her emotions. "Thank you," she whispered.

She was very quiet as he wheeled her up to the house. They paused on the porch while he opened the door. She wheeled past him hesitantly unsure of what she might find. The inside of the house was light and airy. Its furnishings were almost Spartan, and she was glad of that. It would make it easier for her to maneuver through.

"I only had them open the downstairs," Carrick explained from just behind her. "There's a living room, kitchen, a study and the master bedroom and bath. I believe you will be able to access everything, but look through it. There's a couple, Mr. and Mrs. Cooper who live at the end of the lane, they will help you with anything you need."

"Thank you."

He stopped somewhat awkwardly and then drew himself up, looking suddenly, formidably like the royalty he was. "It is I who owe you my gratitude, Annabel. I have never thanked you for saving Cayden's life. For protecting him. I can never repay you."

She looked up at his harshly formal expression. "You owe me nothing. I didn't do it for you. I did it because I love your son and for no other reason." She lifted her chin. "I can't remove what Cayden gave me, but I assume you can." She pointed down to her ankle. "Take it off me. Give it back to him. It's his seal skin, isn't it?"

She saw his shock as he looked down and noticed for the first time that she wore Cayden's anklet, his pelt. It was the one thing no Silkie ever parted with. His dark eyes searched Annabel's face. She knew what power she held, but she gave it up willingly, just as she gave Cayden up. Carrick brushed his hand over her ankle as he murmured the words that would release it.

"I will return it to him."

Annabel nodded and turned her chair away from

him, unable to look at him. After just a brief moment, she heard his steps leave the room, and a few minutes later the sound of him bringing in her cases. He left without another word, and she was relieved. Her composure was gone, shattered just as surely as her heart was shattered.

She had left a letter for Taylor, with a note stuck inside for him to give to Cayden, but she had told neither one where she was. In order to do what was right for Cayden, she had also had to cut her ties with her brother. She heard the ski boat's engines start, heard the sound fade into the distance, leaving behind the wind in the trees, the hum of insects and the lapping of the water against the dock. And when she was sure she was finally quite, quite alone—she cried.

Chapter 14

"Where the hell is she?" It was Taylor Stokes
who yelled at him, but it could just as easily have
been Cayden, who stood right next to Annabel's
brother. Both young men faced Carrick that night in
his study aboard the *Skerry*, their anger radiating
out from them in waves. Carrick looked from one
furious face to the other.

"I must assume you mean Annabel?"

"Where is she, father?" Cayden snarled.

"You dropped her off at Barton's Point this
morning. I have been gone on the ski boat all day. I
am hardly her keeper, Cayden. She's a grown
woman who makes her own decisions."

Cayden took a step forward, his fists clenched
threateningly at his sides. "If you have done
anything to harm her..."

Carrick snorted. "I owe her my gratitude. I
would do nothing to harm her. I might not like the
fact that you were together, but I would do nothing
to harm her."

Taylor studied him with cold, assessing blue
eyes. Cayden couldn't get past his anger and fear for
Annabel at the moment, but her brother had already
moved into logically assessing the situation, and
Carrick knew Taylor was the one around whom he
would need to be cautious. That young man flung a
piece of paper down onto Carrick's desk, and he saw
it was a letter.

"She says she's left. That she's not coming back.
She had to have had help Mr. Clifton. Poppy can't
drive. She wouldn't have been able to get her

suitcases or her other belongings loaded without help."

Carrick leaned back in his chair and smiled. "I think you both underestimate her. She managed to move a raft full of supplies to shore. She managed to drag Cayden up a beach and clean and bandage his wounds. That is hardly a picture of a helpless invalid."

****

Cayden glared at his father. His fury was so great that right now he allowed himself no room for the hurt. That would come later. But he also knew in looking at his father, that neither he nor Taylor would get anything out of the older man. He turned away in disgust, still clutching the note that Taylor had given him. He looked at it one more time.

Dear Cay,

Please don't hate me for what I'm doing. I could bear almost anything, but that. I cannot stay with you. I will not stay with you. This incident with Ciaran showed me more plainly than anything that I can never be the wife you need. I would always be a burden to you and your family, a burden that could end up getting you killed some day because of all the things I can't do on my own. You need someone whole and strong. I have to go away. Please don't try to find me. I will always love you, and it's because I do love you so much that I must go.

I'm sorry.

Bell

Couldn't be the wife he needed? But she was the only wife he wanted.

"Come on, Taylor. You won't get anything out of him. Even if he knows something." Cayden turned back to his father. "I'm leaving with Taylor. I can't stay here."

"Cayden!" At last Carrick showed some reaction. "Son! Please stay, if not for me then for your mother!"

Catriona appeared in the doorway. Her beautiful face was pale and her dark green eyes seemed to glow as she stared at her husband. "If you have nothing to hide, Carrick, then open your mind to me."

He stared at his wife, at the disappointment he saw in her face. She turned her gaze on Cayden and Taylor.

"Go," she commanded them. "I will deal with this right now. There is nothing to be done tonight anyway."

Taylor looked at Cayden who nodded his head once, stiffly, and then they were gone, the door shutting quietly behind them.

****

Catriona Clifton stared at her husband and began to slowly shake her head.

"You have gone too far this time, my love," she scolded him quietly. "Their love makes even ours pale in comparison. If you would but open your eyes and your heart you would see. They are two halves to a whole, and I don't know that one can survive without the other. Try to remember what we were like Carrick!"

Carrick looked at his wife, his expression shuttered and remote. "I have done nothing that I was not asked to do."

"By whom?" she demanded. "By the Council? By whom?"

"By Annabel."

She took a step back, her eyes widening. "I don't believe you. She would never do that."

Carrick gazed steadily at her. "On my honor as your husband, Cat, and the love that we share, I did nothing that Annabel Barton did not ask me to do. I owe her a debt and I will not betray her."

She stared at him and shook her head. "You are

both misguided in this then."

She turned and left, shutting the door behind her with a decisive click.

Carrick stared at the closed door, a frown furrowing his brow. He would not let any doubt in. Separating them was what was best. It was what Annabel wanted. Cayden would adjust eventually. He reached in his pocket and pulled out Cayden's leather anklet. No Silkie gave up his pelt. It was like giving up your life.

He had been willing to do that for Cat. Why should he think Cayden would be so different?

****

Ciaran stood in the shadows, disappearing into their dark depths as he listened to what transpired in his father's study. A small smile was all the satisfaction he allowed himself. So Carrick had taken the human somewhere, he mused, and wouldn't reveal the location. As he slipped back into the dark waters of the bay, Ciaran turned over in his mind all the possibilities for where Carrick could have taken her.

His father might unknowingly have handed him the perfect revenge. If he could find Annabel and get rid of her, it would turn Cayden against Carrick for good. He could make her death look like an accident. Make it look like he wasn't involved in any way. Then once Cayden was out of the way, his father would have no choice, he would have to make Ciaran his heir.

He swam with new purpose now, following the scent of the ski boat and the whiff of Carrick that also clung to it. While his telepathic skills weren't nearly as sharp as his mother's or brother's, he had always had the keenest sense of smell, and it served him well now. It was hours later when he finally emerged, surfacing in a quiet cove and gazing at the new ramp that led from the dock to a house that he remembered well. It was the home of his childhood, and there was a light in the living room window. Even as he watched, he saw a shadow glide in front of the window. Ciaran smiled.

"Thank you, blessed Neptune," he murmured.

Chapter 15

The house was too quiet, or maybe it was just that the emotions screaming inside her head were too loud. Annabel could find no peace here, at least not right now. There were too many memories, too many things to remind her of Cayden. She rolled restlessly from room to room, occupying herself for part of the day by rearranging the refrigerator so that she could reach what she needed, and then beginning work on the kitchen cabinets. She longed to work herself to exhaustion, but she knew she dared not do that. There would be no Taylor or no Cayden to help work out cramps if she overexerted herself to the point of developing muscle spasms.

She had tried to go to sleep, but to no avail. And so it was that in the wee hours of the morning, she still moved around in the living room. A noise outside broke the stillness of the night, but Annabel ignored it as normal sounds that only seemed strange due to her newness to the house. She was sure as she grew accustomed to the house, her nerves would ease.

She rolled the wheelchair to the table where she had left her father's journal and picked it up to read once again the final entry in which he described her as a fighter. She didn't feel much like one right now. In fact, at the moment, it was almost impossible to imagine her life stretching in front of her endlessly with no Cayden. She could not imagine anything that would be closer to hell on earth. And the silence of everything around her mocked her.

It seemed to her that all she and Cayden had

ever had were mere moments stolen out of time. Youth and summer's end had separated them when they were children. Her accident and their parents had assumed that role when they were teenagers. Now she was the one putting a halt to what they had. The question now was where she went from here.

She flipped through that final journal, and stopped once more at an entry that had puzzled her ever since the first time she read it.

Dear Em,

I haven't been entirely truthful with you, either before our marriage or in the years since while I wrote to you here. You have always been my greatest love, and I look forward to seeing you when we meet again. But I have come back once more to visit my other love, obsession really, the sea.

I laughed at my father years ago when he told me eventually I would not be able to deny my ties to it, but I had to, you see. The ocean took his life even before he perished in the storm. I would see how he was pulled by the water. I saw the craving in him to be out there hunting and simply being what he was. I satisfied it for years by sailing, but that was never quite enough. The pull has become so much stronger since your death, and since Poppy went away.

Part of me longs to find my own, but in my heart I think that time has passed for me. I can't recapture what I once denied. And more than that, I can't face the truth that I may be at once more and less human than I ever thought. Now I can only hope my truth is one that will die with me.

She had no idea what he meant. Had he been confused by all the drugs? There had been a veritable pharmacy of them both in the apartment and at the house on the point. It had told her more clearly than words how desperate and disturbed he had become. She couldn't let herself get that way.

Couldn't bear the thought of years of the kind of mental anguish she had seen in her father's journals.

Never doubt I love you. She sent the thought out to Cayden, hoping that somehow he might actually hear her. There was a wealth of despair in it, the despair of a soul so tortured that she could see no light. Not for her, and she could no longer hide it because there was nothing and no one to hide behind. She held the bottle of valium in her hand and looked at it as if she were in a trance. Could it really be this simple? Would it have been this easy for her father if he hadn't been trying to hold out for her? Not allowing herself to think anymore, she undid the cap on the bottle and shook the pills into her hand.

****

When Cayden and Taylor left Carrick's study, Taylor laid a hand on Cayden's shoulder.

"Come to the house with me, man. If we both work on it, we're bound to come up with something. Between the two of us, nobody knows Poppy better than we do."

Cayden looked at him as if he hardly heard him, but he went with Taylor anyway. More than anything else, he knew he had to get off the *Skerry*. He had to get away from his father. Before he completely lost it. In light of his father's refusal to admit his role in Bell's disappearance, Cayden knew that all of the other times he'd thought himself angry at Carrick were nothing compared to now. He was afraid if he stayed, they would end up in a fight to the death either as humans or seals.

They took the launch over to the dock. Taylor jumped out to tie the boat and then waited for Cayden. "Come on, man. Come up to the house. We'll crack open a couple of beers and figure this thing out."

They sat in the kitchen for a long time. Everywhere Cayden looked were reminders of her. As his anger with his father abated, his anger against Bell grew. Did she trust their love so little that she felt she had to leave? What did that say about their relationship? What did it say about him that she didn't think he could handle her exactly as she was? He'd never wanted perfection, only her. Ever since he'd first seen her when she was seven.

He couldn't believe that she had actually left him, and despite his father's insistence, he knew Carrick was involved in some way. He knew no one else but Carrick had helped her. Fuck! He. Knew. It.

"Let's go about this logically," Taylor said as he popped the cap on his second beer. "I can say pretty positively the places I know she *won't* be. She won't be with my mother or my sister Sydney, and she won't be in the city. She sold the apartment there and swore she would never go back."

"What about school? Would she head back there?"

Taylor took a swallow from his beer. "Doubtful. She had decided to sit out a year and I'm pretty sure she didn't renew her lease. On my end, Cayden, I don't know of any place right off hand she might have gone. What about you?"

Cayden toyed with his beer. "I'm pretty sure my father helped her, so I've been trying to think of places he might have taken her. Hotels would be too easy to trace. I figure it's someplace he could adapt to her use, and that leaves only a couple of spots. We keep an apartment in the city, although we rarely use it, and then we also have a home along the Connecticut shore. We haven't used that in years; not since we were boys, but I'm pretty sure my father never sold it. There's an old couple who looks out for the place."

Taylor finished his bottle of beer. "Those sound

like the best possibilities we have. Now, how do we want to go about checking them out?"

Cayden tilted the beer back and took a swig. "Well, you know the city, so it would be a simple matter to give you the address to the apartment and a key. I can call the concierge and let him know you're coming. I'll take the Connecticut house since I know where it is."

"What time do you want to leave?"

"First thing in the morning." Cayden parked the beer on the counter. "I am completely wiped and there's just no fucking way I'm going back to the *Skerry* right now. Can I crash here?"

Taylor's blue eyes, so like Bell's, shone with sympathy. "No prob, my man. Bell's room's right through there, or if that's too much for you, you can stretch it out on the couch, but you're probably a little tall for that."

"I'll use Bell's room. Who knows, it might help me tune in to her."

As he entered the room he realized he could at least inhale her scent. But after turning restlessly in the bed, he began to question his thinking. He couldn't get her out of his head, but it wasn't because he was truly getting any feel for where she'd gone. He just couldn't seem to get to sleep. After tossing and turning for a few more minutes, he finally got to that drowsy point right between waking and sleeping where everything is possible, and both everything and nothing are completely real.

Never doubt I love you.

The thought intruded and he immediately jerked back to full wakefulness. It had happened before, that he'd heard Bell's thoughts, but only at a time when she was in deep emotional distress. He sat up in alarm, unable to shake the feelings that had accompanied the thought more than the thought itself. Despair. Dark and deep. *Jesus!*

"Taylor!" Cayden shouted, jumped out of the bed, pulling on his pants and shirt as quickly as he could. Bell's brother already hurtled down the stairs.

"What's up?" Taylor demanded as he ran his fingers through his hair to scrape it off his face.

"Don't think I'm losing it, but I swear I just heard Bell in my fucking head."

Taylor scrunched his eyes shut for a moment. "Cayden, I'm long past the point where I think anything is impossible when it comes to you and your family. What did she say?"

"It wasn't what she said as much as the feelings that went along with it. It was so hopeless, so filled with despair."

"Damn! I didn't even consider that. And she has all those meds!"

"Consider what, Taylor?"

When Taylor simply stared at him, Cayden snapped, "What, Taylor? What the fuck are you not telling me?"

"Did she tell you how Uncle...our dad died?"

"No. She didn't seem to want to talk about it, so I didn't ask."

"He O.D.'d, man. It was a suicide."

Shit! Cayden hesitated only a second. "Come on! We're going back to the *Skerry*."

"Right now?"

"Damn. Right. I'll make my dad tell me where he took her. He has to!"

They raced down to the launch. Taylor just barely managed to get the boat untied and jump on board before Cayden was pushing the throttle forward and banking the small vessel into a sharp turn away from the dock. When they reached the *Skerry*, Cayden shouted for his mother as he leapt aboard the ship. Catriona came out on deck from her private office. Carrick peered over from the deck above, but he ignored his father for the time being.

"What is it, Cayden?" Catriona asked in concern.

"I want you to try to open your mind to Bell, Momma! Your telepathy is stronger than mine. See if you can hear her thoughts, and even if you can't, try to speak to her with yours! Tell her," he paused and his voice became choked. "Tell her not to do it, Momma. Please!"

"Not to do what?" Carrick asked from above, his voice suddenly clipped and cold, every inch the Silkie Lord.

Cayden ignored his father.

"Tell her... Not. To kill. Herself," he whispered hoarsely. His hands were knotted into fists at his side as he gritted his teeth against the vision that involuntarily sprang into his mind.

Taylor's eyes widened as Carrick suddenly vaulted down from the deck above and landed nimbly on his feet. He grabbed Cayden by the arms. "This is not funny, Cayden, nor is it worthy of you. Is this some kind of a joke? Some sort of ploy to get me to tell you where she is?"

Cayden's eyes were still on his mother. "Please, Momma."

Catriona shook her head. "It's no joke, Carrick. Cayden you know how weak human telepathy is. I need something of hers or I need to be in her room so I can immerse myself in her scent."

"As much as I want to go with you Cay," Taylor said, "I can be more help here. I'll take you to the house," he told Catriona quietly. "You'll find what you need in her room. That's probably why Cayden heard her."

Catriona didn't even hesitate. She ran with Taylor back to the launch and in a moment he'd gunned the motor and sped toward Barton's Point.

Cayden faced his father in desperation, doing something he never thought he would do. He knelt in front of him, his head bowed, and spoke in the old tongue. "I beg you, father. Tell me where she is or take me to her. There is no time to lose! As your son and your heir, I humbly beseech you."

Carrick closed his eyes. "I gave her my word."

"Damn. You." Cayden leaped to his feet snarling, pushed beyond endurance. "Damn you to the deepest depths of the sea! Don't you understand? There is nothing for me without her. If she dies, I will track down Ciaran. I will kill him and then kill myself. I will leave you with no one to carry on your precious Silkie line. No. One."

As Carrick stared into his son's dark, angry eyes, so like his own, his thoughts went back to another time, and another young woman who had faced an intolerable choice. He remembered going after Catriona, and how pale and still she had been when he scooped her up from the floor of the sea. In that moment, he had wanted nothing more than to join her. The fear that he had lost her tortured him. Was he not now doing the very same thing to his own son?

"She's at the house on the Connecticut shore."

Cayden sucked in a deep breath. "I'm taking the ski boat."

"I'll go with you."

"I don't want you with me!" Cayden spat as he spun on his father, ready to fight.

"Nevertheless, I'm coming with you." He reached into his pocket and held Cayden's anklet out to him. "She gave this to me, son. You might need it."

Cayden stared at the pelt and felt as if his entire world had shattered. She had never intended coming away from this alive. Had never intended to come back to him.

****

She stared at the pills in her palm. She could just go to sleep and never wake up again. It wouldn't hurt, and it would end the pain. Annabel started to raise her hand to her mouth when a large, masculine hand grabbed her wrist, twisting until the pills spilled to the floor.

"Oh no you don't! That's way too easy a way out, you pitiful little bitch!"

She looked up in shock to see Cayden's younger brother hovering over her. The two men were startlingly alike, but where Cayden's eyes were warm and gentle, Ciaran's burned with hatred. He released her hands but only so he could scoop her up out of her wheelchair which he then kicked across the room. Annabel was still trying to absorb his presence in the house.

"Wh-what are you doing here?" she stammered.

Ciaran laughed. "Just wanted to see what lengths my father would go to in order to get you away from his precious Cayden." His eyes narrowed as he tossed her onto the couch. "I can see it wasn't far enough. That's the problem with both of them. They're soft. You have the right idea, killing yourself, but why should I let you take the easy way out? There's so much more for me to gain by making Cayden suffer. They'll figure out soon enough where you are, but by the time they arrive? Well, it will simply be too late."

"Please, Ciaran," Annabel said softly. "Let me be. I left him. Isn't that enough for you?"

He laughed at her, and laughed at her struggles to sit up so she could restore some dignity to her inelegantly sprawled form. She had changed earlier into just a t-shirt and her panties when she had tried in vain to get some sleep. He stopped in his tense pacing around the room and looked at her with dark eyes that had lost the sparkle Cayden's had.

"Once it might have been," he spat, "but not anymore. No, not anymore. The only way I will ensure I take my place on the Council of Lords is to be rid of him and my father. Cayden wouldn't fight

183

me before, but he will now. Once you die and he connects it to me? He'll finally give me the fight I've tried goading him into for years."

Annabel cringed. She who had always wanted family couldn't even begin to understand Ciaran's hatred. "Don't do this, Ciaran. I will leave here and go someplace else if you want. Anywhere. Just please give your family a chance to get back to normal, to heal."

"There can be no healing." For just a moment, she swore she saw a wild kind of grief in his dark eyes, but then it was masked once again by his anger. "For seven years, I did everything my father asked. I learned from him, became a model son while Cayden was banished for his failure to honor our traditions. Yet the moment he returned, my father cast me aside as if I was nothing. *Nothing*."

Annabel watched Ciaran's nervous pacing through the living room with alarm. Gone were any thoughts she might have had of wanting to call it quits. His abrupt snatching of the pills from her had woken her from her trance and reignited the fighting spirit within her. Not for herself, but she knew she had to find some way to save both Cayden and his father from Ciaran's wrath.

She pulled herself up and straightened what clothing she had. Her mind worked frantically to find some way to stop him, some way to even delay him, and at the same time she began frantically sending her thoughts out. Cayden had said his mother was telepathic. Perhaps she could reach her.

****

Catriona Clifton sat in the armchair in Annabel's room, while Taylor leaned against the footboard of the bed. He watched as the older woman stroked her fingers over the photo of him and Poppy that had been taken after a dinghy race that summer she was fourteen, before the accident on the

Silkie. Inside he teemed with frustration at the inaction. He would have much preferred going with Cayden and Carrick, but knew he had to help here.

She looked up at him, frustration evident in her expression. "I'm getting nothing."

Taylor looked around the room, his eyes alighting on a small, stuffed seal that sat on top of her bureau. How long had she had that? It seemed like forever. He remembered seeing it when he visited her in the hospital after her accident, and he knew she had taken it to college with her. In fact, he had teased her about it as he sprawled across her bed in the New York apartment while she had rolled around packing her trunk. She had told him it was a gift, and he remembered she seemed defensive about it. Had it been something she'd gotten from Cayden? It was worth a try. Taylor pushed himself up from his lounging position and grabbed the seal.

"Here. Try this. Poppy's had it for years, and it means a lot to her."

****

As soon as Catriona touched the stuffed animal, she felt herself being flooded with Annabel's memories of that summer seven years ago, images that flickered through her brain. She saw the walls and ceiling of a hospital and felt the pain of rehabilitation. But when all of that cleared, she was left with a clean, blank slate. Her shoulders slumped.

"Are you getting anything?" Taylor asked anxiously.

"Memories. But what's happening now?" Catriona shook her head. She started to toss the seal aside and suddenly stiffened. "Oh no! Ciaran's with her!"

Taylor spun around from where he had started to search through the contents of her closet. "What?"

"Ciaran!" Cat's eyes filled. "He's in a murderous

rage. Do you have a cell phone?" At Taylor's nod, she held her hand out. "I have to call Carrick. They have to hurry!"

****

Annabel watched Ciaran continue to pace. Behind him the sky began to lighten as dawn arrived. If she could just find some way to reach him.

"My mother died when I was seven," she whispered, not daring to look at him as he kept up his prowl around the room. "Daddy was the only one left, but not really. I knew all along that what he really wanted was to be with my mother. It was very lonely."

"Shut up!" Ciaran snarled at her.

She ignored him. "The summer I turned fourteen he told me he was sending me to live with my Aunt Helen. I didn't want to. I don't like my aunt, but more than that, I was afraid of what Daddy would do without me there. My accident ruined his plans. He couldn't end it until this year."

Ciaran stopped prowling. "I said shut up! I don't care about your life. I don't care that your father was so weak he killed himself. It means nothing to me."

Annabel looked at him. "It should. You have no idea how lucky you really are Ciaran. You have a family. They won't turn you away. Give them a chance."

For an instant again, she glimpsed pain and loneliness in his dark eyes. But he hid them, masked them with fury. He slapped her. The force of the blow knocked her sideways and made her senses swim for an instant. "Don't patronize me. I've had that for the past seven years. Bones thrown to keep me in my place until the favored son showed back up. Well fuck that! Who knows you're here?"

Before she thought, Annabel answered him honestly, "Just Carrick."

"That won't do at all. I want them both here to

witness this." He picked up the backpack she kept on the back of her chair and rifled through it until he pulled out her cell phone. He flipped it open and punched in a number. "Tell him I'm here. Tell him!"

Annabel's hand shook as she took the phone from him, but it wasn't Carrick who answered, it was Cayden. She sucked in a shaky breath.

"Cay?"

"Bell! We're on our way, darling. Please! Please don't do anything rash."

"Ciaran's here."

"We know..."

Ciaran snatched the phone from her hand. "Don't worry big brother. I took away the pills she was going to swallow rather than face you again. You must be such an amazing lover if your mate would rather kill herself than fuck you. Shall I give her a test drive? See if she likes me any better? Don't snarl, Cayden. Jealousy is such an ugly emotion. I should know." He eyed Annabel with a smirk. "She has such creamy soft skin. You don't like that?

"Are you on your way then? Good. We're going for a swim. It will be just like when we were pups. Maybe you can join us. High tide should be particularly interesting."

Annabel heard Cay shout his brother's name through the phone just as Ciaran clicked the cell shut and tossed it down on the couch. His gaze slipped over her. "I hope you won't be offended. Though I have a reputation for fucking almost anything, I do like it to be able to move underneath me, so I think we'll skip that part."

He pulled her up by her wrists and threw her over his shoulder.

"Don't! Please Ciaran!" Annabel didn't want to beg. She hated feeling helpless.

He carried her down to the boathouse. As he

walked with her slung like a rag doll, he was talking. "The Coopers are wonderful, conscientious caretakers, and one of the things I'm sure they've kept in good working order is the boat we always kept here. It will be the perfect thing to help show you how we really live. After all, if you want to be Cayden's mate, you should learn to share the Silkie lifestyle in every way."

Annabel couldn't say anything. She clutched his shirt in fear that he would drop her. In addition to her fear, her anger built at his treatment. But she refused to let him see just how afraid she was. Her mind worked frantically to decipher what he meant about learning to share Cayden's lifestyle and his references to Cayden with regard to high tide. Whatever he meant, it couldn't be good.

Ciaran took no chances. Once he put her in the boat, he bound her wrists and then tied the end of the rope to the railing along the gunwale. She tested the strength of the knots while he was occupied opening the doors to the boathouse, but she could find no weakness to them. He smiled at her as he jumped into the boat, and for just a moment, his resemblance to Cayden was remarkable enough to take her breath. It was like seeing a mirror image, but she knew that somehow this image had become distorted.

"Don't even attempt to rationalize my actions," he commented with a laugh that rang with spite rather than amusement. It was almost as if he were able to read her thoughts. "I am not some rejected child to be psycho-analyzed so that you can explain away my behavior. The truth is far simpler. I want what Cayden has, except for you of course. One tumble with you would have been enough. I always failed to see why my brother wanted to ally himself with a human and a damaged one at that. Humans are so weak and stupid to begin with."

"Where are you taking me?" Annabel demanded, holding her chin up and staring him straight in the eye.

Ciaran smiled wickedly. "Why we're taking a trip down memory lane. I'm taking you to one of our favorite hangouts from when we were just pups. Of course, you might not like it quite so much at high tide."

He started the engine, and the noise drowned out any further discussion. Annabel began to assess her situation as calmly as she could. She still felt the imprint of Ciaran's hand on her cheek and knew that it would be useless to reason with him. Although she was sure he ultimately meant to kill her, she was pretty sure she was being used as bait for both Carrick and Cayden.

There were not a lot of items in the plus column, she mused dispassionately. She had no shoes, very little clothing, and almost no use of her legs. She was tied to the boat with no apparent way to free herself. On the plus side, if she could get free, she was still a fairly strong swimmer despite her handicap and she could hold her breath for about four minutes. Not a lot to go on, but she refused to be defeatist. She hadn't fought for seven years to lie down and die just yet.

But you were about to swallow a bottle full of pills, her subconscious reminded her. Annabel dismissed it. Things changed. It was no longer just about her. Cayden and Carrick both could be in danger, and though she wasn't sure yet what she could do, she would find some way to help.

High tide, she knew, was somewhere around mid-morning, so there were still at least a couple of hours before whatever Ciaran had planned would happen. It didn't take long to reach their destination. As soon as Annabel saw where they were headed, she also had a good idea of just what

Ciaran had in mind. It was really little more than a rock sticking up out of the water. While it was out of the navigation channel, it was still far enough from shore that Annabel knew it would be difficult for her to swim. She had the feeling, though, that Ciaran was not going to leave swimming as an option.

He moved in as close as he dared and dropped anchor before turning to her with a deceptively gentle smile. "You want so much to be one of us, one of the Silkie? Well, I have brought you to your very own skerry. Unfortunately for you, this one doesn't remain above water at high tide. If you were able to stand up, well it wouldn't be a problem, but I'm afraid not being able to use your legs will be an issue for you."

Annabel looked at the rock and back at Ciaran. "Go to hell!" she spat at him.

He laughed. "Tut, tut, Miss Barton. No wonder your aunt used to despair of you ever developing that Yacht Club panache." He picked up the length of rope he had tied to the gunwale and untied it. "You know, the real beauty to this plan is I don't even have to tie you to anything. I can simply leave you sitting on the rock with your hands tied, and you will be quite helpless with neither arms nor legs to help you swim. Inspired, don't you think?"

"You can't possibly think to succeed," she told him, "not with both Cayden and Carrick on their way."

Ciaran smiled again. "Oh, but I don't intend to sit and just wait for their arrival. I'm going to prepare a few surprises for them as well."

"What are you going to do?" she demanded.

He chuckled. "That would be telling, Miss Barton, and I would hate to ruin the surprise."

"Ciaran." She decided to try one more time. "Don't do this. Your family loves you. Whatever the problem is, talk to them and work it out..."

His dark eyes narrowed furiously.

"Shut up, Annabel. I heard exactly how much my family needs me the night Cayden confronted our father."

Chapter 16

Ciaran left her to sit on the top of the small rocky island. Annabel shivered. Already the seawater inched its way closer and closer. To insure she wouldn't untie herself, he had pulled her wrists behind her to secure them before he'd hauled her off the ski boat and towed her to the skerry. She pleaded with him to reconsider, but he merely looked at her blankly.

"What are you going to do?" she asked as he set her down, trying a different tack. "It's not as if I'll be around to see it anyway," she added.

He smiled. "Oh, you'll see the preparations, just not the outcome, so you'll just have to figure it out for yourself."

Now she watched him, and even with the sun shining down on her, she couldn't prevent the chill that ran through her. It was more than her soaked t-shirt. It was the chill of watching Ciaran coolly prepare to harm his own father and brother. What had driven him to this? Would he have been different had he been the eldest, and Cayden the younger brother? Somehow she doubted it. Even being the heir to the Silkie Lord probably would not have been enough for Ciaran. Something else would have been the problem. Something else would still have led to this moment. There was an inherent rage and jealousy he seemed unwilling or unable to control. And her being human had only exacerbated it.

The water lapped greedily at her toes. She could see it, but not feel it. She shifted in frustration, but dared not move much for fear of overbalancing. Ciaran moved the boat away, far enough that she couldn't see exactly what he was doing. He disappeared over the side.

Annabel scanned the shoreline hoping to see a house, a person—any sign of potential help. But even if she did see someone, she could only imagine what Ciaran might do to anyone who attempted to foil his plans. She looked down. Her feet were covered, and now she could feel the water as it lapped at her calves. It was colder than the water near Barton's Point.

Her glance shifted up and around again, studying the shore and the horizon. Right now she wished fiercely for some miracle, but as she knew firsthand, miracles were in very short supply.

How long did it take to drown? She had never tried to hold her breath beyond four minutes, but should she even try? Wouldn't it be a whole lot easier when the time came to just get it over with? She shook her head. That was too much like swallowing the valiums. She looked around desperately. There must be some way! She didn't want to drown! And no matter her limitations, she wanted to live.

She had always been the best swimmer in all her lessons both at the summer camps and during school in the city. She could remember being stretched out on her back in the pool, listening to the hollow echo of sounds distorted by the water surrounding her ears as she outlasted everyone else in her class in a timed float.

That had been in a pool. Salt water was infinitely more buoyant. Floating was much easier— but without arms or legs? She would have no control. If anything disrupted her balance, she could do nothing to right herself. But what were the alternatives? She couldn't simply sit here and wait for the water to close over her head.

The water undulated around her thighs. It was just a little like sitting in a tub as it filled with water, she thought. Except she couldn't step out of this tub, and she couldn't stop it from filling. That was the most frustrating blow of all, and she knew that Ciaran had said it to taunt her. If she could just stand up, drowning wouldn't even be an issue because the water wouldn't be deep enough then. If she could just stand up. The water moved higher, tickling her fingers and lapping at her waist. Annabel breathed deeply trying to calm her panic.

Ciaran returned.

"How do you like my surprise, Annabel?"

She glared at him, and he laughed.

"I've decided to be generous, to satisfy your curiosity; after all you have just a few more minutes left anyway. As you can imagine, this area, with its hidden rocks has taken a toll on ships over the years. The sea floor is littered with wreckage. Of course, Cayden and my father know this, but I've taken the liberty of rearranging a few things and adding some hazards of my own. First I'll get their boat, and then I'll get them."

"You could not have accomplished so much in so little time!" she exclaimed disbelievingly.

Ciaran smiled at her. "You assume that bringing them here was a spur of the moment decision. You just happened to provide the catalyst. And you'll also be the perfect distraction. They'll be so concerned about getting to you, they'll be careless."

The water washed around her breasts now and she realized with sudden horror that the salt water's very buoyancy was going to play against her. It would cause her to lose her precarious perch on the rock that much sooner.

She turned her face away from him. "Go play your games, Ciaran, and leave me alone."

"Gladly. I will sit and watch you drown. Arms bound and legs useless to save you." He leaned over the gunwale and smiled at her. "Shall I give you a jump start, so to speak?"

Before she quite realized what he was doing, he revved the engines on the boat and pushed the throttle forward. The wake created by the boat buffeted her. Annabel scrabbled with her fingers trying to find something to grab onto, but there was nothing, and with no gripping strength in her lower legs, she could not maintain her perch on the rock. She felt the water close over her head and for just an instant blind panic filled her brain.

Calm. She had to calm down and get control of what parts of her body she could control. Instinctively, she stretched herself out so she could float. There was just one problem, she was face down in the water. She arched her back and forced her face up out of the water much as someone doing the butterfly raises their head for air. As she gasped in a deep breath, she heard the sound of a racing boat engine and realized Cayden and Carrick must be near.

It's a trap! She screamed in her head. She had no sooner thought the words than she heard a horrendous scraping noise and the abrupt cessation of the boat engine. A couple of splashes followed and then to Annabel's horror, she heard an explosion.

She desperately wanted to see what was happening, but she had a much more immediate problem. With her hands behind her back, she couldn't control her position in the water, much less stabilize it, and she was finding it increasingly difficult to get her face up to get a breath.

Relax! The thought came to her and she realized it was from Catriona. *Remember summer camp.*

A sudden vision came to her of sitting with a group of other girls while everyone demonstrated weird things they could do. There was one girl who could contort her fingers and thumbs into odd positions. She used it sometimes to say she'd jammed a finger so she could get out of basketball games. There was another girl who could bend backwards and grab her ankles from behind, and then there was the thing Poppy could do with her shoulders. It had grossed everyone out.

But she had done that just holding her hands behind her, not with her hands tied and she'd been a kid!

Try it!

Annabel relaxed and allowed herself to sink some as she began to roll her shoulders. The rope bit into her wrists, but the water also provided some lubrication and she realized she could twist her hands inside the rope. Slowly, she began to relax even more as the confidence grew within her that she could still do this. She contorted her upper body and twisted, feeling the pop in her shoulders, first her right and then her left. She rolled her shoulders again, opened her eyes and found herself staring at her tied wrists. She brought the knot to her teeth and began working on it as she slowly moved her body to help her tread water.

As she looked around her, she saw the boat Ciaran had used bobbing in the water more than a hundred yards away. Closer by floated the wreckage of Carrick's ski boat. Her frantic eyes saw no humans anywhere. She tried to calm herself. That didn't necessarily mean anything. They could have shifted to seals. They could be under the water. She got her hands free and slowly began to swim toward Ciaran's boat.

She was more than halfway there when he slammed into her, knocking her sideways. Annabel grunted with pain, but he didn't return. He was being pursued, but as far as she could tell, by only one other seal—one with a gold chain. She breathed in relief. Cayden was alive! But where was Carrick? Despite the pain in her ribs, she stopped and turned back toward the wreckage of the ski boat.

What if he was hurt? Annabel turned around and swam back toward the wreckage. He had helped her. All she could think about was the respect she had seen in his intelligent eyes that night when she had talked to him. She could not let anything happen to Carrick. She had lost her own father and had been helpless to save him, but she could help now. As she reached the wreckage, Annabel took a deep breath and dove down into the water beneath.

It was darker than in the coves around Barton Point, but in the light filtering down, she saw Carrick floating beneath the surface. His hair had come loose from its normal ponytail and swirled around his head. He was tangled in what appeared to be a discarded fishing net, so wrapped up in it that she had to believe Ciaran had done it deliberately before his father could transform. He opened his dark eyes as she approached, and she saw the resignation there. He was out of air and so tangled he didn't dare transform. Annabel reached for the knife she saw in his hand and began to cut.

Her lungs burned as she worked. Their eyes met and he shook his head at her, jerking his chin up toward the surface to indicate she should leave him. Annabel looked away from him and continued to cut. The longest she had ever held her breath was four minutes, but she had seen Cayden do it for six. With no watch, she had no idea how long it had been. She only knew that she had to free Carrick, for Cayden and for Catriona.

Spots danced in front of her eyes as she cut the last bonds holding him. He had already gone limp. With the last of her strength, Annabel shoved him upward to the surface. She moved to follow him, but could not. As her consciousness faded, she looked down to see that her feet, her unfeeling, crippled feet had become entangled in net while she worked, without her even knowing because she had no sensation there.

The knife fell from her fingers, drifting slowly to the bottom, and she smiled.

****

Carrick gasped for air, sucking powerful lungs full of the precious oxygen as soon as he broke the surface. He turned to find Annabel and thank her, but she was nowhere to be seen. Had he lost track of time? Had she already swum away? He saw Cayden and Ciaran locked in a fight, seal against seal on top of a rock still jutting from the water. The other boat still bobbed on the waves, empty.

A feeling of dread came back over him as he sucked in air and dove down again. She was there, not far from where he had been, her feet entangled in the mesh. Frantically he swam, down to the bottom where he saw the faint glint of his knife. After picking it up, he cut through the strands that ensnared her. Knowing this was no time for gentleness, he grabbed hold of her hair and pulled her to the surface. As soon as he had her on top of the water, he pinched her nose, tilted back her head and blew a couple of breaths into her mouth.

Swimming strongly now, he pulled her pale, limp body behind him until he reached their old ski boat. He shoved her over the side and into the bottom of the boat and then hauled himself in after her. From a distance, he still heard the sounds of Ciaran and Cayden as they growled and screamed, their bodies slamming into one another, but he couldn't take time to see what was happening. He got down on his hands and knees next to Annabel and continued to work on her. She still had a pulse, but was not breathing. He tried another breath and suddenly, her body jerked. Carrick rolled her to her side, holding her as she began to vomit and cough water from her lungs.

"Annabel!" he called to her. "Don't you dare die on me, girl!"

She continued to cough, and then he heard her suck in a deep breath of air. As he watched, she began to shiver. He checked the storage locker in the small cabin and came back with a couple of thick blankets.

"I have to get your shirt off Annabel!" he said firmly. "Do you understand? Then I'll wrap you in these blankets."

He propped her up and peeled the soaked t-shirt from her. With infinitely gentle hands, he swaddled her in the blankets and carried her below deck to lay her on the narrow berth there.

"I must go help Cayden. Will you be all right?"

She nodded without speaking, her lips still blue and her body trembling with cold and shock.

"We'll be back."

As soon as he got back above deck, he stripped his clothes off and dove into the water, transforming into seal shape as he flew through the water to help. Both Cayden and Ciaran were bloody and beginning to tire. Bursting from the water, he clamped his jaws on Ciaran's throat. Closing his eyes, he drew deeply upon his powers as the Silkie Lord and forced Ciaran and himself both to change back to human form. Cayden, seeing what was happening, transformed as well.

Carrick pressed his hand against Ciaran's forehead and mumbled words in the ancient tongue. His younger son's eyes went vacant and he slumped into Carrick's arms.

"What did you do to him?" Cayden asked, awe in his voice.

Carrick's gaze was sad. "A spell very similar to

one I gave you seven years ago for Annabel's father, except that Ciaran will not awake until I remove it." He looked over at his elder son. "Are you all right?"

Cayden nodded, but his gaze searched the water frantically. "Bell!"

Carrick touched his shoulder. "She's on the ski boat. We need to get her back to the house, maybe to the hospital."

"What's wrong with her?" Cayden's deep voice was sharp.

Carrick looked at his son, feeling a stunned kind of confusion. "She nearly died trying to save me. She had to have been under the water cutting me free for more than five minutes."

"I had started to pass out. When I got to the surface, I looked for her, realized she wasn't with me and went back down. Her feet had become tangled in the same net in which Ciaran trapped me. I cut her loose and then had to resuscitate her."

Cayden stared at his father and swallowed thickly. "Thanks, Dad."

Carrick smiled. "Go to her, Cayden. I'll take care of bringing Ciaran over to the boat. Then we need to get back to the house and call your mother and Taylor."

Chapter 17

Cayden barely paused to dry off and find some pants before he was kneeling next to the berth where Annabel lay. She still looked so pale and still. He stroked the wet curls from her face.

"Bell!" he said softly. "Please be all right!"

Above him he heard thumps and felt the boat shift as Carrick shoved Ciaran over the gunwale, quickly following, and then the sounds of preparation before the engines fired to life.

Cayden stayed below, stroking Bell's face and staring at her wan cheeks. How many times, he wondered, would she have to prove herself before someone sat up and took notice of her? She had saved him. Now she had saved his father, and both times she put her life on the line to do it. Just how in debt did the Silkie need to be to this one frail, damaged human before they said thank you?

He stroked his fingers along her jaw and gently brushed them over her lips. The skin there still had a faint bluish tint to it. He didn't know whether it was from the cold or the lack of oxygen. Either way, he knew that the shock to her system, fragile as it was, could be more than she could take. She needed a hospital, he thought. After tucking the covers around her, Cayden went up the short flight of steps to check on his father.

Above, Carrick pushed the vintage ski boat for all it was worth. Cayden glanced at his brother and saw his father had tied him up.

"I thought you said your spell would keep him knocked out."

Carrick glanced over his shoulder. "It will. Just don't want to take any chances."

"Thanks, Dad," Cayden said. "She would've died without you."

Carrick took a deep breath. "I would have died without her. As soon as I talk to your mother, I'm calling a meeting of the council. Ciaran has to be dealt with, but there's another matter as well."

Cayden waited, saying nothing.

"I'll help you with whatever we must do to clear the way for you and Bell to be together."

Cayden swallowed and nodded. His father had always been willing to admit when he was wrong.

When they reached the house, Cayden carried her inside and back to the bedroom, quickly slipping her underneath the covers and pulling them up around her shoulders.

"Cay?" she whispered hoarsely. "You're all right? Your dad?"

"We're both fine, Bell," he reassured her. "You nearly drowned. I want you to go to the hospital so they can check you out."

"No, please!"

"Honey," he said quietly, "I won't risk it. I can't lose you...not again."

In the end, Carrick called 911, nearly as concerned as his son that Annabel was not bouncing back like she should. While Cayden sat with her, waiting for the ambulance, Carrick used her cell phone to call Taylor. He and Catriona were already on their way by car. Taylor was driving so Cat was the one who actually answered the phone.

"Cat," Carrick said softly.

"Oh Carrick!" she breathed. "I was so concerned! The images that kept hitting me! Are Cayden and Bell all right?"

"Cayden is fine. I have an ambulance coming to take Bell to the hospital."

"What happened?"

He swallowed and said hoarsely, "She nearly died saving my life."

There was a long pause on the other end. "Ciaran?" Catriona asked.

"I have him locked in a sleep spell. Can you send out a message for the Council? I want them to convene as soon as possible, and Cat?"

"Yes?"

"Request the meeting take place aboard the *Skerry*. It will concern Annabel and I don't think she will be in any shape to travel anywhere."

"Oh Carrick! How bad is she?"

"She nearly drowned. I had to resuscitate her."

****

Annabel heard the sirens. She forced her eyes open and met Cayden's dark, worried gaze. She tried to smile reassuringly, but she was so tired. She only vaguely remembered what had happened after she had cut Carrick loose. The rest of the events after that were just flashes that popped into her head out of order. She did remember opening her eyes and seeing Carrick's worried gaze. The memory warmed her.

As the paramedics checked her, she began to tremble again from nervousness. Her gaze sought Cayden's and held it. They moved her to the stretcher and the younger of the two paramedics looked at Carrick. "Are you her father?"

Carrick smiled. "I'm hoping to be. Would you mind if my son and I both ride along with you? We arrived by boat and don't have a car here."

"Not a problem, sir. You can ride up front and your son, I'm guessing, wants to stay with her in back."

Carrick laughed. "Smart man."

Annabel's gaze was confused as she looked at Carrick. As if he sensed her stare, he turned and gently touched her cheek. "Hang in there, Bell, we'll get you well again."

She smiled weakly, and to her embarrassment tears rolled from the corners of her eyes. She turned her head and stared at Cayden, her eyes locking on his velvet brown gaze. She saw scratches and bruises on him that were already beginning to heal. She tried to reach out to touch them, but her arms felt so heavy and she ached all over not only from the physical strain she had undergone but also from the stress.

"Lie still, darling," Cayden admonished her. "You're exhausted."

"You're hurt," she whispered.

"Just scratches," he reassured her. "They'll be gone before you know it."

The next several hours were a blur of light and activity to Annabel. It reminded her too much of seven years ago. She hated hospitals. They were forever associated in her mind with pain. When they would have kept Cayden away from her, she became so upset that the emergency room physician relented. As they hooked her up to a heart monitor, Cayden stood in the corner of the room where she could see him. Her eyes never left his as they attached an I.V. drip.

"Why do I need all this?" she asked hoarsely.

The doctor looked at her, his sandy hair falling over his forehead. "Precautions against some of the common complications with near drownings. We'll monitor you for any arrhythmia, get fluids into you, because believe it or not, dehydration is sometimes a problem, and in a few minutes we'll get you on some respiratory therapy and oxygen."

"Can't I just go home?" Annabel asked miserably.

"Miss Barton, you must be aware as someone who lives with paralysis, your system is much more delicately balanced. Any upset can become a major, life-threatening issue."

Annabel closed her eyes. As if she needed a reminder of how unsuitable she was for someone like Cayden. She turned her head away from both men and stared sightlessly at the wall.

****

Cayden felt his anger stir at the doctor's abrupt manner. While it might have been an honest assessment, its bluntness was more than she needed or could handle at the moment. He stepped forward, his dark eyes hostile.

"Was there really a need for that?" he asked quietly. "You just gave your fragile flower speech to a young woman who held her breath for about five minutes while she cut my father loose from a fishing net!"

The doctor raised his brows and looked once more at Annabel. "My apologies," he said.

Cayden looked at him contemptuously. "It's not me you need to apologize to. That girl is one of the toughest, bravest women I know."

There was a commotion outside the sliding glass door to the treatment room and suddenly Taylor entered his blue eyes frantic. "Cayden? How is she? Did that bastard hurt her?"

The doctor glanced at the new arrival who was so obviously a blood relative of Annabel Barton that he didn't even ask for identification.

"No, but not for want of trying. He'd left her with her hands tied behind her back, sitting on a rock that submerged with the tide!" Cayden stared at her. "I'm still not sure how she got loose."

Taylor actually chuckled. "Loose shoulder joints. I have them too." and he proceeded to demonstrate.

Cayden actually smiled. "I'll be damned. She could have gotten loose that whole time she sat there!"

Taylor looked at his sister, and his face clouded with concern. "No. She had to wait for you all to arrive so your brother couldn't catch her again." He stepped to the side of her bed.

"Poppy?" he called quietly as he softly touched her cheek.

"Take me home, Taylor," she murmured. "I hate hospitals. No one will listen."

A chill went through Cayden as he listened to her slurred words. It reminded him too much of the night he had discovered she was paralyzed. She had been hysterical, but like then she had turned automatically to Taylor. As if he, too, sensed something wrong, Taylor turned to Cayden and motioned him forward.

"We'll get you out of here just as soon as we can, Poppy. The *Skerry* is on its way..."

Annabel turned haunted blue eyes to Cayden. "You should go. Taylor's here. You should go."

Cayden looked up at Taylor. "Leave us for a little while."

Even as Annabel said no, her brother nodded and ducked back out the door.

"Okay, Bell," Cayden said quietly. "What have you thought through and decided without getting any input from anyone else."

"I can't be what you need, Cayden," she said tonelessly. "Surely today proved that to you?"

Cayden took her chin between his thumb and forefingers and leaned over until they were mere inches apart. "What today proved to me is that you are *exactly* what I need, and not only did it prove it to me, you proved it to my father as well. Even as we speak, the Silkie Lords are preparing to gather on the *Skerry*. They will decide Ciaran's fate, but my father has asked them to come here for another reason as well. He wants them to meet you, Bell. He wants them to put aside the ancient prohibitions against our marriage."

"I never said I would marry you." It was a weak, last ditch attempt to make him go away, and they both knew it.

"But you will," he whispered with a smile before he leaned down to kiss her. The steady beeping of the cardiac monitor picked up its pace. Cayden lifted his face and grinned at it and then down at her. "What do you think it would do if I made love to you?"

The beeping speeded up to the point that a nurse stuck her head in the doorway. "Everything all right?"

Annabel smiled weakly.

They kept her overnight. Cayden stayed with her despite their best efforts to remove him.

****

Carrick and Catriona had left with Taylor to return to the house so that they could see to Ciaran and Taylor could get Annabel's belongings packed in preparation to remove them to the *Skerry*.

"Don't you think she'll have something to say about you just up and moving her?" Catriona asked from the doorway.

Taylor grinned at her. "Yes, but if it's already a fait accompli, what can she really do? Sometimes my dear sister is far too stubborn for her own good. I believe this is one of those instances where she will need a strong shove in the right direction."

Catriona tilted her head. "Why?"

Taylor sighed. "She's still convinced that Cayden could do far better than her."

The older woman arched her delicate brows. "That's nonsense. They are soul mates. There can never be anyone else for either of them."

Taylor smiled grimly. "Then let us hope that you, Carrick and Cayden can convince not only the Silkie Lords of that, but also Poppy."

Catriona stared at Taylor. "Tell me something, Taylor."

"What?" he replied absently as he continued to pack her clothing.

"If Annabel were whole again, do you think she would question her suitability to my son?"

Taylor frowned. "You know that's not possible, but hypothetically speaking? No. If she were the Poppy I knew seven years ago, she would never doubt it."

Catriona looked pensive for a moment and then said, "I actually came to tell you that the *Skerry* is at anchor. Carrick has already taken Ciaran out there to have him confined to his cabin."

Sympathy shown in Taylor's steady gaze. "I'm sorry, Catriona. I know this must be hard for you."

Her smile was sad. "I love both my sons, Taylor, not the same because they are not the same people. Yet, I have to wonder if I somehow failed Ciaran in some way."

Taylor zipped the suitcase shut that was in front of him and stood looking down at where his hands rested on it. "I think no matter how much we love some people, there is always a part of them that we can't touch, and it doesn't matter what we do, or how much we do."

"What do you mean?"

"Well my uncle...I mean my father for example. Poppy loved him and would have done anything for him, but she knew there was a part of him that would never be the same again after her mother died. There was a part of him that, no matter what she did, was always going to long for my aunt. It didn't matter how much Poppy loved him. That part of him wouldn't be denied and eventually it caused him to take his own life."

"God!"

Taylor smiled at Catriona. "The rest of us have

had a tougher time adjusting to that than Poppy. I think she's known ever since she was seven that it was just a matter of time. She held him as long as she could."

"And you think the same applies to Ciaran?" Catriona asked softly in a choked voice.

Taylor nodded. "I think there's something inside him that tortures him, and I don't think you or Carrick or Cayden can do anything to help him. Ciaran will either figure it out and conquer it, or he'll give up and let it conquer him."

She looked up at him, and he saw tears filming the deep green eyes. "I pray it will be the former."

"So do I."

Chapter 18

Taylor was amazed at how quickly Carrick Clifton managed to get Poppy moved out of the hospital and aboard the *Skerry*. There was simply an air of command about the man that people paid attention to. The only one not bowled over was his sister. She was angry that they had gone ahead and moved all of her belongings, but Taylor let her ire flow right over him. He looked at her narrowed blue gaze and grinned.

"Look, there is no way I'm going to miss what's happening here. It took Catriona to convince Carrick to let me stay. She gave him some story about how my testimony before the Council could help you and Cayden."

"What if I don't want your interference, Taylor?" Annabel spat. "Everyone seems to think they know what's best for me, but no one asks me. Well, I can tell you right now that if I get an opportunity to talk to these Silkie Lords, I'll tell them to keep their traditions and send me away!"

Taylor's eyes narrowed. "Why the hell would you do that? You love Cayden almost to the point of insanity. I'd give my left testicle, maybe my right one too, if I could find someone to love like that!"

Annabel looked at him, all the anger suddenly draining out of her. "Both testicles?" she laughed. "Wouldn't that rather defeat the purpose?"

Taylor grinned. "Well maybe. At any rate, I want to see these Silkie nobles. The crew tells me the *Skerry* will be absolutely packed. As soon as everyone's on board, we're sailing to some remote bay to keep everyone from being exposed to too many humans. I guess we're a bad influence."

Annabel frowned. "Don't you have to start your new job?"

Taylor looked guilty and blushed.

She sat up abruptly and brushed her long hair out of her face. "Taylor! What have you done? What's going on?"

"Well, I sort of accepted another job offer with a bit more freedom to it."

"And what would that be?"

"Private attorney for the Clifton's and Chief Counsel for Carrick's shipping business. Seems the guy who's held the position for decades is making noises about retiring. Now, if you will just go ahead and shut up and marry Cayden, we'll be one big happy family."

Annabel laughed shortly. "You've forgotten one small thing, haven't you? Tradition forbids Cayden to marry a human."

"So we'll find a loophole."

"You are crazy, Taylor, you know that?"

"I must be. I'm encouraging my sister to marry a seal."

"I heard that."

Taylor and Annabel both turned to see Cayden walk into the room, but it was a Cayden they had never seen before. Gone were the jeans or even the khakis. He was dressed in a flowing green robe, worn somewhat like a kilt and plaid. His hair was loose and a gold circlet with mother of pearl inlay rested around his head.

"Cayden?" Annabel breathed. He was incredibly handsome. The clothing left his chest partially bare along with his muscular legs. She smiled as she noticed one thing had not changed; he was still barefoot and the leather anklet was back where it belonged. She couldn't take her eyes off of him, and when he unexpectedly blushed, she smiled. "You're beautiful."

"Handsome, Poppy," Taylor reminded her. "The guy's already blushing. Don't make it worse. What's with the fancy clothes, Cay?"

"The Council is beginning to arrive. They've brought their wives and families as well. Dad decided to invite them for an extended stay once the business at hand is taken care of. So, I have to put on traditional dress. It's a *feileadh*."

Taylor coughed. "Please tell me there is an exemption for humans. My legs aren't nearly as good looking as yours."

Cayden's dark eyes twinkled. "And I was just thinking how good you might look in royal blue." At Taylor's horrified look, he relented. "You're fine as you are, and it's normal evening attire for dinner. You can use Ciaran's tux. He's not invited. Now go away and leave me with Bell."

****

As soon as Taylor left the stateroom, Cayden sat on the edge of Annabel's bed.

"Hi," he said softly, taking her hand in his own. His dark eyes had grown soft and warm, stirring a familiar heat deep in her belly. "Are you up to putting in an appearance tonight?"

Her eyes skittered away. "I have nothing to wear, Cay."

"My mother has ordered something brought in for you," he responded softly, gently carrying her hand up to his lips. "I would love to have you at my side, but only if you think you're strong enough. Otherwise, you can put off meeting the Council until tomorrow."

"So soon?"

"It's an unpleasant business, the situation with Ciaran, and one they want to get out of the way. Once that's done, then they'll make a decision about us."

"What if they say no, Cay?" Annabel asked.

His expression became cold. "Then I will live my life out as a human. I won't leave you, Bell."

She ducked her head. She could never allow that to happen. Seeing him as he was now only brought home to her that he had a destiny to fulfill. He was a Silkie Lord, and not only was she human, she was a limited human.

"Hey!" he slipped two fingers under her chin and tilted her face up to his. "Don't worry. We'll figure this out."

He lowered his face and kissed her softly on the lips. Her hand fluttered up to touch his cheek and she gave herself over to the taste and the feel of him. When she opened her mouth to him, Cayden growled deep in his throat and immediately deepened the kiss. His hands caressed her shoulders and down her upper arms before slipping down to bracket her ribcage.

"Ow!"

His hands stopped and he looked at her apologetically. "Forgive me, love, I forgot you were bruised."

She sighed. "I will go tonight," she promised him. "See to your guests now, and I will see you later."

When the door shut behind him, Annabel turned on her side and stared at the wall. She no longer had anyone left who would take her away. Carrick now supported the idea of a marriage between her and Cayden. Catriona and Taylor always had. Why could no one see how wrong it would be? She could never be a part of them.

You already are.

Annabel stiffened and rolled over to look around the room. No one was there. It had been a deep, masculine voice that spoke in her head, an older voice. She pushed herself into a sitting position and looked around once again.

Who are you?

You will know when the time is right. Dress yourself and appear tonight.

Annabel shivered. She had no idea who the voice belonged to, but she had easily communicated with him through her thoughts. She reached for her crutches and pulled up so she could stand. She had barely begun to cross the cabin to the bath when Catriona came through the door. She wore filmy robes similar to Cayden's only longer so that the filmy bottom of it struck her around mid-calf. Below that, she saw an anklet like Cayden's and strong, finely made feet.

"I've come to help you bathe and dress."

Annabel's chin lifted. "I can do it on my own."

Catriona stopped and smiled at her. "I know you are capable of doing it on your own, Bell. I would like to help you. I brought along a traditional dress and wanted to fix your hair as well. All of the other women present will be dressed in traditional gowns."

Annabel dropped her head forward, her hair shielding her face. She felt petty.

"It is okay to get help, darling," Catriona said softly. "I have a maid, a young Silkie girl who often helps me. Now I wish to provide the same service for you. I do it because I owe my son's and my husband's lives to you. I do it because you are the woman Cayden loves."

She stepped forward and stroked Annabel's cheek. "You are not being petty, child."

"How do you know what I'm thinking?"

Catriona smiled. "I hear you sometimes, your thoughts, and your memories."

She tilted her head. "Have you always?"

"Not as clearly as I do now, but even when you were just a child, I had a sense of you. At the time I thought it was through Cayden. It became stronger the summer of your fourteenth year. Now I sense that you not only communicate, but you hear as well. Is that correct?"

Annabel nodded slowly. "I think I have talked to Cay this way sometimes. I know I have done so with Carrick. At least, he heard me. And then..."

"Then what?"

"Just before you came in. Someone told me I should come tonight. A man."

Catriona's auburn brow arched. "Really? Not so surprising, I guess. With all of the Silkie Council coming on board, we have more than our fair share of telepaths, one or two who are exceptionally strong."

Catriona began running a bath and then turned to help Annabel disrobe. As her green eyes took in the bruising along Annabel's ribcage, she briefly closed her eyes. "I fear I must also apologize for the treatment you received at the hands of my other son, Bell." She touched the bruises with gentle fingers.

Bell blushed. "It's nothing. I will need your help getting in and out of the bath."

"Of course." Catriona was so smooth with her assistance; it took Annabel a moment to realize she had all but picked her up and put her in the tub. As the older woman helped her wash her hair and sponged her back for her, Annabel relaxed, even finding herself getting somewhat sleepy.

"May I ask you something?"

"Of course, child."

"Have you always been a Silkie? I mean, your coloring is so different from the others, your family and the servants I have seen."

Catriona smiled as she poured water over Annabel's long honey curls to rinse the shampoo from it. "No. I was not. When Carrick and I first met, he was a Silkie and I was a Faerie."

"I thought those were little people who lived under mushrooms."

Catriona laughed. It was a merry, tinkling sound. Their eyes met in the mirror above the tub and both women smiled. "Some of us are. My line was not. Just as some of us are inclined to be good, and others are not only full of mischief, they are downright evil."

"But you are a Silkie now?"

Catriona inclined her head. "I am."

Annabel's brow furrowed as she moved her hands through the bath water absently. "Could I...?" she shook her head. "No. It doesn't matter."

Catriona helped her up until she sat on the edge of the tub, then she wrapped a bath sheet around her, tucking the ends beneath her arms before handing her crutches to her. "Move over to this stool, darling, and I'll dry your hair for you." As Catriona began brushing through her thick hair, she continued. "Did you wonder if you might become one of us?"

"No. That wouldn't be possible. I could never..."

Catriona smiled gently. "Never is a long time, child. In the meantime, there is some small bit of magic I can give you."

"All right."

Catriona placed her hands gently along Annabel's ribs. "From this pain my son did make, take away the hurt and ache. No more bruising let us see, as I will so will it be."

Her eyes met Annabel's in the mirror. Slowly, Annabel loosened the towel. The bruising was gone along with the hurt.

"That is amazing." Annabel breathed.

Catriona laughed. "That's only remnants of what I could do as a Faerie."

****

Cayden was talking with Taylor inside the

ballroom on the *Skerry* when a tingle ran down his spine. He looked up just in time to see Catriona push Bell's wheelchair into the ballroom. He felt as if he'd been punched in the gut. She was beautiful. His mother had dressed her in a deep blue gown, a traditional Silkie dress that brought out the sapphire of her eyes. As a concession to Bell's modesty, he could see the material was draped more heavily than many of the other women whose bodies could be clearly seen through the translucent material. Her sun-streaked curls were gathered loosely at the crown of her head, but then cascaded down her back. It showed off the slender column of her throat and the fragile bones of her shoulders.

"My God!" Taylor breathed. "Poppy?"

Cayden brushed past him. He bowed before the two women. "Momma. Bell."

He lifted her hand and brought it to his lips, smiling slightly against her skin as she blushed. "You're beautiful, Bell."

"Your mother's handiwork." She looked up over her shoulder and smiled at Catriona.

Cayden came around to take the wheelchair from his mother. After kissing her on the cheek he bent near Bell's ear. "God's handiwork, my love. Come, let me introduce you."

He pushed her chair forward into the room. Annabel now felt as if every eye had turned to watch the two of them. Taylor stood next to Catriona and Carrick. She noted that the older man no longer had the leather anklet on. Instead a silky sealskin hung over one shoulder. Annabel looked around the room and saw ten other men similarly garbed in traditional dress with sealskins hanging from their shoulders. All of them wore circlets more ornate than the one Cayden had. Annabel swallowed as she realized that Cay was pushing her toward a man who stood straight and tall at the opposite end of the room. His iron gray hair waved to his shoulders and his eyes were black and piercing. Next to him was another man equally imposing, with black hair and when Annabel looked closely, she realized his eyes were a deep, mesmerizing blue.

Her heart beat heavily as she felt their eyes on her. When they reached the other side of the room, Cayden stopped just a few feet away, and coming around to her side, he bowed to both men and then lifted Annabel's hand.

"Your graces, allow me to present Miss Annabel Barton."

She was unsure what to do. She couldn't curtsy, couldn't do anything.

"Bell, may I present Riordan, King of the Silkie and Faeran, Duke of the Atlantic."

She knew her hand trembled, just as her smile did. When Riordan bowed over her hand, she cringed away in her chair, overwhelmed by his piercing black eyes.

"Back off Rory," the man next to him spoke, and Annabel's eyes instantly swiveled to stare at him. It was the voice she'd heard earlier in the day in her mind. "You're frightening her. She's not used to us, especially not decked out in all this ceremonial garb."

When Riordan chuckled and stood up, Annabel exhaled in relief. The one called Faeran stepped forward. "Don't let the titles scare you. We're not like your human aristocracy. He's Riordan or Rory and you may call me Faeran." He looked at Cayden. "Be a good pup. Go away. I would like to speak with your Bell."

Cayden stiffened, his brows drawing together in a frown.

"Don't puff up at me, boy. I won't hurt her. In ten minutes, you can bring her something to drink out on the bow deck."

Cayden saw the glint in Faeran's eyes and bowed politely. "As you wish your Grace."

"Stuffy puppy," Annabel thought she heard Faeran mumble as Cayden walked away, but she wasn't sure because she was so petrified when the man took hold of the handles on her wheelchair and pushed her out the side doors before turning to guide her toward the bow.

She chafed with frustration and fear. It was a situation she resented, her inability to walk away.

"Ah but then you must listen to me while we discuss a little of your family history."

She clenched her hands in her lap. "It was you!" she accused. "Why were you in my head this afternoon, and what are you doing now? I—I want Cayden."

He stopped pushing her chair, set the brake and came around to stand several feet away, leaning against the rail of the *Skerry*. "Hmm. I thought you were a strong, brave woman. Instead you sound like a spoiled, frightened baby right now. Where is your backbone?"

Pompous ass! Annabel glared at him. "My backbone is right in this fucking chair where it's been for the past seven years."

"Am I supposed to pity you?"

She reached for the brake. "I don't care what you do. I don't care who you are. You are nothing to me. I am not a Silkie. You have no say over me."

"Don't I? Set that brake. I might not control you, but I have a big say in what happens tomorrow to both Ciaran and the request I know Cayden and Carrick will make to allow a marriage between you and your pup."

"Then if you're smart, you and your other lords will tell him no and make me leave."

Is that what you really want?

No! I want to be what he needs. I want to be

219

whole. I want to be the mate he needs.

"What about what he wants? Do you think he doesn't know and you must be the one to decide? Would you be brave enough to be the mate he wants?"

She stopped the chair even as she had begun to turn it away. With her hands still on the wheels, Annabel lowered her head. "I don't know."

Faeran stepped forward and once more took hold of the handles on her chair. "You must give it some thought. If you love him as I think you do, then you must give it some thought Annabel Barton."

He pushed her chair forward slowly. "Tell me about your father. Tell me about Phillip Barton."

"How do you know his name?"

Faeran laughed. "I know."

Annabel looked out over the bay. She could see the lights of the Yacht Club in the distance and the shimmer of reflected light from the boats anchored in the marina. Farther away, the subtler lighting of the big summer houses. Places like Barton's Point.

"It's funny. We only ever spent summers here, but I always have the hardest time picturing Daddy anywhere other than here. I barely remember him in our apartment in the city. It was here that he always seemed to come alive, as if he only marked time until we got to the ocean. I think had it not been for my mother, he would have lived here year round."

"He could have after her death. Why didn't he?"

"He said he wanted me to grow up in the city where I would be exposed to people and culture." She stopped, and her hands clenched in her lap. "But the truth is...I would have been happier here. I always looked at the house here as my home, my room. If it was the place where Daddy came alive, then to me it was the only place where I truly lived. The smell of the ocean, the sound of the waves and the feel of the salt spray, they are what made me feel at home."

"But yet you left for seven years. Why did you not let it heal you?"

She looked over her shoulder at him in confusion. "There was nothing to heal. I am what I am."

He set the brake and came around to crouch next to her. "You have no idea what you really are, girl. No idea at all. And you denied yourself the one thing that would have made the difference."

Annabel drew back from the fierce light in his night dark eyes. *Who are you?*

He stared at her and shook his head. *Not tonight. The time is not yet right.*

"Bell?" Cayden scowled when he saw Faeran crouched next to her. "You said you wouldn't hurt her," he growled.

Faeran stood. "And I have not."

Cayden hovered next to her protectively.

"Take her, pup. Make your introductions, but then let her rest. Tomorrow will be a long day for all of us."

Faeran walked away, his robes molding his broad chest and flowing about his strong thighs.

"Are you all right, Bell?"

"Yes." She looked at him pleadingly. "Must I meet the rest of them?"

Cayden knelt beside her and buried his face in the warm skin of her neck. "Yes, love, but none are as bad as what you've already been through. The rest of the Atlantic lords are not nearly as fierce, and the Pacific lords take a very different approach to things, not nearly as tense."

Chapter 19

The next hour passed in a blur of names and faces that Annabel was positive she would never remember. For her there were only three who stood out from the rest: Carrick, Riordan and Faeran. She felt his eyes on her as Cayden escorted her around to meet them all. She glimpsed Taylor in conversation with him and wondered if he would grill her brother as he had her. When the hour ended, Annabel reached up to put her hand over Cayden's.

"Please, Cay. Take me out of here."

When they reached her cabin, he shut the door behind them. The only light was from the moonlight that came through the windows next to the bed. Annabel sagged with relief.

"You look done in, love. Do you want me to get Momma or a maid to help you?"

"No," she whispered. "I need you, Cayden. Can you stay with me?"

In answer, he picked her up from her chair, carried her to the bed and sat down. His elegant, sensitive hands cradled her, stroked her, and cherished her. His touch comforted her, relaxed her and then aroused her. Fingers brushed along her arms, down her throat and across the diaphanous material of her gown to the aroused points of her nipples. She whimpered.

"That's it, love." His voice was a low purr in her ear.

She twisted in his arms, wrapping hers around his neck and pressing her swollen, aching breasts against his broad chest. He felt her softness and his hands bracketed her waist. She quivered under his hands and heat stabbed his groin making his cock swell and press against her. When her hand slipped down and circled him, he jerked in her grip and moaned. Her hand was like a hot brand searing his nerves as she stroked up and down the velvety skin of his shaft.

"Not yet, Bell. Not quickly. I want to treasure you, touch you, and taste your sweet juices. I want to watch you come for me."

His hands stroked the robe from her body and he laid her on the bed, his eyes devouring the creamy expanse of her skin. She was flawless. He spread her hair out on the pillow, rubbing a silken curl between his thumb and his forefinger. With a gentle, patient touch, he spread her legs and ran his hands along the outside of her thighs, over the crease at thigh and hip and inside to the sensitive flesh of her inner thigh. His dark eyes watched her intently as he stroked along the wet pink lips of her pussy. He pushed and they parted. With a slow, seductive smile he slipped one finger inside of her and worked it lazily in and out. When her breathing accelerated, he added a second finger to the first.

"Feel me, Bell. Feel me."

She twisted and whimpered beneath him. "Please. Cay!"

He smiled again, removed his fingers, coated with her sweet honey and slowly rubbed some of it on each nipple before he touched his fingers to her mouth. Her lips parted and he slid the fingers in, groaning as she sucked the wetness from them.

"Taste yourself, darling. Taste how sweet you are."

Lowering his head, he laved her nipples with his tongue and then knelt between her spread legs, his eyes meeting hers in the moonlight that streamed into her cabin. With his gaze locked on hers, Cayden ran his palms up her thighs, over the smooth skin of her stomach, the indentation of her waist and up to the firm, pale globes of her breasts. His touch was feather light, leaving her gasping for more. With his eyes still locked on hers, he lowered his mouth until he touched her nipples again with his tongue. When she arched upward, he took her softly into his mouth and suckled her. His fingers traced back down over her belly, sliding intimately between her thighs to caress her clitoris.

"Yes," she moaned, her hands twisting in his long hair, her mouth parting in pleasure. But Cayden was nowhere near done. Leaving her nipples, he traced a path with his lips and tongue down to the very core of her. As he thrust a finger deeply inside of her this time, his mouth suckled the swollen bud of flesh nestled in her curls. Whimpers became moans, and then turned to cries of pleasure. His cock throbbed with anticipation, but still he held back, concentrating on pleasuring her. With lips and tongue, fingers thrusting, he brought her again and again to climax until all she could do was shudder wordlessly in his arms. Her cries turned once again to whimpers. He lay next to her, soothing her.

"Shh, Bell. My beautiful Bell."

He felt her tears and stroked them away with his thumbs. "Are you all right? Did I hurt you?"

Her arms twined around his neck. "I want to taste you, Cay. I want to touch you like you've touched me."

He shuddered at her whispered words. Just the idea of her lips wrapping around him was almost more than he could stand. "Bell…"

"Please, Cay. Help me."

He helped her sit, then slid from the bed and stood in front of her. He looked down and simply seeing her beautiful mouth so close to him made his groin tighten even more. She took him in her hands, caressed the length of him and then slowly lowered her mouth, taking the tip of his cock into her mouth. With a husky groan Cayden threaded his fingers through her curls.

"That's it, Bell. Yes. Like that. I love it when you suck me."

He stroked her head, caressed her shoulders and reveled in the nearly unbearable pleasure of her touch. His hips moved in gentle thrusts, but when he looked down to see her, it was all he could do not to push himself all the way in. But it wasn't her mouth he wanted to fuck.

"Lay back, Bell. Lay back and let me bury my cock in you."

He eased her back, watching as her sun bleached curls spilled across the dark sheets. His hands caressed along her thighs, lifting her legs and hooking them around his hips. He growled as a sudden shaft of intense lust rocketed through him. With one hand supporting her bottom, he used his other hand to guide his engorged shaft between the moist folds of her cunt. In one powerful thrust he seated himself inside her and then set up a fast pace as he felt his own climax build.

"Come, Cay," she whispered. "Come in me."

He cried out, holding her hips in place as his body bucked into her, spilling his seed. With his penis still sheathed within her, he turned and took them both down onto the surface of the bed. His hands stroked the bare skin of her back from neck to buttocks. "I love you, Bell. I love you so much."

They curled together. When he heard her breath smooth out into sleep, he shifted them both until he could pull the covers up over the two of them. Love so intense it made him shake poured through him. He couldn't live without her. He knew it, but he had to make the Council believe. More importantly, he had to make her believe it too.

Chapter 20

They sailed during the night. Cayden awoke once when the movement of the boat shifted and smoothed out. Bell rested trustingly against him and he realized they had never spent an entire night in each other's arms. Her fingers were like butterflies against the hair covered skin of his chest, so light he could barely feel them. The covers had slipped off them, and he studied her freely in the dark. His eyes absorbed and memorized every line and curve of her.

She was everything he ever wanted. From the first moment he saw her when they were but children, she had always been the one. Even as a child he'd loved her far more deeply than just a friend. As a teenager, that love exploded into passion he had barely been able to control, and now as an adult, he wanted her as a lover, a friend and the mother of his children. He would sacrifice everything for her if he had to, but they would be together. She was his soul mate, perfect in every way. If only she would realize that.

He lay awake for a long time, simply watching her sleep, seeing the shadows that lay like bruises beneath her lovely eyes. He stroked her hair away from her pale cheeks, feeling guilty now for having kept her awake so long while they made love. She had been through incredible trauma, and he knew her body had limitations, had seen for himself what happened to her when she was pushed beyond those limitations. And she would be pushed today and tomorrow. The council would expect her to be there for Ciaran's hearing later this morning and then again for Cayden and Carrick's appeal tomorrow.

"Just two more days, love, and then I will make sure that you rest. You have my promise on that."

****

Annabel insisted on using her crutches. They had left the bay and were now anchored somewhere in the Atlantic, but the roll of the ship made navigating with crutches a challenge. Cayden slowed his steps to match hers.

"Bell, I can get your chair."

"No." Her chin was tilted at a determined angle. "I will not be wheeled in before your Council."

He opened the doors to the conference room. When she looked at the gathering of dark-haired men, she hesitated. Then her eyes lighted on Ciaran. His stare was hostile. Although her face was pale, her chin went up and her dark blue eyes sparkled with determination. If this gathering of the Silkie nobles couldn't see her worth, then he would gladly give up his pelt for her. She might be running on sheer heart by the end of this, but she would still be there with her chin up.

****

The room was set up with one long table. Riordan sat at the head with Faeran and another man Bell remembered being introduced as Dylan sitting to his right and his left. She quickly realized that the lords of the Atlantic and Pacific were seated on each side. At the opposite end from Riordan was a smaller table at which Ciaran sat between two large, muscular Silkie. Carrick stood when he saw them enter and came to pull out a chair for Annabel to sit. He smiled at her encouragingly as he took her crutches for her and set them against the wall. Briefly, his hand rested on her shoulder. She looked up into his dark eyes; the respect was still there along with something else she couldn't identify.

Riordan cleared his throat. "We have gathered

to hear the charges against Ciaran Clifton, second son of Carrick, Lord of the Northwest Atlantic Quadrant. Faeran please read the charges."

Faeran unrolled a scroll and held it up before him. "Ciaran Clifton, you are charged with the attack on your brother Cayden with the intent to kill. In addition, you are charged with the kidnap and attempted murder of the human, Annabel Barton. Further, you are charged with the plotting and attempted murder of the Silkie Lord, Carrick Clifton." Faeran re-rolled the scroll and looked at Ciaran. "What say you to these charges?"

Ciaran stared defiantly at all of them and mutinously remained silent.

Riordan stared down the length of the table, his eyes narrowed and his thick brows arched. "If you have nothing to say then let us begin. Cayden tell us about the night at what I believe you call 'Bell's Cove'."

Cayden related the events as he remembered them, up to the point where he lost consciousness and reverted back to human form. When he finished, it was Dylan who spoke.

"So, if I understand you correctly, Ciaran's initial attack occurred while you were in human form and he was in seal form?"

"That's correct, my lord."

There were several murmurs from around the table, but they quieted when Faeran spoke. "I would like to hear Annabel's version of this story."

She glanced nervously around at the Silkie Lords. Carrick nodded to her encouragingly and Cayden reached over to cover her hand with his. "Cayden saw him first and shoved me back into the boat right before Ciaran slammed into him. Before he could do anything, Ciaran had slammed into him again, and Cayden cut his leg on the boat propeller."

"Did you know what they were?" one of the

228

Pacific lords asked.

She looked over at him with his slightly slanted liquid brown eyes. "No. Right before Cayden transformed he asked me to remember that no matter what I saw, he loved me. I realized almost immediately what he was, what they both were.

"The fight was terrible. Cayden was already injured and Ciaran was the larger of the two. I yelled at them to stop, but it just kept on and on, the snarls and the sounds of their bodies slamming together. I knew we needed help so I crawled below deck and found the radio. I kept trying radio frequencies trying to reach the *Skerry*."

She looked at Carrick apologetically. "Carrick wouldn't speak to me. I tried to radio again, just in case he still had it on and gave him our location."

"What happened then?" Faeran asked quietly.

"I searched the cabin and found the flare gun and I crawled back on deck. Ciaran hovered over Cayden..." She stopped and swallowed, her eyes closing briefly as she remembered how frightened she had been.

"Go on."

"Cayden was back in human form. He was so still. I was afraid Ciaran would kill him, if he wasn't dead already. I pointed the flare gun at Ciaran and told him I would shoot him if he didn't get away from Cayden."

"And did he?" Dylan inquired.

"Yes. He disappeared into the water."

"So that left you in the boat and Cayden on shore?" Dylan sounded confused. "But I thought when Carrick arrived you were both on shore."

"I swam to him and pulled up onto the beach."

"You entered the water at night knowing Ciaran might be somewhere around?" The question came from Brayden, Lord of the Northeast Atlantic.

Annabel turned her palms up in appeal. "I had

to. Cayden was hurt. I didn't know how badly. I had to go to him."

Carrick interrupted at that point. "When we finally arrived, Annabel was half on top of Cayden, I suppose to shield him, and armed with a spear gun."

"Would you have shot Ciaran?" Faeran asked curiously.

Her hands clenched into fists as she gazed into eyes that reminded her of her own father's. "Without a second thought."

"Tell us when you next saw Ciaran." Riordan commanded.

"I was staying at the Clifton's house along the Connecticut shore. It was late and I hadn't been able to sleep. I was sitting in my chair when he broke into the house."

"Tell them what you were about to do, Poppy," Ciaran taunted. "Tell them how I knocked the pills from your hands!"

"Silence!" Riordan roared and Annabel saw without any doubt the authority he had so far wielded with such casualness. He turned to Annabel. "Is this true?"

"It is true."

"So he saved your life?"

"Only because he would not let me take the easy way out, as he called it," she retorted. "He bound my hands and carried me on board an old ski boat before taking me out to a rock that would disappear below the sea at high tide. That's where he dumped me with my hands tied behind my back to wait for the water to rise and drown me."

She described how the water rose while Ciaran worked on other booby traps.

"But how did you finally get loose? Did Cayden and Carrick free you?"

"No. Catriona did."

There were several looks of confusion around

the table, although Annabel noticed Faeran wasn't one of them. His expression was serious, but not unkind as he said. "You must explain. We were told that Catriona and your brother were at your house and came up by car."

Annabel looked around at all of them. "I heard her thoughts. Is that unusual? I have spoken to Carrick that way, and I think also Cayden, though not as clearly."

Brayden, who sat next to her, touched her arm. She turned to look at him questioningly, barely registering the fact that his eyes were also a deep, mesmerizing blue.

Can you hear me now?

Yes. Just like I hear Faeran.

When Brayden's head suddenly swiveled to Faeran, the Silkie noble smiled ever so slightly.

"Catriona reminded me of an amusing situation from my childhood, and I simply tried to do again what she helped me to remember."

"And what was that?" Brayden prompted.

"I rotated my shoulders and arms and slipped them over my head until they were in front of me. Then I used my teeth to untie the rope."

Riordan smiled at her. "You are a very resourceful and determined young woman, but we will talk more about that tomorrow. Right now you must tell us what you saw of Ciaran."

She told them about him slamming into her as she tried to reach the boat and what she saw of Ciaran and Cayden locked in battle. Then she told of looking for Carrick and finding him entangled in fishing net below.

Annabel's shoulders slumped a bit as she finished. Cayden put his arm around her and she leaned her head against him. "I'm sorry, my lords. I fear that is all that I can tell you."

Cayden stood and looked toward Riordan,

Faeran and Dylan. "I beg your indulgence, your graces. Please allow me to take Bell back to her cabin. She is still not completely recovered and needs to rest."

Riordan nodded. "We have heard what we need to hear from both of you. Carrick can fill in the gaps and Ciaran if he chooses."

When Cayden brought her crutches to her, Annabel looked up at him and whispered, "I'm cramping. You'll have to carry me."

He lifted her effortlessly. "It's all right, Bell."

She lifted her pale face to the Silkie lords. "Thank you for hearing me. I'm sorry..."

Her voice trailed off and her mouth tightened with the pain of a cramp arcing down her thigh and into her calf. Cayden waited no longer, he spun on his heel and hurried out of the room, directing a crew member standing at the door to find Taylor to help.

****

Carrick watched Cayden and Annabel leave, worry furrowing his brow. He could still not completely resign himself to allowing them to be together, but he also could deny them no longer. It was plain even to him that they belonged together, but it brought him no joy. He could see no happy ending when she was so limited.

"Lord Carrick, perhaps you would relate more of this tale to us?"

He stared sadly at his younger son. Ciaran still wore a look of anger and defiance, but Carrick also saw the hurt that lay beneath it. No one would win in this situation, not Ciaran, Cayden, Annabel, and especially not he and Catriona. Any way around it, they would lose a son. And if he could not get the Council to accept Cayden and Annabel, then he and Cat could very well lose both sons.

"The cove had been booby trapped," he began

232

and continued to recount what he could remember of the ski boat hitting an object and exploding just as he and Cayden managed to jump clear. Ciaran had then been on him while he was dazed from the blast, dragging him down and tangling him in the net below water. It had made it impossible for him to transform. He spared nothing in explaining how Annabel had come after him, freeing him and nearly sacrificing herself to do so.

Finally, he explained how he had gone to Cayden's aid, overpowering Ciaran and forcing him to change. At last he finished. For a moment he was silent and then he looked up and around the council.

"I cannot condone what Ciaran has done. I can't even begin to understand it. Yet, he is my son. What kind of father would I be if I didn't look at all of you now and humbly beg you to at least spare his life? It would break his mother's heart, and mine too, to have this day end with his death. I must refuse to make a decision on this, but I beg you to spare him."

Riordan's dark eyes were sad. "It brings us no joy either. We are all kin, and we must fight to preserve our kind. When any one of us leaves the fold or puts himself beyond redemption, it must be a tragedy for all of us. Remove Ciaran to his cabin until we have discussed this."

"I would go with my son."

Riordan nodded. "Return in one hour. We will pass judgment."

****

Cayden and Taylor both massaged her, and Taylor had already slipped her painkillers, but Annabel's cries could still be heard throughout the ship as they fought to ease the cramps knotting the muscles in her legs. Catriona stroked her hair and tried to soothe her. From the doorway, Carrick watched in horror.

"What's wrong with her?"

"Her body has been through too much and she's had no time to recover," Cayden snapped. "My God, father, it's been only two days since Ciaran's attack, since she nearly died saving you! It would tax even the strongest of us. She cannot appear before the Council tomorrow. She cannot!"

"She must! If you are to have any chance to make your petition, she must!"

Cayden saw the agony in Annabel's face. "I'll live as a human."

"No!" Carrick and Catriona spoke simultaneously, but it was his mother who continued. "Please Cayden. Before this day is over, I will lose one son. I cannot bear to lose you both. Don't ask it of me."

"I. Will. Be. Ready." Annabel got out between clenched teeth. Her eyes held a glazed look that told them the painkillers had kicked in. Her screams subsided to whimpers, tears leaking from the corners of her eyes and rolling along her temples and into her sweat dampened hair. She swallowed and looked at Catriona's pale face. "Momma," she slurred through the haze of the drugs.

Catriona frowned as she stroked her hand across her forehead and wiped the tears from her face. When she looked up at her husband, she saw her own pain reflected in the lean planes of his face. This was as hard or harder on him.

"She'll sleep now," Taylor said. "The longer she does the better. It will help her recover."

Carrick's nostrils flared. "It's time to go back."

****

Ciaran stood before the Council of Silkie Lords, flanked by his guards. Behind him stood Carrick, Catriona and Cayden. Riordan stood up, his gray hair flowing and his dark eyes sad. He spoke formally in the old language.

"Ciaran Clifton, we have listened to the words of

your father and brother and to the words of the human, Annabel. We have heard the pleas of your father, and felt those of your mother. You, however, have refused to tell us anything with which we could either condemn or condone. I give you one last chance."

Ciaran looked around at all of them. "I have nothing to say in my defense. I will accept whatever is your judgment."

Faeran and Dylan stood, coming around to where Ciaran stood while Riordan finished his pronouncement. "We have heard your parents and will not put you to death, but we hereby sentence you to live as a human until such time you can prove you have developed compassion, understanding and some love for others to balance out the warrior instincts you have in abundance. Remove his sealskin."

Short of a death sentence, taking a pelt was the most severe form of punishment.

Faeran bent, murmuring softly as he moved his hand gracefully around Ciaran's ankle. The leather bracelet fell into his hand. He stood once more and gave it to Catriona whose beautiful green eyes filled with unshed tears. She cradled the pelt as if it were Ciaran that she held.

"You must keep it safe for him in the hope that he will earn it back and be able to take his rightful place among us once more." Faeran's deep blue eyes were somber.

"You will come with his grace and me now, Ciaran," Dylan told him quietly. Ciaran nodded. For just a moment, his dark brown eyes turned to his mother and father. It was the first sign he had shown that he felt anything at all. There was a flash of vulnerability and then it was gone, a bitter brightness taking its place.

"I'm ready."

"Where are you taking him?" Catriona asked quietly.

Faeran's jaw was tight and for a moment it looked like he would ignore her question. Finally, he replied, "He will be set adrift in a boat with three days of food and water. After that he is on his own."

She nodded, and then stepped hastily forward to hug him tightly. "Be safe, my son," she whispered brokenly.

He squeezed her tightly and then turned and left with Faeran and Dylan.

Chapter 21

It was dark when she awakened, and Annabel wasn't quite sure what it was that roused her. Perhaps it was the dream, a wonderful dream in which she swam and played in the water as fluidly as any of the seals that surrounded her. They accepted her as one of their own and allowed her to play and sleep in the sun with them. She had no physical limitations, but then she realized that she not only swam with them, she was one of them.

She stared at the ceiling. It was an old dream; one she first had as a child. Then it had been a fantasy, now it was a taunt. To be able to move with no limitations? Wishful thinking.

Is it? Or does your subconscious not already know?

She froze, and then slowly reached over to switch on the lamp next to the bed.

No. I am not in your room, but I do wish to speak with you. May I?

It's the middle of the night.

Yes, but the time is now right.

She sighed. *Very well, your grace.*

The cabin door opened quietly and Faeran, Duke of the Atlantic stepped inside. His overpowering presence at once made the cabin seem small. With a casual glance at his surroundings, he spotted the chair next to the bed and lowered his large frame into it. He no longer wore traditional Silkie garb, now dressed in khakis and a tee shirt that loudly proclaimed "I got shucked at Stan's Clam Bar."

Annabel hid a small smile.

Faeran looked down suspiciously. "Is it the shirt? Carrick was very willing to let me borrow it. Perhaps too willing I now think."

She giggled. Carrick had to have done it on purpose. Faeran smiled and leaned back comfortably. "Ah, if it makes you laugh, then it is well worth the expense to my ego."

It was an interesting thing to say, as if he cared what she thought or how she felt.

I do.

Annabel glared. "Stop it, your grace! I don't understand all of your Silkie ways, but it seems pretty rude to me to keep barging right into my own personal thoughts."

He inclined his dark head. "My apologies. My brother Brayden and I wished to speak to you before tomorrow. There are things you must know."

She remembered Brayden. He'd sat next to her earlier in the day. She vaguely recalled that the two men looked similar, but she had been so nervous at the time that was all she could recall. She lifted still slightly sleep muddled eyes to Faeran. "Is he here, too?"

Faeran nodded. "Waiting outside."

Annabel sat up. "Could you hand me my robe, please?"

Faeran looked confused.

"You're sitting on it."

He leaned forward, pulled the thin silk wrap from behind his back and handed it to her. "Do you need any help?"

She scowled at him. "Hand me my crutches, then go outside and get Lord Brayden while I get out of bed."

He inclined his head with a faint quirk of his wide, mobile mouth at her imperious tone. He stood up with a bow. "I'll take that as a no. As you wish, my lady."

She looked up at him, startled. "Why do you say that?"

He merely smiled and let himself out of the cabin.

She watched him go with a frown. He spoke in rhymes and riddles she didn't understand, and she particularly didn't understand why the two men wanted to speak to her in the middle of the night. As nervous as they made her, she wasn't frightened, didn't believe she had any reason to be scared. Belting the robe around her waist, Annabel used her crutches to get to her wheelchair. Once she had settled herself in it, she wheeled over to the cabin door and opened it.

Faeran and Brayden stood just outside, talking quietly. Their heads turned at the same time toward her and she saw then how much they looked alike.

"Where do you wish to speak, my lords?" she asked quietly.

The two men looked at each other, and then Faeran spoke. "We would prefer your cabin for now."

He opened the door and Annabel wheeled herself back in. With a deft turn of the wheel, she spun her chair to face them. "Don't you think it's enough that I will be called before your Council again? Do you also have to drag me from my sleep?"

Faeran stood near the door, his arms crossed across his chest. Brayden crouched next to her. "I'm going to ask you to keep an open mind Annabel, just like Cayden asked of you when he had to reveal what he was."

She looked suspiciously from Brayden, over his shoulder to the man leaning against the door. Her smile was nervous now. "Look, I've accepted the fact that the Silkie are more than just a myth, but I don't know how many more surprises I can stand."

Brayden took her hand and looked gently into her deep blue eyes. "We don't often use family names among us, since we tend to view ourselves as part of one large family, but that doesn't mean we don't have them."

"You mean like the name Clifton."

"Yes. Carrick uses his family name among the humans, so you have heard his. But we were not introduced to you in that way because where we are from often tells us more about another Silkie than a family name would."

She blinked in confusion as she once more glanced from one to the other. "So, you got me out of bed in the middle of the night to tell me your last name?"

Don't be catty. Faeran's eyes narrowed dangerously.

"I'm not being catty. I'm exhausted."

"Bell," Brayden drew her attention back to him. "Our last name is Barton. Like yours."

"Okay," she said in a sarcastically perky voice, "so we have the same last name. An interesting coincidence. Barton isn't exactly as common as Smith, but I suppose it was a possibility. You seem to forget, though, Annabel—human. Brayden and Faeran—Silkies. Now that we have that settled, can I go back to bed? Maybe tomorrow I can get you an invitation to the family reunion. Oh. I forgot. I have no family other than Taylor."

The two men looked at each other and Faeran slowly came forward. "Taylor is your cousin."

"My half-brother. Daddy had a wild weekend with Taylor's mother before he married my mother."

"Faeran?" Brayden was asking a question and Annabel had no idea at all what it was.

"We'll deal with him separately. We must take care of her first before the Council meets today."

Now Annabel grew alarmed. She didn't like the turn of their conversation. Exactly how did they intend to take care of her?

Faeran snorted in disgust. "We tried easing her into this. That was our mistake. She managed to take in who and what Cayden was without going to pieces, surely we can take the same direct approach with this." Impatiently, he pulled his shirt over his head and came toward her bare-chested.

"What the hell are you doing?" she demanded, brows drawing together as she prepared to spin her chair way and lock herself in the bathroom.

"Stop!" He commanded. "I am merely showing you a mark which I believe you will find familiar."

He pointed to a spot on his left flank, just above the waistline of his pants. Exasperated, she turned her head to look at it and then without even thinking, grasped the waist of his pants and pulled him closer. There, just above the waistband were three moles that formed a perfect triangle. While she stared, Brayden stripped off his shirt and stepped up to her, revealing the same mark. Involuntarily, her hand dropped to her own side. Her heart beat heavily in her chest, and she flew back to a scene from her childhood.

"Look, Daddy!" Poppy pointed to her father's side. "You have the same spots on you that I do!" They were sailing on the bay at the time.

He laughed. "My father had them too. He told me they were a mark of royalty. We are the lords of the sea!"

Poppy laughed. "That's silly. We would have to live in the sea then and we can't do that."

Phillip knelt next to her and tilted his head. "No. We can't. Can we, Poppy darling?"

Annabel closed her eyes and leaned back in her wheelchair. "This is why you kept saying the time was not right. You had to show me this. Then surely you must also know I have this same mark. That my father did, too. Who are you?"

"Your uncles."

She opened her eyes and glared at them. "You lie! My father would have told me!"

"He didn't know, at least not who his family were." Faeran said. "His father, your grandfather, mated without permission with the human Mary Taylor. Phillip was the result. Taurent lived with them until he thought Phillip would be old enough to understand, and he tried to convince him to come away with him to sea, but your father rejected him, and Taurent left. He was killed in a hurricane as he tried to return to *his* father... Riordan."

"The king?" At Bray's nod, Bell protested, "but he's not old enough! That would make him my great-grandfather! Are you my father's brothers?"

Brayden shook his head. "His uncles. When Taurent was lost, Riordan married again to our mother. So that would make us..."

"Great-uncles."

Brayden and Faeran both nodded as if everything had been perfectly explained.

"Is this some kind of joke?" Annabel's chin trembled and she pressed her lips together to stop it. She wasn't comforted. Instead they made her furious. "You want me to believe I am one of you?"

"You are one of us, Annabel Barton."

"Then why am I in this chair?" she demanded furiously. "I've seen how quickly Cayden heals! If I am one of you...why didn't I?"

Her voice ended as a whisper, a quiet plea to understand that hung in the silent room.

Both men crouched next to her, one on each side, but it was Faeran who spoke. "Come with us, Annabel. Trust us. Let us show you. Your body couldn't do what it didn't know. Come with us and let us show you how the sea can change you."

Brayden touched her arm. "We'll have you back in time for the Council."

She touched the mark on her flank. Taylor had

it too. Did that mean?

Yes. But we will deal with him later. It's you we must show first.

"Riordan?"

"He doesn't know yet."

A wild hope surged through her, the hope that she could change the future she had seen lying ahead of her. For years, she had hoped just to have enough movement and control to be able to use crutches. But what if there was more?"

"You'll show me how to change?"

Brayden nodded.

"But what if I'm paralyzed as a seal?"

"You swim now, don't you?"

Slowly she nodded, the hope once again gaining ground. It was the one thing she was able to hang onto since the accident, the ability to swim. She always felt more at home in the water. It was the place where she could still be graceful and able, where she could be equal.

"Come with us, little Bell," Faeran said. "Let us show you what you can be and help you shift."

God! It was like someone had just held a bag full of wishes in front of her. When she nodded, Faeran, Duke of the Atlantic smiled. He picked her up and carried her from the cabin, with Brayden right in front of them. They took her down to the launch. As Annabel looked around, she realized they had returned to the area around Barton's point since Ciaran had been set adrift. She could see the lights of the Yacht Club, and silhouetted against the night sky, she could see the house. Her house, her father's house, his grandmother's house.

"Can we do this by the dock below my house? I feel at home there."

Faeran smiled down at her. "Of course."

****

Cayden awoke at the sound of the launch.

243

Rolling over he looked out the window by his bed to see it speeding away. He recognized the towering forms of Faeran and Brayden, and then to his horror, he saw Bell sitting in the back of the launch, her gold streaked hair blowing in the breeze.

What the fuck?

He leaped to his feet and raced out of the cabin. They had taken Bell. Without waiting to alert anyone, he stripped off his boxer shorts and dove over the side of the *Skerry*, transforming as he did so. What were they doing? They were Riordan's sons. Royalty. What did they want with Bell? Was this some trick to separate the two of them? Cayden nearly panicked at the idea. He would not lose her again. He could not. He shot through the water like a torpedo, but he was no match for the ski boat.

****

Her nerves got the better of her as they tied the launch up at her dock. When Faeran offered her a hand, she shrank back.

"I can't do this. What if I'm like this..." she gestured to her legs, "if I transform?"

Brayden knelt next to her. "We will be right there with you. You must not fear it."

Faeran began stripping off his clothing. "You are our blood. We will protect you and help you."

She averted her eyes from his taut, muscular body. "Do I have to..."

Faeran arched a brow at her. "What is it you say? Get naked?" He laughed at her shocked expression. "Only in the purest sense of the words."

She swallowed. "Then look the other way and let me get in the water."

They nodded, amused by a modesty that was foreign to them. Annabel took off her wrap and the silky nightgown she had underneath it. After maneuvering her way to the gunwale, she perched briefly on the side and then leaned forward to dive in. As she acclimated to the water, she heard two more splashes.

"Come to where it's a little shallower."

Faeran stroked lazily on his side, and then stood up. With gentle hands, he grasped her waist and set her on her feet.

"Can you stand with my support?"

"Yes."

There was a loud splash and suddenly Cayden came toward them.

"Let her go. What the hell are you doing?"

Faeran looked at his brother. "Silence him and bind him. Now that he is here, let him watch, but I do not want his interference."

"My lord?" Annabel looked over shoulder at him. "Please."

His deep blue eyes gentled. "We will not hurt him, Bell. We only make sure that he does not interfere."

She was vaguely aware of Brayden stopping Cayden with a slow pushing motion of his hand. At the words he murmured in the ancient tongue, Cayden was suddenly without voice or movement. He stood silently by, a witness powerless to do anything else. Faeran turned to look at him.

"Watch pup. When you have witnessed, then we will release you. If you still have a quarrel with me, then I will gladly do battle."

Cayden's eyes blazed angrily from his lean face, but Faeran ignored him.

"Close your eyes Bell, remember the dream that awoke you. Think of the mark you bear, the mark your father and his father and his father before him all bear. You are one of us. You have only to wish it so."

Annabel tuned out everything but his softly spoken words and the gentle sucking sounds of the water lapping against the dock. She remembered the dream, swimming and playing with the seals. Her family. Heat began to course through her from her head down through her limbs until she could swear she felt something even in her toes.

Faeran continued to speak, but his words now were in a language she didn't know. She felt his hands shift so that one touched her head and the other he placed flat against her chest, just above her heart. When he spoke again, she understood him.

"We are here who hold you dear. Take what we offer, discard your fear. Now draw upon the blood of old and create a Silkie in our mold."

With infinitely gentle hands he pushed her forward into the water. Instinctively, Annabel snatched a breath and then moved out of his arms, swimming as she always had using her hips and thighs to propel her through the water, but it was so much faster than before! She spun and twisted, leaped and then dived, skimming across the bottom. As she looked to her side, she laughed. Faeran glided along with her, a smile on his face and his blue eyes sparkling and luminescent. She surfaced, treading water easily, even her legs were moving freely and with feeling. Faeran surfaced next to her and smiled at her as he tilted his head.

"Well?"

She laughed. "But nothing is different! I am still as I was, except I can move my legs."

He laughed loudly. "No, you simply see as we see. Look down at your reflection in the water."

Curious, Annabel did just that, but it was not the familiar outline of her face and her long damp hair that she saw. Instead, it was the sleek outline of two seals, the larger one Faeran, and a smaller, lighter seal. Was...was that *her*? Her eyes darted back up to Faeran again and then back down to their reflections.

"I'm a seal."

"A Silkie. Not an ordinary seal, little Bell. You are a Silkie. You are a true daughter of your royal lineage."

She looked up to see Cayden several yards away. He looked transfixed.

Release him.

In a moment. Play with him by all means, but you must come back to me to let me help you change back this first time. Then I will teach you the words. You have only to say them in your head. At first, it will take you longer, require more concentration, but then you will soon be able to do it faster and with less forethought.

"Release him, please."

He nodded.

In an instant, Cayden changed. He shot through the water to her, diving down and then back up, brushing against her, blowing bubbles around her in welcome, in courtship that she had only dimly understood before. What she had thought simply amusing as a human, she now realized he had done as part of the mating ritual, as a way to express his care and tenderness. She looked up to find Faeran had returned to the boat. He and Brayden had both transformed, and now idly sat watching the two of them.

Swim with me.

Cay! I'm whole. Like this I'm whole.

He laid his cheek against her. *I have so many questions, Bell…*

Not now. Swim with me. Make love to me.

They swam to the beach where she had napped with him as a child, and found him again as a teen. They hauled out, to human eyes just two seals playing in the moonlight. To each other, they were Cayden and Annabel. As the water lapped around their entwined bodies, he kissed her and caressed her. They were both too hungry, too excited to wait for long.

"Bell," he breathed against her. "I'm afraid I'll hurt you."

"No. It's different like this. I'm different. I can move like I can't when I'm human, but I still see us both in human form."

He stroked her hair back from her face. "Crazy, isn't it?"

Gently he turned her over until she lay prone. He raised her hips, kneeling behind her as he stroked his shaft between her thighs. She moaned, pressing against him at the very moment he thrust into her. They came together wildly. Cayden gloried in the way she met him thrust for thrust. Her hands curled into the coarse sand of the beach. Pushing the wet strands of her hair to one side, he bent over her running his tongue up along the line of her spine to the nape of her neck. He nipped her with his teeth, but instead of protesting, she raised up into him. She sat in his lap and he continued to thrust, but now his hands were free to roam over her breasts and down between her legs. When he pressed his fingers against her clit, she cried out and his own cry of completion echoed across the water and along the beach, carrying in the night air.

Faeran and Brayden waited patiently for their return. When they saw them both approaching, the two men dove into the water.

While Cayden transformed, Brayden and Faeran held Bell between them.

Are you ready, little Bell? Faeran smiled at her.

Yes, but scared.

Why?

I have such freedom like this. I don't want to go back, to be confined.

Give it time, child. Because you are whole as a Silkie, there's hope that you can become so in human form.

248

I'm ready.

"Take from her this Silkie shape and leave her with a sealskin cape."

Disappointment flooded her as she realized immediately that her legs would no longer support her. Cayden was there in an instant to hold her and soothe her. As she calmed down, she realized she did feel stronger. Brayden handed her a heavy pelt.

"You must keep it safe and keep it with you always," he told her. "Without it, you cannot transform. If you allow someone to possess it, then they hold you hostage."

She fingered the pelt, stroking it and seeing in the first light of dawn that it had a golden tint to it, as if it had been bleached by the sun. She held it against her as Cayden lifted her into the boat. She continued to stare at it as he helped her with her clothing. After Brayden and Faeran were dressed, Cayden opened a storage box beneath one of the seats and pulled out a pair of swimming trunks. He grinned at Annabel.

"You will have to start squirreling clothes around different places like the rest of us."

"Clothes and crutches?"

He touched her cheek. "Give it time. We'll make it work. The biggest hurdle is behind us. Your Silkie blood will open the door for us to be together, love."

Annabel picked up the pelt again and laid it across her lap. She stroked it for a moment and then looked up at all three men. "What about Taylor?"

Faeran frowned. "First things first. We must get things squared away with Riordan and the rest of the council. You will let me do the talking, Bell."

Cayden looked at the rising sun. "I think we should get back. There are only a few hours until the Council meets."

Faeran and Brayden looked at one another, but it was Brayden who spoke. "I believe our father will be in for a surprise."

Cayden arched a brow. "Along with the rest of us?"

The other two men just laughed.

"You have no idea," Brayden told him with a smile.

Chapter 22

"Why is everyone skulking around here like there's some big secret?" Taylor demanded a couple of hours later as he finished the coffee he had brought to Annabel's cabin. "And you, Poppy. You look like the cat that ate the canary."

"Sorry." She yawned.

"Didn't you sleep last night?" He demanded in the tone of someone about to give a lecture.

She munched hungrily on a piece of toast. "I slept. Some."

"Poppy! You'll make yourself sick."

She laughed. "Don't lecture. I feel fine, Taylor. Better than fine. I...well I'll tell you after the Council meets. Now get out. I need to get dressed."

When the door shut behind him, Annabel grabbed her crutches and walked into the bathroom. She stripped off her robe, staring at the leather thong around her waist. Faeran had told her he would change it to an anklet later, after the Council, but for now it would allow her to keep her pelt with her and keep it hidden. She was quickly realizing that Faeran and Brayden both had a flair for the dramatic. They had convinced Cayden to go in with Carrick and allow them to accompany Annabel. Dress was traditional, Faeran explained, and as a member of the nobility, she could choose to wear her pelt pinned to her shoulder if it was her wish.

He grinned at her then. "It will be as you say, my lady."

Annabel smiled slowly. "Oh what the hell. Let's make a statement."

A few minutes later, they stood outside the doors to the conference room. Everyone else had gone in. Faeran was "listening" to what was being said while Brayden pinned the pelt to her shoulder.

"I love a woman with guts enough to be bold. Too bad you're my niece."

"Great niece."

"Don't remind me."

"How old are you two anyway?"

Faeran scowled. "About the equivalent of thirty-five. The pup there is thirty, give or take a few human years."

She looked them both up and down. "You don't look that old, but then Great-grandpa Rory hardly looks his age either."

Brayden snickered. "Oh that will go over well. I'll have you know, we mature early, then age very slowly. Are you ready?"

Annabel straightened on her crutches and as she moved her left leg forward, she felt her toes grip the deck. She halted abruptly. With conscious thought she tried to wiggle her toes—nothing—but as she moved her right foot forward, she felt again the movement of her toes. She halted again. Her breathing had suddenly quickened.

"Bell? What is it?" Faeran touched her arm. Concern darkened his midnight blue eyes, so similar to her own.

She swallowed as she turned to him, her own eyes wide as she filled with a mixture of hope and fear. "I felt my toes move."

Both men looked down at her feet. "Can you wiggle them?"

"No. But when I stepped forward, I felt them move."

"Show us." Brayden ordered.

As she stepped forward, they grinned. "They did move." Faeran confirmed. "Give me those damn crutches. If they're moving on their own, let's see how you do with just us supporting you."

She was a little unsteady, but as they tested her a few feet down the deck, she gained confidence. "I think I can do it if you two will help." She looked up from one to the other and burst into tears.

"Here! Stop that!" Brayden growled, glancing around uneasily. "No tears. It makes me nervous, and you'll make your face splotchy."

Faeran wiped them away with the pads of his thumbs. "Ignore the pup. No finesse. Now, chin up. You are going to blow them away."

As they approached the conference door, Faeran reached out to fling it wide and they marched in with Annabel between them. As she saw the faces of the council, the faces of Carrick and Catriona, she smiled, but there was really only one face she wanted to find. Cayden came toward her slowly, watching her progress on the arms of Faeran and Brayden.

"Bell?" he whispered. "You're walking?"

She nodded. "Not much, but it's better than yesterday."

His glance skittered From Faeran to Brayden. "Thank you."

Riordan stood, but his eyes were locked on the pelt hanging from Annabel's shoulder. He scowled at her, and then turned icy dark eyes on Cayden and Carrick. "What is the meaning of this? You would parade her before this Council as if the outcome were already certain?"

His voice began to rise. Dylan stood at his side, also frowning, but his gaze was locked solely on Annabel. "Who are you, human?" he snapped.

Though her fingers trembled on Faeran's and Brayden's arms at the fury of the two men before her, she raised her chin and faced them calmly.

"I am Annabel Barton, daughter of Phillip,

granddaughter of Taurent, and your great-granddaughter, King Riordan."

Each word she spoke rocked the Silkie Lords seated around the table. Riordan's eyes shifted to Faeran. "Is this the truth, Faeran? You have examined this human? She bears the mark?"

Faeran smiled and touched Annabel's pelt. "No human, father. A Silkie, a true Silkie of the sea, and yes, she bears the mark. A great-granddaughter." His eyes shifted to Dylan. "A great-niece."

As Brayden stepped back, Cayden took her right hand, carried it to his lips and then wrapped it securely around his forearm. "Lean on me."

She smiled up at him. *I love you!*

Cayden turned to Riordan. "Your grace, I humbly beg you for your great-granddaughter's hand in marriage." He looked from his parents to the men around the table. "A true mating of Silkie royalty."

Riordan stared hard at his eldest and youngest sons. "I should like to hear this tale, and I believe there is one other person who should also hear it. Have the human, Taylor Sto—Barton brought into our midst."

Cayden helped Annabel to a chair, his hands never leaving her as he stroked her arm and held her hand. It would have been so easy to lose herself in his eyes, and she thought back once again to their lovemaking last night. Even now, the memory of that wild, earthy mating on the beach sent a shiver of desire through her. When she dared to look at Cayden, she saw the same heat flaring in his eyes.

Soon, he promised. *We'll swim to a favorite beach of mine. I'll take you again as a Silkie takes his mate.*

The door opened, and Taylor stepped in, flanked by Faeran and Brayden. Seen together like this, the similarity was unmistakable.

"Be seated, Taylor Barton," Riordan

commanded.

Taylor took the seat next to Annabel. When he looked at her with questions flooding his deep blue eyes, she simply smiled and turned her attention back to Riordan. The Silkie king now regarded his eldest and youngest sons severely.

"I do not care for surprises, yet you two have always completely ignored that fact. Now, I would like to know how you ascertained the relationship."

Faeran cleared his throat. "Brayden was the first to remark upon Bell's name. Although I pointed out that Barton was not an uncommon name among humans, it did rouse my interest, particularly in light of her relationship with Lord Cayden. Taylor actually supplied me with the name of their father, and then I knew."

He looked at his father apologetically. "I must beg your forgiveness, but I was just a child at the time Taurent died. I went to see the house on the point where he had lived for all those years. I met Phillip who simply thought I was a boy vacationing here for the summer."

He turned to Annabel then. "I must ask your forgiveness as well, for I believe it was my visit that reminded Phillip of who he was. We talked of the Silkie, but your father rejected the idea yet again. When he turned his back on us and our ways, Phillip became despondent."

Annabel felt Taylor grow increasingly tense as he sat next to her. She reached out to cover his clenched fist with her hand and squeezed lightly. He looked at her and she saw reflected in his eyes all of the doubts and fears that she had felt last night.

Riordan looked at all of them. "I cannot see any impediment to marriage between Cayden, son of Carrick, Lord of the Atlantic and my great-granddaughter, Annabel Barton."

Cayden leaned over, turned her face toward him

and kissed her softly. As he nuzzled her ear, he whispered. "I will love you forever, my beautiful Annabel Lee."

****

Taylor stared at the gathering of Silkies watching from the upper deck of the *Skerry*. "Are you sure about this?" he asked his newly found uncles. "Do I really have to bare my ass to everyone?"

Brayden snorted and even Faeran smiled slightly.

"Unless you plan on being the only seal wearing board shorts," Brayden snickered, "you'll need to give them the full Monty."

Taylor looked over his shoulder to where Poppy stood next to Cayden. Poppy stood. It still blew his mind. Well shit. If she had enough guts to do this, he could too. As soon as he stripped off his shorts he dove off the *Skerry's* stern.

Faeran and Brayden surfaced on either side of him.

"Tread water. Close your eyes so you can concentrate, and I want you to picture watching Cayden change."

Taylor would never forget that; it had blown his mind. Now it was him. As he felt Faeran's hands on his head and chest, Taylor's breathing accelerated.

"Relax."

Shit, this was really happening! Feeling as if everything inside him had scrambled and unscrambled, Taylor suddenly found himself shooting off beneath the water. The speed was incredible, like skimming over the water in his racing skiff. Only this time the water flowed over and around him just like the wind kissed him while sailing.

Not too long, pup, Faeran cautioned. *This time's just for show so you can prove you're one of us.*

Surface and I'll help you change back.

The tingle of the change barely registered as he shook back his hair and looked up to see Poppy and Cay smiling down and waving at him. He looked around at everyone. They all smiled at him, and he realized suddenly that he'd turn in to a *squid* if it meant he could call all these people family.

Epilogue

Annabel had plenty of offers to escort her to the bow of the *Skerry* the following month for Riordan's blessing on their marriage, but she turned every single one of them down. As Cayden stood next to his father and watched her, he understood why. With her chin lifted and her honey brown hair pulled up and back so that her curls still cascaded down her back, she looked positively regal in her traditional Silkie gown as she walked—alone—between the parted gathering of guests to take his outstretched hand.

He took just one more moment to gaze upon her, feeling his breath quicken and his cock jerk. God! The pale blue, diaphanous material left almost nothing to the imagination. He could see the aroused pink tips of her nipples along with the shadowy cleft of her sex. He could already smell the arousal in the air around him. Silkies loved sex. While he'd gotten permission to consummate their marriage privately, Cayden knew there would very likely be an orgy going on outside.

He smiled and pulled her forward, hoping like hell that King Rory would hurry up with the blessing part so that he and Annabel could get on to the consummation part. When he looked into her dark blue eyes, he saw the same desire reflected there.

You know where I want to go?

Cayden cocked an eyebrow at her. "Our cove," he whispered. "We'll take the *Belle* and spend the night there. And this time there won't be any interruptions."

She smiled at him in such a way he was grateful for once that his *feileadh* hid a lot more than her dress did.

A word about the author...

From the moment Rhett walked out on Scarlett, Laura's been hooked on romance. Deciding truth really is stranger than fiction, though, she chose a career path in journalism. Laura now teaches English and has returned to her first love—writing fiction.

She lives with her husband and son in central North Carolina along with a menagerie of animals that includes two rowdy Jack Russells and a gentle white mare named Tweed. When she's not reading or writing, Laura enjoys riding, photography, and baking the best darned carrot cake you've ever tasted.

Thank you for purchasing
this Wild Rose Press publication.
For other wonderful stories of romance,
please visit our on-line bookstore at
www.thewildrosepress.com.

For questions or more information
contact us at
info@thewildrosepress.com.

The Wild Rose Press
www.TheWildRosePress.com